THE ANIMAL HOUSE

'In the Middle Ages, women like you were gagged to stop them from arguing. The implement in question was called a Scold's Bridle. It was a piece of metal that fitted over the tongue, preventing it from moving, and was held in place by straps around the neck and head.' His smile chilled her. 'I actually own a replica of the Scold's Bridle, you know. I've been told it's extremely uncomfortable to wear.'

She stared up at him, aghast. 'You wouldn't dare.'

'Keep arguing and you'll find out.'

'This isn't the Middle Ages!'

'No,' he said harshly. 'But this is my house and my rules apply here. Now come downstairs with me and let me see you in this outfit.'

THE ANIMAL HOUSE

Cat Scarlett

This book is a work of fiction.
In real life, make sure you practise safe, sane and
consensual sex.

First published in 2004 by
Nexus
Thames Wharf Studios
Rainville Road
London W6 9HA

www.nexus-books.co.uk

Typeset by TW Typesetting, Plymouth, Devon

Printed and bound by
Clays Ltd, St Ives PLC

ISBN 0 352 33877 6

You'll notice that we have introduced a set of symbols onto our book jackets, so that you can tell at a glance what fetishes each of our brand new novels contains. Here's the key – enjoy!

cp (traditional)

cp (modern)

spanking

restraint/bondage

rope bondage/hojojutsu

latex/rubber/leather/enclosure

fem dom

willing captivity

medical

period setting

uniforms

sex rituals

One

The beautiful redhead with the bored green eyes fanned
herself with her train ticket, glancing idly around at her
fellow passengers in the half-empty compartment. The
sticky afternoon heat seemed to be intensifying as the
train sped down through the centre of France, passing
vine-green valleys and sun-scorched plateaux on its way
to the Côte D'Azur. But at least the tanned young
couple opposite her seemed to be enjoying their journey.
The athletic-looking man and the girlish brunette had
been kissing and whispering to each other ever since
they got on at Paris. Violetta watched them for a few
moments, then looked away, surprised by her own
arousal as the man reached over and quite openly
squeezed his girlfriend's breast.

Violetta uncrossed her long bare legs and straightened
up with a sigh, too restless even to watch the flash of
passing countryside at her elbow. She glanced down at
her ticket once again and then put it away in her
handbag. The chateau must be quite near the coast. She
hoped they had a swimming pool at this place; her skin
was already prickling with the heat and she fancied a
few lengths of breaststroke before dinner. Though, with
so little idea of what to expect when she arrived,
Violetta almost regretted accepting this mysterious free
holiday. Yet it was odd how the ticket had arrived,
forced through her letterbox last month without any

1

explanation. The hand-written note stapled to the ticket informed Violetta that she had won a fortnight's holiday in the South of France, yet she had no recollection of entering any such competition. It was probably a case of mistaken identity, she had decided in the end, but there was no harm in taking advantage of someone else's mistake. It could not have arrived at a better time, after all. She had slogged her guts out in the office this year and deserved several weeks of time out in the sun.

The young couple opposite were getting a little carried away, she thought, trying to hide her smile as she watched them from under her lashes. He looked German, fairly attractive and obviously used to working out, blond head shaved to fine stubble and one muscular tanned arm stretched around the girl's waist as she giggled, rubbing her body provocatively against him. Violetta could not help noticing the growing bulge in his jeans and flushed in sudden embarrassment when the brunette's hand dropped to cup it, splayed fingers pressing and stroking the thickening flesh beneath.

Her face hot, Violetta looked away down the train and realised with a shock that she was being watched. Her observer was a lithe dark-haired man sitting several seats away, one leg crossed casually over his knee and with dark glasses masking his expression. Probably in his late thirties, he was wearing an expensive suit and appeared to be a business executive of some kind. Yet even when she fixed him with a cold stare, irritated by his unashamed scrutiny, the man continued to watch her. His sardonic smile suggested to Violetta that he too had noticed the courting couple and was laughing at her red-faced embarrassment.

Stung by his amusement, Violetta swung her gaze back to the couple opposite. It might be ridiculous to respond to a stranger's silent taunt like this, but she felt oddly determined to continue watching them now.

Under the flimsy cover of a denim jacket laid across his lap, the young brunette seemed to have unzipped her boyfriend's jeans and slipped her whole hand inside. The man's smile gradually disappeared, his eyes closed and his head fell back against the upholstered seat. As her hand continued to work inside his jeans, his breathing quickened.

Violetta shifted uncomfortably and crossed her legs, unable to prevent her moist crotch from leaking into her panties. The man in dark glasses smiled again as she did so and she angrily uncrossed her legs, feeling the moisture creep down her bare thighs. Damn him!

Apparently oblivious to the eyes of their audience, the young couple continued to fondle each other. As their train curved into the next bend at an incredible speed, sunlight flashed in gold bars across his gleaming shaven head and down the shadowy ravine of her cleavage. Violetta felt dazed by the heat. Yet she could not take her eyes off them, smothering a gasp when she saw one of the man's hands push upwards under the girl's short white dress. Quickly and expertly, he pulled down her panties, as the puckered line of material across the top of each thigh indicated. Then his hand moved between her legs, his mouth nuzzling the girl's throat as he muttered something incoherent. Violetta expected her to protest or push him away, but the girl writhed enjoyably at his touch, a faint sheen of perspiration glossing her upper lip.

For one moment, the young man looked up over the girl's heaving body and met Violetta's gaze. She would have looked away but something prevented her. She was not sure what it was, but she burnt inwardly with shame when he flashed her a wolfish smile, his eyes slipping down over her long bare legs with obvious admiration. The athletic-looking young man seemed to be taking even more pleasure from her voyeurism.

Shocked, Violetta glanced hurriedly about the half-empty compartment. Nobody except herself and the man in dark glasses appeared to have noticed what they were doing. For a moment, she considered leaving her seat until the young couple had finished. She could wander down to the dining car and grab another of those bitter tasting coffees, or perhaps stretch her legs for the next fifteen minutes or so – anything to escape the tangible sexual tension in the compartment. Yet those watchful dark glasses were still trained relentlessly on her face and for some reason she found herself determined not to move. She did not want the man behind them to leave the train laughing at her prudish reactions. So Violetta decided not to flinch or look away, whatever she saw over the next few minutes. It was as though some challenge had been thrown down between them, an unspoken test of her sophistication, and the man in the dark glasses had dared her not to fail it.

The young man lifted the brunette from her seat, tanned biceps bulging with exertion, and pulled her forcibly down onto his lap. The girl gave a sharp cry which he muffled with his hand, holding her still in that position. Pushing his jacket to the floor, the man deftly arranged the folds of her dress to cover them from prying eyes, although it was obvious from the girl's flushed and glazed expression that she had just been penetrated. Gripping her by the hips, he started to jerk her back and forth on his lap in an age-old rhythm. Facing Violetta, the young brunette rocked helplessly with the motion like a rag doll. Her mouth had fallen slightly open, her lips moist and pink as she tried not to pant. It was clear that her orgasm was not far away and even the young man's low grunts could no longer be disguised.

The train slowed as it approached the dark mouth of a tunnel and some of the other passengers began to notice the unusual sounds from their part of the carriage. A well-dressed old gentlemen further along the compartment lowered his financial newspaper for a moment, his eyes narrowed on the brunette's flushed cheeks. Yet he made no attempt to stop them. A heavy woman sitting two seats down from him cleared her throat in noisy approbation but equally said nothing. It was as if the other passengers tacitly approved of this lewd public display.

Violetta caught a glimpse of the woman's fingers rubbing furtively at her crotch and turned to stare out of the window, horrified. Once more she felt the tell-tale fluid seeping between her own legs and struggled to keep command of herself. There was no need for her to react in such a knee-jerk manner to the young couple's sexual activity. She was not an animal, lost to instinct and genetic necessity. She was an intelligent woman and all her physical reactions were controllable by the mind.

When she looked back, the man in the dark glasses was smiling again and Violetta knew that she had failed some unspoken test. Illogical though it was, that knowledge made her angry and she rose disdainfully to her feet, heading along the narrow aisle towards the toilet cubicle outside the carriage. As she passed the man in the dark glasses, her head held high, he too rose and followed close behind her until they had both left the carriage.

It was darker in the swaying passageway between compartments. Violetta fumbled for the toilet door and felt the man in the dark glasses lean past her to turn the handle.

'*Après vous, mademoiselle*,' he said softly, his eyes on her face.

'*Merci.*'

But as she tried to close the door, he stepped neatly inside as well. Taken by surprise, Violetta stopped and stared round at him. 'What do you think you're doing?' she demanded in English.

The man locked the toilet door behind them and gave her an assured smile, not bothering to remove his dark glasses. Close up, she could see that he was indeed an extremely attractive man but one she would never wish to anger. The broad shoulders and lithe body spoke of a strict physical regime and the cut of his suit might be casual but it was undoubtedly expensive. So this was a man of means who believed in the ethics of self-discipline, she thought, and there was a certain inflexibility to his smile that warned Violetta not to cross him unless she wanted to live dangerously. The dying strip lighting above their heads flickered on and off, lending a sinister touch to her reflection in the dark glasses which watched her so closely.

He stepped closer in the confined space and lifted one hand to stroke a few loose strands of red hair away from her face, an oddly intimate gesture which made her shiver with anticipation.

'Beautiful,' he murmured in English, his accent attractively husky. 'A little naive for my tastes, perhaps, but otherwise exquisite.'

She stared up at him, swallowing hard. 'What do you want?'

'Precisely what you think I want.'

'I'll scream . . .'

'I don't think so, *mademoiselle*.'

Still smiling implacably, the man in dark glasses lifted Violetta without any sign of effort and rested her bottom against the cold metal of the sink basin, reaching down to yank at the hem of her short skirt. She gasped as it slid easily upwards, revealing her long bare thighs and the tiny patch of material covering her sex. Her cheeks burnt with shame at his laughter, only too aware that her excitement showed in the tiny beads of fluid caught on the lace thong. He parted her legs, tearing the fragile material as he did so, and stepped between them in one movement.

He unzipped his trousers and pulled out an enormous penis, its red head swollen and already lubricated by a dribble of pre-come. This he rubbed between her exposed cunt lips, appearing to enjoy the way she squirmed with embarrassment at her own weakness. It was an horrific admission that she did not know this man's name, yet the former convent girl was not even struggling as he held her lightly poised against the metal sink, legs spread wide for his scrutiny. She did not want to consider how low she had stooped, having sex with a stranger in the toilet cubicle of a train.

His smile was dry. 'I can't hear you screaming.'

'You bastard!'

But if she had expected her insult to anger him, she had been mistaken. His smile merely broadened and the man in dark glasses leant forward, shoving his penis up inside her without further preamble. Violetta grunted at the unexpectedly sudden entry but knew she was easily wet enough to take him, juices soon running down her inner thighs and soaking the thin material of her skirt. There was no longer any pretence that she did not want him. Her head fell back as he began to thrust himself into her, hands scrabbling at the sink surround for a more secure position, her buttocks slithering dangerously on the cool metal sink at each rattling bend of the train. She hated herself for submitting to his callous treatment but at the same time something inside her thrilled at being held and forced with such disdain. It was almost as if this was what she had wanted as soon as their eyes met: no preliminaries, just this brutal wordless penetration at which the stranger seemed to excel.

Not wanting to look up into the blankness of those dark glasses, she tried to keep control by staring over his shoulder at the grey metallic wall instead. But soon enough Violetta wished that she was wearing dark glasses too, to lend her a much-needed sense of anonymity. It was bad enough to be accepting sex from a stranger but when she could not even see the expression in his eyes, it made her feel even more vulnerable. Yet that potential for danger only served to increase Violetta's excitement. Her eyes began to close and, much to her shame, she heard herself beginning to pant as his thrusts increased, her fingers clawing at his shoulders in the expensive suit as if to urge him on. The stranger responded without speaking. His hands tightened their iron grip on her legs, holding her just behind the knees and forcing her legs up and apart so that he could penetrate her more deeply.

The train's loudspeaker system crackled into life above their heads, its distant foreign instructions lost as the stranger repeatedly shoved himself up to the hilt inside her and Violetta found herself crying out, her face flushed with the frenzy of an impending orgasm. The stranger replied with a deep guttural grunt, his whole body straining as he pumped himself rhythmically in and out between her legs. Then the thick meat of his penis seemed to swell even larger inside her, stretching her fleshy walls until it was almost painful for her to take his full length. The veins were standing out on his tanned forehead as he too cried out, suddenly thrusting as far as he could go into her slick channel and holding himself there for one long agonised groan.

Violetta held the stranger close, squeezing her sweat-dampened thighs around him in an effort to keep the momentum going. She was still eager to feel him begin to thrust again, and it was only when he abruptly withdrew, releasing her legs and tidying his rumpled suit, that she realised the man in dark glasses must have ejaculated inside her. Furious that he had finished before she had reached her orgasm, her entire body trembling as it came slowly back from the brink of ecstasy, Violetta stared up at the man in disbelief.

'But you can't stop. I haven't come yet.'

'Did you not hear the announcement, *mademoiselle*?' The man seemed totally oblivious to her feelings, waving her aside so he could wash his hands in the basin. 'The train is about to arrive in Nice.'

Drying his hands meticulously on a white cotton handkerchief which he then replaced in his pocket, the stranger looked down at her with a sardonic expression. His hands were well-groomed, she noticed, each fingernail perfectly clean and polished. In spite of his muscular arms and shoulders, he was clearly no labourer, this expensively dressed Frenchman. Even though she was still angry with him for finishing before she was ready, her curiosity had been aroused and she could not stop staring at him. Much to her frustration, however, those dark glasses still concealed the man's eyes from her.

'Surely you did not expect me to continue fucking you once the train was standing in the station?'

Before she could reply, the tannoy crackled again and this time Violetta could feel the train beginning to slow considerably. The brakes were being applied as they approached the station and now she could make out a few familiar words from the hiss and crackle of the speakers. Grudgingly, she accepted that he was probably right. The high-speed train must be coming into the station at Nice and soon it would be impossible to make an exit from the toilet cubicle without arousing suspicion. He might not have any sexual manners, she thought, but at least he showed a necessary grasp of discretion.

Immaculate and composed, the man in dark glasses inclined his head slightly before opening the toilet door to leave.

'Thank you for an entertaining fuck, *mademoiselle*. I knew that such an inviting mouth would not disappoint me.'

Gasping at his infernal cheek, Violetta only refrained from raising her voice in an angry reply when she saw the corridor outside the toilet cubicle was already crowded with passengers for disembarkation. He clicked the door shut behind him and she leapt forwards, hurriedly snapping the lock back into place before anyone else could come in and find her half-dressed.

She really did not have time for anything but to have a quick wee and then tidy herself up, but she simply could not resist bringing herself to orgasm. The stranger's fast and brutal penetration had aroused her beyond the point of endurance and she would die of frustration if she did not quickly finish what he had started. Slipping a hand between her warm semen-soaked thighs, she rubbed her erect clitoris with tiny circular movements, closing her eyes as the sensations began to build again. It did not matter that about twenty people were pressed together in the corridor outside the toilet cubicle. There were no prying eyes in here to witness her secret act of masturbation.

Aching for release, she pushed her index finger deep inside herself and revelled in the sensation of fullness as it was swallowed up by those heavy inner lips. Although Violetta had been to bed with several lovers since leaving convent school, she was still pretty tight down there and proud of the fact. Moaning silently as her warm fragrant juices began to flow again, Violetta pushed her thumb inside as well. She could smell the stranger's semen on her fingers and lifted them to her lips, wishing he was still pulsing inside her. As her tongue lapped at her spunk-covered fingertips, the sensations in her cunt began to intensify and she knew that she was nearly ready to come. What she really wanted was that thick purple-headed penis which had stretched her muscular walls so completely and driven deep towards the neck of her womb as he came. But in its absence her own fingers would have to suffice. Violetta closed her eyes. In her imagination, she was lying on a grassy bank and the man was kneeling above her, pushing her legs wide open as he penetrated her fully. His penis thrust in and out slowly and smoothly, never hurrying, taking her gradually to greater and greater heights of pleasure.

Eventually, his imaginary fingers moved down to stroke her tense clitoris and Violetta gasped as the flush deepened in her cheeks and she began to reach orgasm, her whole body twisting in agonised pleasure.

After her high-pitched cries had finally died away and her legs had stopped shaking, Violetta realised that the train had come to a halt. There was an odd silence outside the door and when she had rearranged her clothes, splashed her face with cold water and slid discreetly out of the cubicle, she found the train deserted and the platform empty. All the other passengers must have disembarked while she was bringing herself to an intense climax. What must they have heard from her cubicle, though? She could hardly look the guard in the eye as he helped her climb down out of the compartment with her suitcase, her cheeks hot with shame as she realised how wantonly she had behaved – and with a complete stranger!

Much to her relief, though Violetta glanced about for him more than once as she picked her way through the busy sunlit station to the waiting taxi rank, the man in dark glasses was nowhere to be seen.

The chateau itself was far more imposing than she had anticipated from the bare invitation card, an isolated building hidden away in a dry hillside grove and surrounded by the funereal Mediterranean spikes of cypress and pine. Row after row of shuttered windows declared that people were at rest, and her arrival at such a moment was nothing short of an embarrassing intrusion. The whole place looked highly exclusive and far beyond what she would normally have been able to afford. She should have been ecstatic, looking forward to two weeks of sunshine and pampering, absolutely free, but as the taxi pulled away in a swirl of dust and

11

disappeared back towards the main road to Nice, Violetta listened to the sound of cicadas singing invisibly in the thick afternoon heat and felt her throat tighten with unexpected apprehension. The gravelled drive outside the chateau was empty of cars and there was no sound from behind those forbidding shutters.

Thrown off balance by the unexpected silence, Violetta put her suitcase down on the gravel and stood nervously beside it, biting her lip. This was not how she had imagined the first day of her summer holiday. Perhaps there had been some mistake with her invitation. Nobody had come out to greet her, after all. This could be the wrong place. And even if there had not been any mistake, what if nobody at this chateau spoke English? Her command of the French language was extremely limited and it would be a pretty hellish two weeks if she could not understand her hosts and they could not understand her, free holiday or not.

Just as she was beginning to consider the long walk back towards Nice, there was a loud clattering above her and one of the shutters on the first floor was thrown open. A busty young brunette with a cheeky grin gave her a cheerful wave out of the window, calling down to her in perfect English.

'Hello! You must be Violetta. I'm sorry I wasn't downstairs to greet you when you arrived, but I had a sudden call of nature.' She giggled. 'You must be bursting yourself, actually. It's quite a long drive from the station. Why don't you come in and freshen up?'

'Thanks. And what's your name?'

The brunette smiled down at her. 'Mandy. I'm the receptionist.'

'But you're English.'

'I love working abroad. It's always a challenge, it can really stretch you. Last summer I was out in Germany, helping to run a guest house.' The receptionist giggled again, a slight flush in her cheeks as she leant dangerously far out of the window. Violetta could see that the other girl was wearing too much eye make-up and that her low-cut blouse made no pretence of covering her cleavage. But she seemed friendly enough. 'Remind me to tell you about that before you leave. Some of those young German lads . . .'

'Careful!'

Mandy stopped herself in time as she nearly overbalanced, laughing and hanging breathlessly onto the shutter. 'Oops, silly me! I had a few glasses of wine at lunch and it's made me all woozy. Look, I'll come straight down so we can talk properly. The main door's open, just give it a shove. You'll find a little washroom on your right behind the stairs.'

It was cool and dark inside the chateau. Violetta's heels echoed on the red and gold tiles of the entrance hall as she pushed the door open, left her suitcase at the foot of the stairs and hurried towards the narrow door of the washroom. Mandy had been right. She was absolutely bursting for the toilet and it was such a relief to let go at last, staring around at the small dim washroom with its vase of musky scented flowers on the windowsill and old yellowish shutters keeping out the light. Their toilet paper was the cheap stuff that came in flat sheet packs rather than rolls – rough to the touch and not particularly absorbent – and she guessed the chateau's drain system must be too old-fashioned to handle the softer modern variety. When she stood up afterwards, Violetta used the cheap paper to wipe away traces of that stranger's semen from her swollen outer lips and the tops of her thighs. It was intended to be an act of contrition, harsh and self-condemnatory. But there was a terrible secret pleasure in touching herself there again, and Violetta reddened at the memory of what she had done on the train, pressing and rubbing the rough toilet paper between her legs until she was sore.

She had to learn to control her sexuality before it landed her in trouble. That much was clear from the way she had just allowed a complete stranger to enjoy her body. But why on earth had she behaved so out of character? Perhaps she had been affected by the heat or the intoxicating Mediterranean sunlight flashing through the train windows, or perhaps it was the excitement of foreign travel after too many summers spent in the English rain. There were many possible explanations for her behaviour but none that made any real sense to her. Violetta had always prided herself on an iron self-restraint when it came to sexual activity. To lose her head like that, to hand herself over to a stranger, could only mean that her control was slipping. The man in the dark glasses must have been some sort of magician, she thought ruefully, to seduce her so thoroughly without even a struggle.

Mandy was waiting for her in the magnificent entrance hall when she emerged from the washroom. The pretty young receptionist, dressed smartly in her white blouse, short black skirt and neat heels, led Violetta to a small shady office at the back of the chateau. The heat in there was claustrophobic and the other girl puffed her cheeks out exaggeratedly, flicking the switch on an electric fan to allow air to circulate. Violetta settled down in one of the comfortable office chairs and glanced around herself curiously. Compared to the rest of the ancient chateau, the office seemed oddly modern: state-of-the-art computers, fax machines, a photocopier and one large display board with graphs, computer read-outs and various memos pinned across it. Mandy rifled through a metal filing cabinet, finally producing a stapled document which she put down in front of Violetta.

'That's a translation of the holiday contract you need to sign before we can book you in. We keep one copy, you hold onto the other. It contains everything you need to know for your stay here – all the usual boring rules and regulations, conditions of insurance, consent forms, and so on. Just sign your name on the back page and I'll show you up to your room.'

Violetta frowned, weighing the thick document in her hand. 'Could I read it and let you have it back later?'

'Of course, if you think that's necessary. But I can't let you look around the chateau or have your key until it's been signed.' The receptionist shrugged apologetically. 'Rule of the house, I'm afraid.'

Crestfallen, Violetta glanced through the many-paged document. She disliked putting her name to anything without having checked it properly beforehand. But the chateau office was stifling and she was dying to step out of these creased travelling clothes and relax under a cool shower at last.

'Most of this looks fairly straightforward, but why do I need to sign a consent form?'

'It's standard policy for our guests,' Mandy explained, perching beside her on the desk to look down at the document. As she crossed her legs, making herself more comfortable, the short black skirt slid up to reveal white thighs. 'Some of the chateau activities can become a little . . . physically demanding. So we prefer you to give consent for your limits to be challenged.'

'Challenged?'

'Do you know your own limits, Violetta?'

'Yes.'

The receptionist smiled. 'Honestly?'

Violetta remembered the man on the train, his arrogant hands tearing her lace thong before he entered her, and shook her head.

'I didn't think so,' Mandy murmured, watching her confusion with a sympathetic smile. 'None of our guests really understand their limits when they first arrive. That's why it's such a pleasure to work here. It's so amazing to see the alteration in people after just one or two weeks at the chateau. Especially the women.'

15

'The women?'

The receptionist laid a gentle hand on Violetta's thigh. 'There's nothing better than a man when you're in the right mood, but there are moments when what you really need is something gentler, less demanding. Don't you agree?'

'I've never exactly . . . not with a woman . . .' Violetta found herself blushing hotly and looked away, extremely aware of the other girl's hand burning into the pale skin of her thigh. She was beginning to feel a little out of her depth in this strange, intimidating chateau. Her tone was flustered. 'But you don't have to explain. I can guess what you mean.'

Mandy stared at her incredulously. 'You've never had sex with a woman? But didn't you go to a convent school?'

'How on earth did you know that?'

'Oh, I don't know.' The receptionist waved her hand vaguely towards the filing cabinet, not meeting her eyes. 'Maybe I saw it in your file or somebody mentioned it to me. No, actually, I was only guessing. I don't want to be rude but you look like a convent school girl. You know, like butter wouldn't melt in your mouth.'

'I'm not that innocent!'

'Aren't you? I'm glad to hear it. Innocence can be so . . . frustrating.' Mandy's voice dropped to a soft thoughtful purr. The hand on Violetta's thigh slid even higher, moving beneath the thin material of her skirt. The warm chestnut-coloured eyes slipped restlessly over Violetta's high full breasts and the shadowy gap between her thighs as they parted slightly under the pressure of her fingers. The chateau receptionist began to breathe quickly and unevenly, as though she were becoming sexually excited. 'But perhaps I'm being unfair to you, Violetta. When did you last do something naughty, then?'

Violetta knew she ought to stop the other English girl touching her so intimately. But the afternoon was so hot and her limbs felt achingly heavy as she allowed those searching fingers to move higher beneath her skirt. There was no harm in it, after all. She had certainly heard stories about how the convent school girls had touched each other after lights out, but Violetta herself had never gone further than the odd kiss and cuddle with her best friends, though she had often longed to but was too embarrassed to suggest it. It was odd to see another woman's hands stroking her thighs now, but she was curious to know how it would feel to have them brush against her love lips or maybe even tease her eager clitoris. She sighed and let her thighs fall wider apart under the short skirt, unaware of how provocative she looked.

It was not long before Violetta relaxed even further and let her mind drift away from respectable thoughts. Prompted once again to confess her most recent naughtiness, the memories of her sexual encounter on the train came tumbling back through her mind and, flushed and stammering, she told Mandy how she had accepted a stranger's spunk deep inside her belly and never even asked his name. As Violetta described the pulsating head of his penis and how the man in dark glasses had entered her so brutally, without conversation or foreplay, the other girl fingered her sex until those tormented inner lips were soaking wet and crying out to be penetrated.

'You enjoyed his brutality?'

'Yes.'

'Even the sordid nature of what you did? Used by a total stranger, in a public toilet on a train?'

Violetta nodded, embarrassed to admit the depths of her own depravity but somehow glad that she had done so at last. 'Do you think that's wrong? To have enjoyed it so much?'

'Nothing is wrong so long as it gives you pleasure and upsets nobody. So, it gave you pleasure, the way this stranger fucked you?' Those clever fingers continued to stroke along the slippery edge of her lips, making Violetta want to scream with frustration. 'Did you wish he had gone even further?'

'Further?'

'Slapped you, beaten you, hurt you?'

Violetta was shocked, staring up at the other girl with astonished eyes. 'Of course not. Why would I enjoy that sort of violence?'

'You have no experience of pleasurable pain?'

'I don't even understand what you mean by that. Though it sounds like a contradiction in terms,' Violetta murmured, looking away. She did not want the receptionist to stop touching her, though she was a little worried in case this situation flared out of her control and she found herself in dangerous new territory. Although Mandy seemed harmless enough, after that incident on the train she had to be careful not to give herself so entirely to another person. But the other girl's fingers began to move deeper, stroking just inside her fleshy channel and making her groan under her breath, her whole body alive with the need to be filled. Violetta ached with that need. The heated flush on her cheeks was spreading to her throat and breasts. It was becoming impossible to think straight, though she kept trying.

'Isn't pain just . . . well, painful?'

Mandy smiled indulgently down at her as if she were a child who had just said something terribly amusing. Then she leant forward and pinched her love lips twice, rather hard, watching the way Violetta's body jerked in helpless reaction and strained upwards, eager for more.

'I'm sorry. Did that hurt?' she asked solicitously,

'Yes . . . no . . . I don't know.'

The other girl gurgled with laughter at her confusion. 'Now do you see what I mean? It can be hard to know where pain ends and pleasure begins. That's why you need to sign the consent form, Violetta. Because sometimes people mistakenly refuse what their bodies need for the greatest pleasure. Do you understand what I'm saying?'

Those fingers tortured her exquisitely. 'Yes, I think so.'

Mandy gave her the ball point pen again and folded back the papers to the correct page. 'Sign there, then, at the bottom of the page.'

'Right now?'

'Yes. Then I can take you up to your bedroom and you can . . . freshen up . . . after your long journey.'

Freshen up? Violetta stared down at the page, pen poised in her hand as she skimmed briefly through the small print. *Guests need to give their full consent to all chateau procedures, regardless of* . . . Images of lying on a clean white sheet, her fingers between her legs as she masturbated to a satisfying climax, spun dizzily through her mind. *Any breach of contract shall result in immediate punishment* . . . Mandy's lips were on the back of her neck, flicking across the warm salty skin as her fingers continued to work between her damp thighs, and it was becoming increasingly difficult to concentrate on the printed word. *All such punishments to be administered by the chateau owner or his staff as he sees fit and notwithstanding* . . .

Her palms sweating with excitement, Violetta could no longer focus on the chateau contract. Without bothering to finish reading its long-winded translation, she signed her name with a flourish at the bottom of the final page and handed the document back to the receptionist. Only then did she allow her legs to fall open for better access, and she let out a long satisfied gasp of pleasure as one, two, three of the receptionist's fingers pushed past those swollen lips to stretch her soaking hole. That was precisely what she had needed, Violetta thought, suspecting that Mandy must be psychic. She closed her eyes, arched sensuously back in her chair and wondered why she had never let another woman touch her like this before.

For the next few moments the two girls seemed locked together on a river of shimmering light. It was as though somebody had thrown open all the shutters in the chateau so that wave after wave of heavy golden sunlight had come flooding over both of them. Mandy's murmured words of appreciation barely reached Violetta, she was so lost in the warm liquid sensations between her thighs. Her juices were flowing so strongly, she thought dreamily, they must be absolutely soaking the other girl's hand and wrist. That image electrified her. Pushing beneath her top, Violetta found her own nipples and toyed with their taut peaks, her mouth opening in an ecstatic moan. Her climax was not far away, but she was in no hurry this time. There was no train coming into the station here, no curious passengers crowding outside the door, no brutal stranger finishing before she was ready. She could hold back and wait and let those sensations well up inside her until her entire body was bursting like a dam, longing for that great wave to crash down over her breasts and plunge deep into the hot maelstrom of her belly.

An amused cough broke her concentration and brought her slamming back down to earth. 'I hope I'm not interrupting anything?'

Somebody had come silently into the room while they were entranced and caught them on the verge of orgasm. The receptionist leapt away from her side as though she had burnt her fingers, hurriedly retreating behind her desk. Red-faced and embarrassed, Violetta dragged down the hem of her skirt and covered her breasts with a shaking hand before turning to look at the intruder, her eyes darkening in shock at what she saw. It had been the voice of a man behind them in the shadowy office, but what she actually saw when she turned was the head of an adult stag, strong male antlers towering above a man's body, lithe and muscular in tight black jeans and T-shirt. She stood up, knocking over her chair and backing away in immediate fear.

Angry and disorientated, Violetta suddenly realised it was a man wearing a mask, complete with fur and antlers, fastened at his throat with a strong leather strap. This was no supernatural being but a trickster, a practical joker who was watching her reaction with every sign of amusement. She could even see the man's eyes glittering through slits in his mask, and then heard his soft laughter as he examined her dishevelled appearance from head to foot.

'You must be Violetta. I apologise for disturbing your ... erm ... rest. But I have some very important documents to collect,' the man said smoothly, coming further into the office and closing the door.

'How do you know my name?' She stared at the man in an accusing manner. 'And don't you ever knock before coming into a room?'

'*Jamais, mademoiselle,*' he replied impassively. 'Not when the room belongs to me, no.'

Mandy had bent to rearrange the papers on her desk but she looked up at their brief exchange, a high colour in her cheeks. 'Violetta,' she said with strained politeness, no longer meeting her eyes. 'This is the owner of the chateau. He will be organising your holiday activities over the next two weeks. Guests are requested to address him simply as "Stag".'

'Stag?' Violetta echoed in disbelief.

The chateau owner walked to the desk and searched rapidly through a pile of loose papers. Sinking back into her seat, she examined his hands and wrists from under lowered lashes, noting the tough line of his bones and sinews. The skin on the back of his hands was a weathered golden brown, presumably the result of many summers spent outdoors in the sun. But he was not old. Somewhere in his late thirties and still extremely fit, to judge by the way his body moved under those black jeans. Once he had found the documents he had come for, the man tucked them under his arm and leant against the side of the desk, watching her. The antlered head tilted to one side as though he were examining some unusual specimen. Now that she could see them more clearly, Violetta thought his antlers looked threatening, almost sinister. She could not help shrinking away and was humiliated to hear, only slightly muffled by the mask, the sound of the man's laughter. Embarrassed at the thought of what he must have witnessed when the door opened, Violetta crossed her legs tightly and saw his gaze slide down their length with sudden intensity.

'The stag is my animal of choice, the mask I have chosen to wear. Did my appearance frighten you, *mademoiselle*?' His accent was strongly French, almost exaggeratedly so, though his command of English seemed impeccable. 'That was not my intention, I assure you.'

'Then why wear a mask?'

'It is the custom at this chateau for all guests and staff to adopt the mask of an animal or bird. We have found it useful for preserving identity and releasing inhibitions.'

'Perhaps I like my inhibitions.'

He shrugged. 'But you are on holiday here, *mademoiselle*. Why would you need any inhibitions? You are free to indulge yourself during your stay. Nobody will comment on your tastes or desires.'

Violetta glanced towards Mandy for a reassuring nod or smile, but the pretty receptionist had turned away and was replacing her signed contract in the filing cabinet. It was clear there would be no support from that area. She cleared her throat, trying to shake off her embarrassment at having been caught with another woman's fingers between her legs. This enigmatic Frenchman must have seen what they were doing when he walked into the room. There was the sound of a smile behind every word he said and, in spite of that obscuring mask, Violetta felt sure the chateau owner was secretly laughing at her.

'So what sort of mask would I have to wear?'

'That depends entirely on you. Each guest or member of staff is given the mask which seems most appropriate for their character. But that is not important at this stage. First you must earn the right to wear a mask.'

'Earn it?'

She could see the dark eyes glittering sardonically at her through the eye slits of his own mask. 'Everyone here works hard for their mask, as I'm sure our lovely receptionist here will confirm. The journey to enlightenment contains many pitfalls and punishments. But once you have earned the right to wear a mask, it will be presented to you.'

'I'm not sure I like the sound of being punished,' she said doubtfully. 'What sort of punishments do you normally give out?'

'Again, that depends on the misdemeanour.'

She shrugged. 'OK, let's say I do something mildly wrong. I spill some red wine on your carpet or break a glass at dinner. What might I expect as a punishment?'

'You might be made to perform some task around the chateau. Some simple cleaning or cooking, for example.' He paused, watching her face. 'Or you might be spanked, *mademoiselle*.'

She coloured at the thought of being spanked, but Violetta merely nodded, turning to watch Mandy as the receptionist threw open the shutters and flooded the office with sunlight. She did not want to appear inexperienced in front of the chateau owner. She had been spanked a few times in the past, lightly on her bottom, but only in jest. Somehow, she had the impression that this masked Frenchman did nothing 'in jest'.

'I expect that I could handle a few whacks. But what if I did something worse?' She looked across at the receptionist and was rewarded with a bright smile. 'Do the physical punishments stop at spanking?'

'Not always.'

She stared at the other girl for a moment. 'What else, then?'

'You might be caned.'

'By whom?'

Mandy bit her lip and glanced nervously across at the chateau owner, as though unsure how to answer that last question. The room fell oddly silent for a few moments. Could she take the cane without flinching? Violetta doubted it, though they must think she was much more experienced than she really was, otherwise they would never have suggested it. But her mouth was dry, hands clasped tightly in her lap as she remembered what she and Mandy had been doing when the owner walked in. No wonder his eyes kept moving over her body with such languorous heat. She had only arrived at the chateau less than an hour ago and already she was behaving like a slut. What on earth must he think of her? Then the man in the antlered mask stirred, walking towards the open shutters and closing them again. The small office darkened as the shutters folded back in on themselves and he moved back into the centre of the room, shadows swaying across the walls.

'I would normally administer the cane myself, *ma belle*,' he said softly. 'If the crime was serious enough to merit my attention.'

There was a lengthy silence while Violetta digested that information. She had heard in the past that a caning was extremely painful, and had even received the odd stroke at her convent school from some of the older, more zealous nuns, but it would be quite a different thing to take a caning from this man. Unable to stop herself, Violetta glanced down at his hands and then wished she had not done so. They frightened her. Large, strong and with long, elegantly tanned fingers, those were the hands of a man who could do severe damage with a cane. They reminded her of the stranger on the train, the man in dark glasses, whose hands had pushed her legs so forcibly apart before he entered her. To her eternal shame, she felt her nipples begin to stiffen and turned away before the chateau owner could see her reaction. The last thing Violetta wanted was for this Frenchman to suspect that she found the idea of being caned sexually arousing.

'I'd better not misbehave, then,' she said lightly.

Two

For the third time, the scented bar of soap slipped through Mandy's fingers and disappeared under the white bubbles of the bath water. Sighing, the young and slightly flushed receptionist scrabbled to retrieve it but it was no use. The blasted thing must have slithered further down between her legs and out of reach. After another few moments of searching, she gave up the hunt and stretched out in the hot bath water, closing her tired blue eyes. It did not matter, anyway. Her body was clean enough. Nothing had happened today to make her dirty, after all. Not since her naughty little game with that new girl, Violetta, had been so rudely interrupted by Stag. He had taken Violetta away before Mandy had managed to discover and explore the pale English beauty only slightly concealed beneath those provocative clothes. But that was his prerogative as the boss at the chateau, she considered with an air of resignation, and it would be stupid to argue with a man like that. Stupid and potentially dangerous, as his receptionist knew only too well.

Mandy wondered for a moment whether Stag would break this new girl in himself. She was certainly beautiful enough. It rarely happened, but there had been odd whispers ever since her name had been shortlisted and Mandy suspected that Stag had some hidden agenda in inviting Violetta to the chateau. After all, it would not be the first time he had done the honours for a new girl himself, she thought wryly.

When she herself first came to the chateau, Stag had allowed his former personal assistant Sophie to undress and spank her for the first time, but the greater delight of introducing Mandy to the special chateau regime had been reserved for himself. It was rumoured that he preferred English girls to all other nationalities. Mandy was not sure why that should be, but Stag had often commented on the interesting whiteness of her buttocks and breasts. She suspected it increased his pleasure to see such pale skin tormented into bright red weals under the cane. The marks did not show quite so well on the firm tanned buttocks of those continental girls who tended to frequent the chateau during the summer months.

She had been at the chateau for three years now, and during that time she had seen many young women saunter through those doors at the beginning of their holidays, arrogant and self-assured, only to walk out with a humbler step once Stag had finished with them. He was a master of the art and the girls who came here never forgot their training.

Mandy herself would never be able to erase that first incredible day from her memory. She had already considered herself quite submissive when she answered his advertisement for a receptionist, but Stag had taught her in a few brutal hours to what depths a submissive must sink in pursuit of perfect compliance. She still fell short of the required standard, she knew that, always hitting some internal barrier which prevented her from reaching perfection. But there were days when she triumphantly pleased both herself and her masters, revelling in their humiliating games and choosing the pleasure of debasement whenever it was offered to her, and she knew to whom she owed those vital skills. Only a true master could provide such deep and lasting training in the art of submission, and it was Stag who had shown her how to achieve that level on her very first day.

On her arrival, he had taken her to the punishment room, situated in the former cellars of the chateau, a place where many applicants before Mandy had failed to reach his minimum standard of submissiveness. She had been wearing exactly what the advertisement had stipulated: a white blouse and short black skirt. She had chosen not to wear anything beneath them, however, a choice he had applauded with some amusement, his eyes dwelling on those prominent nipples showing through her thin silk blouse.

'So you are a slut by nature, *chérie*,' he had murmured, walking around her as though admiring a new purchase. 'Such qualities are always pleasing in a new applicant. But sluttishness is not the only necessity for this job. We are here today to ascertain if you are submissive enough to join us here at the chateau.'

'I think so, *monsieur*,' Mandy stuttered in bad French.

'You are not required to think,' he countered sharply. 'Thought is an impertinence in a submissive. You will merely obey orders.'

'Yes, *monsieur*.'

'And you will address me as master.'

'Yes, master.'

Stag smiled, leaning closer. 'That is better, *chérie*. Much better indeed. Perhaps you may be allowed to remain here after all, assuming you are able to pass our initiation tests.'

Mandy shivered as his finger trailed across her cheek. 'I am eager to try, master,' she whispered.

Stag smiled at her unquestioning compliance, turning to produce a shapeless black piece of material from an adjacent table. She was puzzled until he held it up and she suddenly realised what it was: an eyeless hood with a drawstring neck fastening.

He continued to smile as he approached her again, watching her expression turn from bewilderment to fear. 'Come now, do not shake your head. The hood is a vital part of your training, *chérie*. In time you will learn to appreciate its subtle effect, trust me.'

'I'm scared . . .'

He hesitated, lifting the hood above her head. 'You refuse it?'

Mandy swallowed, recognising the warning note in his voice and fearing what it might mean. She badly wanted to join the staff at the chateau and learn more about her own submissive nature. This was merely the first test of many, she reminded herself sternly, and it would be counterproductive to back out at such an early stage. She had known what to expect when she replied to his advertisement, so she could hardly refuse to accept his terms now. So the pink-cheeked English girl lifted her head and looked up at her tormenter with as much courage as she could summon.

'No, please. I do want to wear the hood.'

'Good,' he muttered, and slid the hood down over her face. The black material was rough against her skin and Mandy felt an age-old panic rise inside her as the drawstring began to tighten. But the hood was not as tight as she had feared, merely closing around her throat to prevent it from falling off as she moved. No light was able to filter through the thick material, however, except for the odd flicker as she turned her head from side to side, searching for something familiar in the darkness.

His laughter was soft as Mandy struggled to control her panic, choking a little as the hood pressed against her lipsticked mouth.

'Keep still. There is no restraint.'

'I can't breathe . . .'

'Don't be so melodramatic. It is all in your mind. You must try and relax or the hood will soon become your master. You have much to learn, *chérie*, if you think I would harm you in any way.'

'Please . . .'

'You want me to remove it?'

She felt his hand grasping the thick hood, poised to lift it away from her face, and suddenly realised what she risked losing here.

'No. I'm sorry, master. I was panicking.'

'That's better. Now take my hand and follow me. Take care not to fall.' When she did as he ordered, Stag led her slowly across the punishment room and pushed her forward across something long and hard. 'Lean over this table and support yourself on your hands so that I can examine you more fully. Hurry now, I have other girls to see.'

Mandy could still remember her fear as she heard rather than saw the man walk around her, his feet echoing against the cold stone floor. As he stopped beside her motionless body at one point, she felt his hands cup her bare breasts through the thin silk blouse, lifting and weighing them experimentally. Her nipples stiffened instinctively at his touch and there was a corresponding rush of liquid warmth between her thighs. As if sensing that hidden reaction, his murmured praise brought heat to her cheeks, then he continued to move unhurriedly around her body. In the stifling darkness of the hood, Mandy felt as though she were being stalked by a powerful and relentless predator. The thought nearly made her panic again and she fought to keep control of her fear. But when he paused again, this time standing directly behind her, she could not prevent a tiny gasp of surprise as his hands lifted her short skirt and she felt cool air across her thighs.

'Relax, *chérie*. This is all completely routine.'

Lying in her bath now, Mandy recalled how his hands had first caressed her exposed bottom and then slipped between those parted legs to check her level of arousal

Once again she felt that initial excitement rising inside and settled back in the bubbles to enjoy her moment of nostalgia. Turning the whole world white, steam misted the mirrored walls of the bathroom as her fingers moved secretly below the water to touch herself. As usual when she remembered the day of her interview at the chateau, it did not take long for her to become fully aroused. That first session in the punishment room had proved such a special occasion for her.

Stag had spanked her naked bottom gently, warming her unaccustomed cheeks with his large hands so that she found his restraint almost frustrating and began to long for a more stringent contact. Stag, reading her physical responses accurately, had laughed and then abandoned her for a moment. When he came back to her side, it was with something hard and sharp in his hands which whooshed through the air a few times before biting down once into the tender skin of her bottom, making her cry aloud in agony and clutch at the table beneath her.

'Did that hurt?' he had asked solicitously.

'Yes, master,' Mandy managed to gasp, still writhing from that fierce single blow.

'Don't upset yourself too much, *chérie*. Since this is only an interview, you will receive no more than three strokes this time.'

'Three?' Her voice was high with pain and disbelief. 'But I don't think I can take another like that.'

'You dislike the cane? How unfortunate.'

Much to her astonishment, his hands abruptly released the black hood without bothering to administer any further punishment. The rough material scratched her face and neck as it was pulled away. Mandy stared around herself in the empty punishment room, blinking at the sudden light as her tormentor stepped away from the table, a long thin piece of wood flexed like a curved bow in his hands. When he gestured to the door at the far end of the room, her disappointment became real and palpable. She had prepared her mind and body for many weeks before coming to the chateau and this was not how she had expected her interview to end.

Her failure seemed final and non-negotiable. Stag gave her a polite smile as Mandy straightened up, rubbing her sore bottom, but he had obviously lost interest in her as a candidate.

'Thank you for your co-operation but I'm afraid you are not suitable for this position, *chérie*. You will find the stairs to your left outside that door. Please send in the next applicant as you leave.'

'I don't understand.'

'The cane is a necessary instrument of training and correction. If you are unable to learn to enjoy its administration, however painful, then you will be of no use to us here at the chateau.'

Mandy stared up at him, aghast. It was as she had suspected. The interview had been going so well and now she had blown it with her pathetic cowardice. Her dream of living at the chateau and learning to develop her submissive side was in danger of being ruined by this one obstacle. At all costs, she had to persuade this man that she was the right woman for the job.

'Please, master. Let me try the cane again.'

Brooding, the dark antlers dipped as he tilted his head to consider her plea. 'There is no point, *chérie*. I do not wish to waste any more time on someone so wholly unsuited to our regime.'

'I won't let you down again,' she whispered. 'Just give me one more chance to prove myself.'

Now, in the warmth of the bath, Mandy feverishly rubbed her clitoris as she remembered how Stag had bent her forwards over the table again with a rough hand, administering the last two strokes of the cane without any warning. She recalled the terrible whistling sound as the cane descended and then that explosion of pain which began in her buttocks and radiated instantly to every corner of her body, jerking her limbs as though she had suffered an electric shock. This time she wisely made no sound except to groan slightly as he moved away, her buttocks stinging and still trembling with the aftershock when her tormentor finally allowed Mandy to rise and drag down her short skirt to cover herself.

Stag had seemed more pleased with her reaction second time around, and – after moistly fingering her sex for a few delicious moments after the caning – had sent her to await his verdict outside. He had then seen five other candidates before eventually offering Mandy the job of chateau receptionist, though she suspected that Stag had made his choice earlier in the day and had merely been amusing himself with those other girls. But his heartless arrogance had excited her on that occasion just as it still had the power to excite her today. In fact, her body was reeling with glorious sensory pleasure as her fingers sought out that bud of arousal between her legs, teasing it until she experienced wave after wave of breathtaking orgasms that left her body tensed for more and her face bright red.

Mandy was still groaning in the bath at the point of a final orgasm, legs drawn up to her chest, when she heard shouts and the door to the bathroom burst open. Shocked, the receptionist struggled to get out of the bath tub but it was too late. There were two masked men in her bathroom, yanking at her wrists and ankles as they lifted her out of the scented bubble bath, her nude body still dripping, and stretched her out on the damp tiled floor. Recognising their animal masks immediately, she relaxed into their forceful hands and even managed to enjoy the last throes of her orgasm, for she knew these two men would not seriously mark her skin unless she begged them to, which she was ashamed to admit she had often done in the past. It was only Horse and Jackal who had burst into her private bathroom, regulars at the chateau during the summer months and predictable enough in their sexual proclivities. Both of them were insatiable dominants, and one of their favourite games during the quiet siesta period was to abuse and torment poor Mandy until she could bear it no longer and rewarded them with a noisy but satisfying climax.

The two men bent over her slick naked body and taunted her ruthlessly, pinching her nipples with cruel fingers. 'Why are you in the bath again, Pig Girl? Have you done something dirty today? I hope you weren't touching yourself down there.'

'Please. I haven't been naughty. I swear it!'

Mandy sobbed like a little girl in their arms and begged them not to hurt her too badly, though without holding out much hope of a last-minute reprieve. The two masked men seemed in the mood to administer a beating this afternoon and it was unlikely that her tearful cries would be able to persuade them otherwise.

Horse stood above her threateningly, his hands on his hips in the tight blue denim jeans.

'You can't help being naughty, Pig Girl. It comes naturally to a dirty girl like you. Now stop making all that noise or I'll block up your mouth with soap. You're hurting my ears.'

'I'm sorry, master.'

'No lies now, Pig Girl.' Jackal dragged her soaking body to her knees, his fingers tight on her arm as he ignored her moans of discomfort and pulled her head level with his crotch. 'We hear a new girl arrived at the chateau today and you've already dipped your fingers in her honey pot. Is that true?'

Surprised, Mandy stared at the ugly bulge in his jeans, directly in a line with her mouth as she knelt before him.

'Yes, master,' she stammered.

There was an odd brief silence as the two men looked at each other over Mandy's head, then she heard Jackal give a low whistle behind his mask. Horse slapped her from behind and told her to stop lying, at which she breathlessly replied that she was telling the truth. The larger man stepped forward, brutally sandwiching her between their two pairs of legs, and repeated the other man's question as if she could not be trusted to tell the truth. But at the end, he added curiously, 'And did she taste good, this new girl?'

'Delicious,' she managed to say honestly before another slap silenced her, this time around the face. Reacting automatically, she dodged the next blow and was caught by Jackal's swift hand who ruthlessly held her in place while his friend continued the punishment until she was yelping with pain. Swaying there on the floor between them, still on her knees, Mandy stared up at the two masked men in bewilderment. Her face stung from their unusually heavy-handed blows.

'Did I do wrong to touch the new girl, masters?'

'We didn't expect you to do anything else. You're nothing but a filthy slut, Pig Girl,' Jackal said, leering down at her.

Horse came forward and pressed her face into his friend's crotch until she could hardly breathe. 'He's right, Pig Girl. You can always be relied upon to behave like a whore, can't you?'

'Yes, masters,' she moaned.

Leaning over the wet surround of the bath, Jackal pulled out the plug and watched the scented water drain slowly away. 'Look at that!' he exclaimed in mock anger, dragging Mandy across the floor and forcing her head against the cold enamel of the bath tub. 'You dirty little pig, you've left a tide-mark all the way round the bath. You must clean that filth away immediately or you will be beaten until you can't stand.'

'But I don't have a cloth,' she cried piteously.

Jackal pulled her up by the hair and bent her further forward into the bath itself, shoving her naked breasts against the enamelled sides. 'Stop that pathetic whining. You can use your enormous titties, Pig Girl. They're nice and wet, and easily large enough for the job.'

'Yes!' Horse shouted, pushing her further inside the bath and forcing her to keep rubbing until her back ached and the tops of her thighs burnt from the pain of holding that awkward position. 'Keep rubbing those tits against the bath and get all that dirt cleaned off, girl. Before we give you the caning of your life!'

Her nipples stung and burnt terribly as Mandy found her breasts being rubbed and ground against the enamel like two giant flannels, but there was no point trying to escape before the two masked men had finished taking their pleasure with her. She had tried that once or twice in the past, and the punishment had always been worse than the games they played while she was still willing to be their sex slave. Besides which, she had to accept that this degradation was exciting her tremendously. Her sex was already moistening at the thought of how badly the two men were treating her, and the fact that their fingers had thoroughly explored her inner wetness and knew what a willing slut she was only served to heighten her pleasure and make her hope for more. They had threatened to cane her and she knew how much her skin ached to be mistreated under the cane's severity of touch. It was a fire which Stag had lit inside her at their first meeting, his cruelty teaching her to both fear and desire the kiss of the cane against her buttocks and breasts.

Mandy would never be a perfect submissive – her masters had made that abundantly clear on several occasions. Nevertheless, she possessed the ability to enjoy this painful humiliation without completely losing herself in it. And there was never any danger that Stag would ask her to leave the chateau, she thought wryly, rubbing her breasts fiercely against the side of the bath and howling at the pain it inflicted. Mandy's eagerness to reach and push beyond her own limits of endurance made her popular with the dominants who frequented the chateau, and everyone knew it, including Stag.

Horse dragged on her hair, smiling at her breathless grimace. 'Are you finding it difficult to clean the bath, Pig Girl?'

'No, master.'

'Perhaps you need a little encouragement?'

Mandy shook her head, but her despairing groan was muffled as Horse shoved her back inside the slippery bath tub. She found herself twisted sideways, legs kicked apart by Jackal as the other man laughed and squeezed her round the waist. She felt the calluses on his fingertips press into her soft skin and knew there would be bruises there later. She heard whispers but could not catch the words properly. The men must be planning some further torture for her, she thought, her skin clammy with fear and excitement. There was an odd scrabbling noise behind her, then a sudden dull blow landed on her buttocks, followed by another, and then another, each stroke making her squeal aloud at the discomfort. It hurt, there was no denying that, but what on earth were the men using to beat her? Mandy managed to turn her head to one side long enough to catch sight of a white plastic toilet brush being brandished by Horse before it came down hard on her backside again. She jerked in shock and unsuccessfully tried to wriggle away from the next blow, yelping as the stiff plastic bristles ground against the tops of her thighs. The pain from each blow radiated from her fleshy buttocks down towards her knees and up the full length of her spine. The slight dampness of the bristles added an extra frisson of delight to her degradation and it was not long before the men were openly taunting her for enjoying the experience.

'Look at that face! The filthy slut's loving every minute of it.'

'Beat her harder!'

'You do it.' Horse passed the toilet brush to Jackal, bending to examine her sore breasts. 'I want to check the little whore's doing a good job of cleaning this bath.'

Mandy cried aloud as his fingers squeezed and scraped her erect nipples, hot and red-raw from rubbing against the enamel sides of the bath. Jackal's strong right arm came down with force upon her aching buttocks, wielding the toilet brush with the expertise of a master. Her cries were ignored, however. The two men seemed utterly determined to punish her for that act of masturbation they had disturbed, or maybe for playing with the new girl before they had even seen her. This was certainly not the quiet afternoon bath she had expected when she came upstairs with Violetta earlier.

But at least she could be sure the toilet brush would not mark her fair skin. Stag did not allow the girls to be marked without his express permission, though it did occasionally happen by accident. Still, the severe discomfort of her breasts being ground against the hard bath was almost as bad as any caning. She would need to anoint herself with several thick layers of cream after the men had finished tormenting her. Yet, in spite of her physical pain, Mandy could not help raising her buttocks and pushing them back against his crotch, her whole body arching like a cat on heat in the hope that the masked man might take pity on her and enter her burning sex. It must be nearly three days since she had last been mounted and penetrated, Mandy realised with sudden frustration, which explained why she was even more eager to be taken than usual. The men at the chateau had been too busy with the other guests to bother with the receptionist, though those girls had left now and it was only herself and Violetta in residence until next week, when a young Swiss German girl was due to arrive. Which meant there would be plenty of sex to go round for the next few days, she thought hungrily, and lifted her smooth full buttocks towards Jackal, softly begging him to enter her. She could feel the warm juices beginning to trickle out of her gaping sex and down the inside of her thighs. She did not believe he would be able to resist such an open invitation.

But Jackal merely laughed, slapping his hand across the tender skin of her buttocks where the toilet brush had struck her. 'Your mind is a sewer, Pig Girl. Perhaps you should clean the toilet bowl too.'

'No!' she yelled, dragged away from the bath tub by her wet hair. 'I won't do it. That's disgusting.'

'You love it!'

Horse tripped her up and she sprawled helplessly across the open toilet seat, moaning at their arrant cruelty. His laughter merely added to Mandy's anguish, demonstrating once again how little these men cared about her feelings. Yet she knew how much their vicious behaviour excited her and began to long for more stringent punishments, once again experiencing a strange pleasure at her own debasement. As if he had sensed her thoughts, Jackal straddled her body and pushed her head directly into the toilet bowl, ordering her to sniff and lick at the white sides like a dog. The two men howled above her in pure delight as she obeyed, her head thrust deep inside the toilet and her moans echoing around the smelly bowl.

'Clean it, Piggy!'

'Lick harder, you slut. Make that bowl shine!'

This new punishment was hell, she thought dizzily. For a start, the toilet bowl stank. Her neck ached from the uncomfortable position and her fingers slipped painfully on the wet enamel as she tried to stop herself from being forced any deeper inside. But Mandy did not dare refuse in case a worse punishment was to follow. She did not wish to add more pain to the misery of a sore bottom and thighs where they had struck her with the toilet brush. It was better to obey without question and escape a harder beating. Her tongue lapped abjectly at the toilet bowl and under the foulness of the curved rim as their hands tangled in her hair, pushing the chateau receptionist further inside the toilet in their desire to watch her suffer greater torments.

'What's her name, this new girl?'

'Violetta,' she stammered, her voice echoing in the bowl.

The two men muttered something to each other above her head but she could hear none of their words, trapped inside the stinking toilet bowl. After another few moments of ferocious licking, one of them dragged her out and allowed her to wipe her face with a clean flannel. Mandy sagged against the toilet in relief, though she knew her ordeal was far from over. Her poor tongue was almost as sore as her bottom now. But at least she could breathe the cleaner air of the bathroom again.

'Has Stag broken her in yet?'

'No, master.'

'Not even using the cane?'

Mandy scrabbled to her knees on the tiled bathroom floor, frowning at their questions. The two men seemed oddly interested in Violetta, but it was impossible to tell what they were thinking behind those masks. She did not want to betray her own interest, in case it earned her another beating, but she was certainly curious to know why this new girl should be so special.

'I'm not sure, master. Would you like me to ask?'

Horse slapped her so that she fell backwards on the damp tiles, surprised and winded. His voice was hard.

'You keep your mouth shut and mind your own business.'

'Yes, master.'

Jackal bent over her prostrate weeping form and turned her easily in his hands, exploring the damp channel between her legs.

'The slut is excited,' he said. 'Should we take her now?'

40

'Not yet,' Horse muttered.

There was a rummaging noise in the bathroom cabinet, then Mandy shrieked as she felt a large finger probing between her buttock cheeks. The cleft was slick enough with sweat after her exertions but she did not yet feel ready to be penetrated there. Mandy tried to fight the two men off, but the thought of the brutality to come merely served to intensify her own excitement until her sex was awash with hot fluids and her lips hung down, swollen and incredibly sensitive. Clearly unconvinced by her struggles, Horse gave a cruel laugh and took her buttocks in both hands, spreading them widely apart. Then she felt his probing finger again, this time pressing against the tightly clenched ring of her anus until the muscle gave way.

Her low moan of humiliation seemed to amuse Horse, for he withdrew his finger immediately and stood laughing above her helpless body.

'I just need a little lubricant . . .'

She stiffened, feeling his fingers drive into the swollen channel of her sex and scoop out some of her fluids. There was a brief pause, then she felt him kneeling behind her body and spreading her buttocks again.

'No!' she squealed.

'Silence, Piggy,' he said sharply, slapping her full buttocks until they jiggled beneath his hands. Then he gave another firm push inwards and Mandy jerked up in shock as something cold and hard penetrated her anus. It was not wide enough to stretch her, but it was longer than she had expected. Still, the man's murmur of satisfaction indicated that she had pleased him in some way. 'There . . . that's perfectly placed. Now stand up and face me.'

Mandy obeyed and struggled to her feet, almost slipping on the damp tiles and supporting herself on the towel rail in an attempt not to dislodge whatever he had shoved into her anus. It was slightly uncomfortable, clenching down on the object to hold it still, but she realised that to lose it now would be to incur terrible wrath. Jackal helped her to turn round slowly and face Horse, the back of her knees pressed against the cold toilet bowl.

'What is it?' she whispered.

'That slipped so snugly up inside your arse? A toothbrush.'

Mandy stared up at the two masked men, perplexed by their laughter. 'A toothbrush?'

'You're going to use it to clean this toilet seat, Pig Girl.'

Jackal nodded. 'And in exactly that position, please. Squatting and facing us while you do it.'

'I can't!'

'You prefer to receive the cane?' Horse put his hands on his hips and stared down at her, his eyes glittering darkly through the mask holes. 'The punishment room is free. We can take you there straight away.'

His hard words brought Mandy to her senses and she shook her head, trembling as she lowered herself a little further until she could feel the rim of the toilet seat against the top of her thighs.

'I will obey, masters.'

By tilting her hips slightly, and wiggling first to the left and then to the right, she soon found she was able to press the protruding toothbrush against the toilet seat in such a way that it mimicked a cleaning action. The men applauded her efforts, standing above her like two forbidding sentinels as they checked how well she was performing her bathroom duties. It was one of their favourite pastimes at the chateau, finding new and ever more unusual ways to humiliate the pink-cheeked English receptionist.

Today they had chosen a particularly effective method of ensuring her humiliation. After less than a minute of this exercise, Mandy was dismayed to feel her thighs beginning to ache and burn, even her well-toned muscles tiring rapidly in that uncomfortable position, and she longed to straighten up and stretch them out properly. Horse and Jackal would never allow her to escape this punishment so lightly, of course, so she breathed hard through her gritted teeth instead and tried to concentrate on those tiny wiggling motions of her bottom and hips which would manoeuvre the toothbrush back and forth across the toilet seat. Once or twice she felt the toothbrush begin to slip and had to pause for a few seconds, clenching her anal ring tightly on the slim brush shaft before it loosened irrevocably and earned her a vicious caning. But luckily it never slipped out entirely and she was able to complete the exercise without a single reprimand.

'Well done, Pig Girl,' Jackal said admiringly, slapping her plump buttocks as he turned her around and removed the toothbrush. Her skin stung slightly as the bulbous end popped out of her anal ring, but it was not as painful as a proper buggering would have been. Her legs trembled with excitement at the thought of being bent over the bath and penetrated in the rear, though it was not permissible to ask for such a thing at the chateau. She would simply have to be humble, she reminded herself, and not risk a less pleasant punishment. If the two men wanted to take her that way, they would do so.

Horse muttered something incomprehensible under his breath which made Mandy suspect the taller man was disappointed not to have an excuse to punish her more severely. But he too slapped her buttocks without malice and gave a nod of approval on inspecting the clean toilet seat.

'Not bad for a filthy little slut.'

'Thank you, master.'

'Now you may have your reward.'

Horse unzipped his jeans and produced a thick purplish cock. The veins on it began to stand out, its one pale eye already weeping fluid, as the man massaged it to a full erection. Mandy's mouth began to water as she watched him, only too aware that the other man was standing behind her now with his own cock liberated in his hand. Nor did she have long to wait for the promised reward. Horse dragged her along the tiled floor on her knees until she was precisely below his crotch, head tipped obediently upwards to receive his sex. His hand applied an instant and unforgiving pressure on the back of her head so that she found herself impaled on his cock within seconds, unable even to draw breath before the thick shaft was lodged deep in her throat.

'Suck,' he said harshly.

Aware that a caning might yet lie in store for her if she could not perform this task to his complete satisfaction, the pink-faced receptionist hollowed her cheeks around his length and sucked it like a lollipop, his hairy ball-sack pressed rhythmically against her lips and chin. An excess of saliva dribbled from the corners of her mouth, but her hands were too busy to wipe it away, carefully holding Horse by the buttocks as he thrust into her throat. She knew it was vital to control the depth of his thrusts without disturbing the man's rhythm. Her knees began to hurt on the cold tiled floor, but her experience at pleasuring the men of the chateau in this way was soon evident. His breathing quickened to a series of soft grunts and Mandy suddenly realised he was not far off his climax.

Suddenly she felt the heavy crack of a belt landing on her buttocks and yelped at the unexpected pain. Unable to turn her head to see the next blow, she heard it cut almost soundlessly through the air before landing in an explosion of agony across her naked backside. Jackal must have removed his belt and was amusing himself by hurting her with it. They liked to do that sometimes, the masked men of the chateau. Catch her off guard with a belt or a cane. But however much she might be writhing beneath his blows, Mandy could not avoid the sticky sensation of arousal trickling down her thighs. They were right – she loved it, and there was no point trying to deny her own addiction to this pain.

Yet if that addiction had existed before she came to the chateau, it had only been in embryo form. Mandy had not been aware of it, at least. It was Stag who had brought it out in her, had shown her how much pleasure could be gained from the cut of a cane or the kiss of the whip. It was an acquired taste, though, Mandy thought hazily, straining to lift her buttocks for the belt without removing her mouth from Horse's shaft. It had taken her many weeks to learn how to take that pain and shift it to a new place inside, as if the body no longer felt it and it had been absorbed by the brain instead, as a pleasurable rather than painful thing. It was not an easy lesson to learn and the slightest distraction could still make her waver, even though Mandy had considered herself quite inured to pain when she first arrived at the chateau. Someone as untouched as Violetta, she thought wryly, would face a long and arduous journey from innocence to experience.

Horse gripped her cruelly by the hair and thrust deep inside as he came, spurt after warm spurt filling her throat and making her gag. She should have been racked with shame at this debasement, down on her knees in the nude, swallowing down several thick mouthfuls of spunk whilst being flayed from behind by a man wearing the mask of a jackal. Yet the final strokes of his belt came down on pure burning skin, her entire body alight with pleasure as Mandy slipped two fingers between her legs and, ignoring their shouts of rage, brought herself to a rapid and deeply satisfying orgasm.

Three

Listening in silence outside the bathroom door, left slightly ajar so she could not avoid catching glimpses of what was happening within, Violetta clutched her dressing-gown tightly around her chest and flushed scarlet. It was the height of prurience, to be standing here like some grubby Peeping Tom instead of running back to her bedroom at once, but she simply could not help herself. There was a compulsive quality about it. She had never heard cries as fiercely stimulating as those which were emanating from the naked English receptionist, down on her knees in the bathroom, fellating one man and – with apparent enjoyment – allowing the other to beat her with his leather belt.

She could not imagine herself ever behaving in such a wanton fashion, though it was true that her sex had begun to moisten whilst listening to Mandy's moans of pained delight under the belt. But that was purely a biological reaction, Violetta reminded herself grimly, and not an indication that she desired similar treatment at the hands of those men. She was determined not to become the same sort of woman as her mother, who had taken such pleasure in the punishment and exploitation of her body by strangers. It had been one of the worst days of Violetta's life, discovering that the woman who had given birth to her was little better than a glorified whore, performing on the screen for thousands of male worshippers. Having been brought up alone in a convent, unaware of who her mother really was, the shock had nearly made her reject sex forever. But after a few months she became slowly reconciled to the truth and no longer woke quite so often in the night, sweating and with her skin electrified from some sexual dream, hating herself for being prey to such sordid thoughts. But Violetta had forced herself to steer clear of men who might abuse her, fearing that her mother's blood ran in her own veins and she might actually end up enjoying their cruelty. So staying on at this chateau, where apparently sensible young women like Mandy could accept terrible punishments in the name of pleasure, was potentially the most dangerous choice Violetta had ever made. She feared what might come churning to the surface if these men tried their sexual games on her, especially Stag, whose dark antlers held such a terrifying fascination for her.

There had been times in the past when, after a friendly slap on the bottom from a boyfriend, she had found herself yearning for a harder touch and wondered if she was indeed her mother's daughter. Scared of turning out the same, Violetta had always frowned immediately and told the man to stop it. But there was no hiding that reaction from herself and, listening to that girl's excited groans from the bathroom, she knew only too well that something deep inside her could not help softening and weakening at the thought that she too might debase herself in front of these strangers.

She had been intending to take a bath after her long trip but she could not venture into the bathroom now. Yet she still felt uncomfortably sticky. Slipping a hand beneath her dressing gown, Violetta cupped those swollen lips between her legs in an attempt to stem the flow of juice. But it was no use. She had become so aroused by what she had overheard that her inner thighs were soaked. Violetta could not help remembering what

47

she had glimpsed through the half-open bathroom door: that naked, pink-skinned receptionist on her knees and the two masked men above her, the taller man feeding his engorged shaft into her pretty mouth while the other came down hard on her buttocks with a thick leather belt. She could still hear the long muffled cries of the girl, cries which told her Mandy was enjoying every second of her torment, difficult to believe though it seemed.

Lingering for a moment over those hidden lips, Violetta's fingers rubbed and squeezed her flesh as if trying to dry it, though the pleasure of touching herself was enough to make her sigh and lean her hot face against the wall. She did not want to admit it, the shame was almost too much to bear, but she was masturbating . . . right here, on the upper landing of the chateau, where anyone might walk past and see her. For some reason, the very fact that her lewd public display might be disturbed at any moment only intensified the pleasure for her. She ought to return to her room, she knew that, but her desire was too strong to resist. Her mind kept returning to that image of Mandy on her knees, her lips wrapped around the Horse's penis and her reddened buttocks raised for each stroke of the belt. It was almost as if the chateau receptionist was so eager to be hurt that she was actively inviting the Jackal-headed man to beat her harder.

Could pain really be so close to pleasure? Violetta wondered. She closed her eyes as her fingers moved faster between her legs. She tried to imagine how it would feel to be in that girl's place, kneeling to suck a stranger's penis while the vicious leather of a man's belt slashed down repeatedly on her tender bottom. It would hurt and humiliate Violetta to accept that sort of debasement. Yet the mere thought of suffering such indignities aroused her as nothing else had ever aroused her before.

Her dressing gown appeared to have fallen open, exposing her naked body underneath to all onlookers, but she was caught in the grip of an urgent need and no longer cared. Her legs widened as she supported herself against the wall, fingers massaging and pinching her damp sex as Violetta imagined her head being pulled back forcibly and a thick penis rammed into her throat. The high cries of ecstasy from the bathroom dimly told her that Mandy had reached her orgasm, lost in the same throes of passion, and Violetta found herself climaxing suddenly and fiercely as well, one hand clawing at the wall as she nearly lost her balance.

Panting and staggering, she gripped the edges of her gown together and turned back towards the safety of her room. Before she could reach her door, there was a sudden creaking sound and Violetta spun, horrified to see the antlered mask of Stag appear at the head of the stairs. She backed away but there was nowhere to hide. Besides, he had already seen her.

The enigmatic chateau owner was heading straight towards where Violetta stood frozen, softly clapping his hands as if applauding her.

'*Bien fait, ma belle,*' he murmured appreciatively. 'That was an excellent performance.'

'I don't know what you're talking about,' she stammered.

Stag pointed drily at the far end of the corridor. 'There are closed circuit cameras on all floors of the chateau. For security reasons, of course, though they come in handy on other occasions too.'

'I don't believe you.'

'I'm afraid it's true, *chérie*. Your little moment of pleasure was captured for posterity on the camera outside the bathroom door.' He laughed at her expression of horror. 'Now, don't look so worried. No one besides myself need ever see that tape. It will be kept in my private collection.'

Her cheeks hot with shame, Violetta did not know where to look. The chateau owner must have been sitting in a chair somewhere, watching every gesture as she masturbated herself to a violent orgasm.

'What an appalling thing to do. You should have turned off the camera as soon as you realised –'

'That you were fingering your own cunt?'

Her hand itched to slap his smiling face but Violetta feared he might just strike her back. She tried to edge past him, still holding her head high, in spite of the terrible feelings of humiliation churning in her stomach, but he grabbed at her wrist and would not release her. Her voice shook slightly, betraying her unease around this darkly threatening man.

'You must excuse me. I have to change before dinner.'

'Not yet,' he said silkily.

'Please,' she pleaded. 'I can't go downstairs in my dressing gown.'

'Take it off, then.'

'Look, I've already embarrassed myself in front of your bloody cameras! Isn't that enough for you? Let go of my arm.'

His eyes met hers through the narrow slits in his mask, then Stag slowly uncurled his fingers and released her. She had spoken more sharply than she had intended, but it seemed to have had the right effect.

'You are going to be a difficult project for me, Violetta. I realised that as soon as –' Stag stopped himself, turning his head away, though not before she had caught a secret smile on his face. When he continued, however, his voice sounded smooth and carefully controlled. 'As soon as you arrived at the chateau. You have that sort of face, *chérie* – stubborn, wilful, disobedient.'

'I don't like taking orders,' she admitted.

'So I gather.'

'I went to a convent school. The nuns there used to say I had a problem with authority.'

His smile was wry. 'Observant women, clearly.'

Violetta folded her arms across her chest, keeping the silk dressing gown clamped tightly shut. There was something about the man that made her feel nervous in his presence, especially when she was completely nude under this wispy scrap of material and they both knew it. She found him very attractive, that was patently clear from her physical reactions every time he appeared. Yet he was making no attempt to take advantage of her weakness.

From under discreetly lowered lashes, Violetta watched him in silent bewilderment. What precisely did this strange man want with her? she wondered. His invitation and the free train ticket across France had been issued with some definite purpose, but what was it? Her presence here continued to be a mystery, but one which she would need to uncover before it was too late and she fell under the spell of this place, as Mandy appeared to have done. Already she could feel herself becoming aroused again, hot-faced and breathless, simply because he was inspecting the contours of her body through the revealing material of this dressing gown.

'I'm sorry,' she insisted, moving past him towards her bedroom door. 'I really do need to change.'

His eyes flickered over her. 'What size are you?'

'Why?'

'I have something downstairs which would suit you perfectly. In fact, you could almost say it's been waiting for you to wear it.'

She tensed instinctively at the suggestion, shaking her head as the man held out a hand to her. 'That's very kind of you. But I brought a whole suitcase of clothes.'

'Humour me,' he murmured persuasively, not dropping his hand.

'I'd prefer to wear jeans tonight, thank you.'

Without warning, his arm snaked around her waist and dragged her close against his chest. Alarmed by his

51

sudden proximity, Violetta tried to back away, looking up into the darkness of his eyes behind the mask, but his grip was too strong for her. She managed to get to arms' length but no further, his fingers like iron bands about her wrists. His laughter demonstrated that he was enjoying her helpless struggles. As she was unable to hold the dressing gown closed, both sides soon fell open and she saw his gaze wander down her exposed body. To her shame, Violetta felt her nipples stiffen under his scrutiny and opened her mouth to protest at this humiliating treatment. But, before she could speak, Stag shook his head and jerked her towards him, his face frighteningly close to hers.

'In the Middle Ages, women like you were gagged to stop them from arguing. The implement in question was called a Scold's Bridle. It was a piece of metal which fitted over the tongue, preventing it from moving, and was held in place by straps around the neck and head.' His smile chilled her. 'I actually own a replica of the Scold's Bridle, you know. I've been told it's extremely uncomfortable to wear.'

She stared up at him, aghast. 'You wouldn't dare.'

'Keep arguing and you'll find out.'

'This isn't the Middle Ages!'

'No,' he said harshly. 'But this is my house and my rules apply here. Now come downstairs with me and let me see you in this outfit.'

Stag dragged her downstairs without another word, her dressing gown flapping open and her breasts bouncing uncomfortably as she tripped behind him. It had been clear when she arrived that this was not a man to cross, but Violetta had not expected his treatment of her to be quite so forceful. It was as if the man had two distinct sides to his personality – one was the suave host of the chateau, always poised and polite, and the other was this brutal creature now jerking her along the corridor like a rag doll, his mood implacable. It was no act, either. There had been a moment there when his sophisticated veneer had fallen away and she had seen the cruelty beneath. That glimpse of his true nature had terrified her and she had longed to pull out of his grip and run away from the chateau, far away into the anonymous depths of the countryside where he would never find her. But she knew the opportunity for escape had disappeared as soon as she signed that deceptively simple contract in his office. She was alone here now, an outsider on his territory, and he was the one who held all the advantages. It was a frightening thought.

Violetta's face burnt as she considered what Stag had said to her and the manner in which he had said it. She sensed that he was perfectly serious about making her wear a Scold's Bridle. Even though her body was embarrassingly exposed as he threw open the door to a second concealed staircase and began pulling her down the narrow unlit steps, she dared not say another word in case she found herself gagged with a cold strip of metal.

Trembling with anticipation of what was to come, Violetta wondered whether the pretty chateau reception-ist had ever suffered that fate, silenced by the Scold's Bridle. She doubted it, though. Mandy seemed far more biddable a girl than she was and would probably never need to be threatened with such a grim punishment. Not for the first time in her life, Violetta suddenly wished she did not possess this wilful nature or her independent spirit. Many men had admired that fiery temperament of hers, but she suspected it was precisely the sort of quality which would get her into trouble here. And so far as any confrontation between herself and Stag was concerned, if she could not learn to accept the French-man's authority, this might end up being a case of the irresistible force meeting the immovable object.

The long narrow room which they had entered was low-ceilinged and oddly windowless. Violetta guessed it must once have been the chateau cellars, a useful place to store row after row of ancient bottles of wine from the local vineyards, but it had since been converted into some sort of recreation area. She shivered as her bare feet met cold stone underfoot, though Stag himself seemed unbothered by the drop in temperature. Still controlled by his iron grip on her arm, she could not help gazing curiously about herself as the masked man dragged her through the low arched door. At the far end of the room, a huge film screen dominated the entire wall and there was another situated directly above them on the ceiling. There were several small tables around the room, which looked rather like exercise benches with movable parts and padded surfaces. Along each side of the long room ran wall racks hung with bizarre implements: some were familiar to her, like leather whips and canes, while she could only guess at the use of others, strange contraptions of metal or leather which she hoped would never be used on her.

Her eyes scanned the wall racks for a glimpse of this infamous Scold's Bridle, but to her relief she could not see it. Perhaps he had been lying when he threatened her with it. Violetta glanced at his forbidding profile, the dark antlers turned to observe her changing expressions, and realised with a sinking heart that he had not been lying. Just because she could not see the Scold's Bridle hanging on the walls of his modern torture chamber, that did not mean it was not being kept somewhere else in his chateau. Possibly on some other unfortunate female who had made the mistake of arguing with him, she thought shakily.

He released her arm and Violetta rubbed it ruefully, certain there would soon be bruises developing there.

'This is the outfit,' he said sharply, gesturing towards a table on which were displayed what appeared to be several pieces of bright red rubber. 'Put it on. I want to see you in it.'

She ran her hands hesitantly over the tiny shreds of material, unused to their strange rubbery feel. 'But it's –'

'Rubber. That's correct.'

'Indecent,' she corrected him hoarsely, her face suddenly hot again as she realised he expected her to strip right there in front of him. 'The skirt's far too small, for a start. I'll never fit into it.'

'There's an art to wearing rubber, *chérie*. You will learn as you go along.'

'You can't make me do this.'

There was a moment of silence, then Stag turned away and crossed to one of the wall racks in an unhurried fashion. His hand hovered above the arranged implements for some time before finally deciding on a thin highly polished cane. When he came back to her, his shoes echoing on the stone floor, the Frenchman was experimentally flexing the cane between both hands. His strange eyes glittered at her through the slits in the mask.

'You signed a contract in my office a few hours ago. Do you remember? For the next fortnight, you belong to me. Body and soul.'

'But I didn't realise –'

'What that contract would entail? You are a grown woman, *chérie*, and you signed it of your own free will.' His laughter was muffled by the mask. 'If you are now reconsidering your position, that is unfortunate, since I refuse to release you from our agreement.'

'You bastard!' she spat.

His voice hardened and he stepped closer. 'Put on the rubber or you will taste the cane, Violetta.'

Her head bent to avoid meeting his gaze across the room, Violetta fiddled with her thong before his final inspection. She had to admit that he was right: the outfit was not as impossible to wear as she had imagined. With the help of a judicious amount of talcum powder, these tiny pieces of red rubber had stretched around her hips and breasts to form a skin-tight corset and an even skimpier thong below it. Her embarrassment, however, was more acute now than when she had been forced to strip off her dressing gown while he watched, and wriggle nude into these absurdly tight scraps of rubber. To be honest, Violetta had worn far less on beaches in the past, but the rubber lent such a dangerously exotic air to her outfit that she felt herself flush nearly the same colour as the corset.

It was odd how clothes could have such a powerful impact on the psyche, she thought, eyeing herself warily in the mirror. For as soon as she had strapped on the high red stilettos which accompanied this outfit and straightened to examine her reflection, Violetta had felt as though she had never seen herself before. The stranger facing her in the mirror looked like some creature from another world: shiny, erotic, willing to be abused. Automatically, she had sucked in her stomach to accommodate the rubber gripping her hips like a second skin. Her shoulders were pulled right back, thrusting her chest out at a jauntier angle than usual. The stilettos seemed to have added an extra few inches to an already provocatively long pair of legs. Her entire body seemed to possess a sharp new sexuality which she had never noticed before: her hipbones stuck out above a concave belly, her buttocks swayed enticingly as she turned to inspect the thong, and the breasts which had always looked too full were so restricted they seemed to jut out of the smooth moulded bodice, all pertness and red curving sheen.

She no longer recognised in herself the same Violetta who had arrived at the chateau that morning. A pale, rather uninteresting young woman had been replaced by this astonishing vision, strapped into a hour-glass corset and poised on high scarlet heels, her lips moistly open and her large green eyes fixed on her own reflection. Even the red hair, tumbled loose over her bare white shoulders, did not clash with the rubber as she had expected but, on the contrary, seemed to complement it precisely.

'I knew it would suit you, *chérie*. Such a tiny waist, perfect for the corset style, and those huge eyes . . . just the right degree of vulnerability. The change is *incroyable, n'est-ce pas*?'

Violetta started nervously at the sound of his voice, so absorbed by her transformation that she had almost forgotten his presence in the room. For a moment she did not understand what Stag had been saying. Her head was spinning and she could barely speak.

'I beg your pardon?'

'Utterly incredible,' he repeated. 'You look like a different woman.'

'Yes . . .'

He sounded satisfied by her reaction, his tone less harsh. 'You see how easy it can be when you do not argue, *ma belle*?'

Lost in a sort of daze, Violetta pushed a stray lock of red hair from her forehead and glanced up at him through her lashes. Those antlers were oddly mesmerising, his dark eyes watching her with an unreadable expression. Her stomach turned over as she realised she found the Frenchman more than attractive. The effect he was already having on her could not be denied, even after spending only a few short hours in his chateau. In this tight corset and high heels she did not merely feel sexy – that was too shallow a description for it. Instead, she felt like a sexual object, something to be put on public display, to be used and admired. She had seen pictures of women in corsets and similar clothes before and had always pitied them. Yet now that she herself was encased in rubber, her buttocks exposed to the cool air and her breasts high as a young girl's, she experienced a real frisson of excitement as his eyes moved slowly over her body.

Flushed and dizzy, Violetta tried not to stare at the cruel bulge in his jeans, her skin prickling with the awareness that he was clearly enjoying this sight of her in rubber. She had a sudden vision of herself kneeling before him, exactly as Mandy had knelt on the tiled bathroom floor, with her head back and his penis entering her mouth. Her barely hidden sex, its hairs peeping out from either side of the red rubber thong, became damp as she imagined how Stag might use the cane on her as he had threatened earlier. Yet how much would it really hurt to be caned? Something like that must leave terrible marks on the skin. What if she embarrassed herself by crying out after the first stroke and begging him to stop? Violetta's glance fell on the cane, now lying abandoned on the padded bench beside them, but her fear of the pain it offered only seemed to add to the moisture between her legs. But when she looked up, she realised he was watching every expression on her face. His laughter suggested he knew only too well what was on her mind and Violetta turned abruptly away, her cheeks hot with shame at her thoughts.

He took her waist in his hands and measured it, that antlered head disturbingly close. 'Such delicate bones. Small as a bird.'

'My mother was petite as well.'

His eyes glittered as he stared down at her. 'Your mother? Was she as beautiful as you, Violetta?'

'I really d-don't . . .'

To her embarrassment, she found herself stammering, unable to reply to his question. Disengaging herself from his hands, Violetta pulled away and shook her head. She did not want to discuss her mother's sordid history with a stranger. Especially one with hard, searching eyes and a mind which seemed to read her own so effortlessly, she reminded herself strictly.

To her surprise, Stag dropped the subject without probing any further, though he drew her inexorably back towards him. This time she did not resist. There was no point angering him and, besides, she was genuinely tempted to find out what those demanding hands would feel like moving over her body. As if he could read her most intimate thoughts, Stag gently caressed the back of her neck, his voice low and purring as his eyes dropped to examine the curves of her body in that shiny corset.

'Keep your secrets, *chérie*. I am in no hurry to learn them.'

When she made the mistake of moaning under his touch, Stag's fingers became cruel, tightening abruptly around the soft white flesh of her throat and bruising it. That moan seemed to have been taken as a sign of her compliance – a sign he had obviously been waiting for. Without any further hesitation, the Frenchman gripped her neck and bent her forwards over the padded table. His body pressed up against hers from behind and she felt that bulge at his groin swell and harden. The excitement she had first experienced when putting on the rubber corset began to grow, filling her with an almost feverish anticipation of his next move. Was he planning to take her like this, quickly and brutally, her body bent over a table beneath him like some sort of inanimate sex toy? The sheer humiliation of such a possibility took Violetta's breath away, yet she seemed frozen in that position, almost as though she were deliberately inviting the man to go further.

He holds me as a male swan holds a female, she thought dizzily, her eyes closing on a strange wave of pleasure as his other hand moved swiftly and accurately between her legs. His fingers were so skilled, Violetta guessed he must have touched many other women in this way. She could feel the rubber thong pulled tight against her sex lips, grinding into her clitoris, that whole area becoming unbearably sensitised until it was almost painful. What he was doing to her down there was appalling. She ought to push the enigmatic chateau owner away, slap his face, demand to know why he was insulting her in this outrageous fashion. Yet Violetta could say nothing, unable either to stop him or turn away. She felt as if she had been driven down here by her own insatiable curiosity, to this long dark room with its terrifying wall racks, these old-fashioned instruments of torture, by some force which she could neither understand nor control, and it was impossible for her to leave until she had tasted at least a little of what this isolated chateau had to offer.

Violetta was not sure what to expect, but she did not have to wait long to find out. He reached forwards and, with an intense feeling of dread, she watched him pick up the cane. His fingers loosed their grip on her throat but, as Stag stepped back from the bench, cane in hand, it became clear that she herself was supposed to remain in this position he had chosen for her. Without any warning, his feet kicked her legs further apart, so that the rubber dragged painfully at her sex lips, and Violetta found her buttocks rising instinctively as she fought to keep her balance.

'What are you going to do?' she whispered.

He did not reply to that but asked another question instead. 'Have you ever been caned?'

'No.'

'Hit with a belt?'

'No.'

'Perhaps you have been spanked, then?'

Her face hot with shame, remembering many secret occasions when she had ached for the touch of a man's hand on her bottom, Violetta shook her head in mute denial.

'But you have desired it, perhaps?'

'No,' she said hurriedly.

. His laughter told her he had sensed that she was lying. 'You seem oddly inexperienced, *ma belle*. I cannot

60

believe you have not played at least a few of these games.'

'I told you, I went to a convent school.'

He paused, his breathing quickening. 'I had forgotten. So you slept in a dormitory there? With the other convent girls?'

'Yes.'

'Did you never share a bed with any of these girls? Did none of them dare to touch you here?'

His hand curved around her breast in the rubber corset and she moaned silently, unable to prevent her whole body from trembling at his touch. As if the Frenchman knew that she was starting to weaken, his hand dropped even lower, slipping along the firm line of the corset until it found the core of her wetness, stroking the tight rubber strip between her legs.

'Or perhaps here?'

She was shaking her head, but a soft groan betrayed her excitement as a memory of one night in the dormitory came back to her and his hand was abruptly withdrawn. He moved further back from her body and she could hear a change in his breathing. The Frenchman sounded almost as excited as she was, though his voice was carefully neutral.

'You are lying to me, *chérie*.'

'No.'

'I dislike lies intensely. From now on, there must be nothing but honesty between us. Pure, unadulterated honesty. Do you understand?'

'But I wasn't lying . . .'

It had never occurred to Violetta that this provocative little game could be manoeuvred so far out of her own hands, but those naive illusions of the convent school upbringing were about to be shattered. There was no longer to be any suggestion that she was in control of what happened in the chateau. He was the master here and he was determined to demonstrate his power. She

61

only recognised the whistling sound of the cane mere seconds before it struck her, and her entire body jerked in shock at the white-hot strip of agony that was beginning to pulse across the top of her exposed thighs. She jumped up immediately and her hands went straight to her bottom, in a gesture of fear and protection. He had given her the cane – just once, admittedly – but that one stroke was enough for Violetta to know that she could not handle another such lightning bolt of pain.

'That hurt!'

He was smiling behind that dark antlered mask. 'Naturally it hurt, *chérie*. Pain is the whole point of the exercise.'

'Don't do that again!'

There was a frightening moment of stillness in the room as Stag stood motionless and watched her through the narrow eye slits, the cane still balanced in his hands. But he did not react with anger, as she had expected. Instead, his voice seemed deceptively silky.

'You are afraid, *ma belle*?'

'No,' she said, biting her lip. 'I just didn't like it.'

'Because it hurt?'

'Yes.'

Stag looked at her, his eyes glittering. 'So you are afraid of the pain.'

'I didn't say that.'

'Prove it.'

Violetta suddenly realised she had walked into a trap of her own making and, to judge by the Frenchman's taunting laughter, he knew it too. She stared over his shoulder at the closed door, wondering if it was locked and how quickly she could reach it. Her bottom was aching terribly from the cane stroke and she was starting to doubt her ability to go through with this unusual 'holiday'. It had seemed a good idea when she signed the contract, something which might loosen her conservative approach to life and make it easier for her to enjoy herself with men. But she had not anticipated how agonising this course of punishments would turn out to be. Now he was staring down at her from behind that antlered mask and she felt her cheeks burn at her own weakness. Could this man see through her carefully constructed façade of independence and strength to the submissive streak beneath?

'How am I meant to prove it?'

He held out the cane. 'Kiss it,' he said softly. 'Then bend over and take two more strokes.'

Violetta was struggling with a crazy desire to obey him, but her bottom was still throbbing from that first powerful stroke.

'I can't,' she said hoarsely.

'You should stop underestimating yourself, *ma belle*. You are not used to the necessary pain of submission. Your skin is still tender. But if you trust me, you will soon learn to enjoy the cane . . . even crave it.'

'No!'

His voice hardened. 'I don't want to lose my temper with you, Violetta, but I am growing tired of your constant refusals.'

The door to the room opened and they both turned. It was Mandy who came towards them, now dressed decorously in a short black skirt and white shirt. There was no sign of the greedy young woman Violetta had seen on her knees in the bathroom, less than an hour ago, sucking voraciously on a masked man's penis while she enjoyed a beating from another man's belt. It seemed more like a dream now though, especially with Mandy's cool business-like nod at herself and Stag. She was holding a light blue folder in her hand, which she opened as she reached them, handing several documents to the chateau owner and then swinging herself up onto the padded bench as if it were the most natural place to sit. The efficient young receptionist did not even glance at Violetta's tight rubber corset, her eyes fixed on Stag.

'Some papers for you to sign, sir,' Mandy murmured discreetly. 'And next week's menu. I hope it meets with your satisfaction.'

'I'm sure it will,' Stag said dryly.

The receptionist's eyes flickered sideways at Violetta, then away again almost immediately. Her expression was slightly coy as she looked at her boss. 'I haven't interrupted anything, have I?'

'As a matter of fact,' he replied, signing the papers with a flourish and handing them back to her. 'I was just trying to persuade our guest that the pleasures of the cane are worth the pain it brings. But perhaps you are in a better position to persuade her.'

'You mean, a woman's touch . . .?'

'Can be so much lighter than a man's, yes,' the Frenchman finished for her, and took Violetta's arm with a cruel grip. But instead of pulling her towards him, he passed her to Mandy in the same way that he had passed her those signed documents, so casual that Violetta thought the Frenchman must have lost interest in her at last. The immense relief she felt when he handed her over was mingled with an odd sort of distress. She might have escaped the cane for the time being, but something inside her was disappointed that she had failed his test so completely. They had only met that morning, yet already Violetta loathed the idea that this enigmatic man might consider her a coward, too scared to rise to his challenge.

Her face flushing delicately, she remembered Mandy's lightness of touch and could hardly bring herself to look into the other girl's eyes. The sensations Violetta had experienced before Stag walked into the office that morning had opened her mind for the first time to the possibility of finding pleasure in a woman's arms, but that did not mean she was keen to repeat what they had done together. Everything still felt too new, too powerful for her to handle. Yet she did not pull away when

Mandy's fingers moved unerringly between her legs, slipping beneath the thin damp strip of rubber and toying with her erect clitoris. It had become a physical necessity to be touched there, Violetta told herself desperately, having suffered in silent frustration for the past hour as the Frenchman had stroked and caned her rubber-bound body but not made any move to satisfy her growing excitement. It might not be his strong fingers pinching and caressing her sex lips, but at least the pretty receptionist seemed to have guessed how Violetta was suffering and was making a fair attempt to relieve her.

Stag leant against the padded bench, his arms folded across his powerful chest, and watched them both with open amusement.

'I could never tire of this sight, *mes petites*. To watch two women make love to each other is to sample one of life's true pleasures.'

Sinking to her knees on the stone floor, Mandy did not hesitate even for a moment but pushed her face directly into the damp cleft between Violetta's legs and, in spite of their audience, Violetta found her slim thighs parting instinctively. She dared not look up at Stag, realising it must look as though she were accustomed to such intimate attention from another woman, and fearing his laughter.

That gesture was clearly the encouragement Mandy had been waiting for. Within seconds, the rubber thong had been pushed aside and the girl's tongue snaked out, lapping without any restraint at the warm quivering flesh before her. It seemed that, for the second time that day, the chateau receptionist had gone down on her knees to give pleasure, placing herself without any outward sign of shame in what was a totally subservient position. It ought not to have gone any further. Yet the sensation was simply too incredible to resist. Indeed, Violetta soon found her fingers tangling in the short

65

chestnut hair below her, fighting an aggressive desire to drag her closer. It had not taken much to rekindle that passionate hunger she had experienced earlier today, even though she had promised herself – much to her present shame – never to give in to such feelings again. That promise had not lasted more than a few hours, she thought hazily.

Whilst licking at those swollen sex lips, Mandy's hand had dropped between her own legs, hitching up the short black skirt and reaching unerringly for her own clitoris. This hot little scenario was exactly what she needed to relieve herself for the third time that morning. Her own vagina was slick with excitement after the beating she had received at Jackal's hands and, although she had climaxed several times in the bathroom, it had not been enough. She admitted to herself that she was a greedy little slut before dipping two fingers into the honeyed mouth of her cunt to further lubricate her aching flesh as she masturbated. It gave the receptionist extra pleasure to hear Violetta suddenly cry out above her, understanding exactly how it must feel for their new guest to have a woman kneeling between her legs.

In response to that cry, Mandy's tongue worked even harder, licking in short hard flicks from the clitoris to the soaking entrance of the girl's vagina, and more slowly and teasingly around those pouting inner lips, following the contours with loving attention. They were full and pink, precisely how Mandy liked them, and had that warm musky scent that only an aroused female could exude. She was acutely aware of Stag's eyes on them all the time and concentrated hard on keeping her performance at a high level. There would surely be some reward later if she succeeded in bringing Violetta to orgasm, and besides, Mandy always hated to disappoint her master. Stag was a strict disciplinarian and a formidable sexual partner, but it was neither fear of another caning nor the desire to feel him inside her that made the receptionist work so hard to please him. Few things in life gave Mandy more delight than simply to gain her master's approval.

Her body arching and stretching the skin-tight rubber corset, Violetta realised she was coming. She closed her eyes on a violent wave of pleasure and heard somebody grunting from a long way off. It was only as the orgasm subsided and her spread thighs began to tremble that she realised it had been herself who had grunted so viscerally. She felt dizzy and confused by the astonishing strength of that orgasm. Her body no longer seemed to belong to her.

Before she realised what was happening, Mandy had straightened and was bending her gently over the padded bench. Her hands gripped the soft edges of the bench for support and her legs widened automatically, still trembling as if she were about to fall. Violetta just had time to glance up at Stag's watchful masked figure before that terrible whistling sound came again and she found herself jerking like a marionette whose strings have been cut, her mouth opening on a hoarse cry. The back of her thighs stung and throbbed with a white-hot pain. The cane!

'No!'

Mandy pushed her back down onto the bench.

'Stay still.'

'Please don't . . .'

'Silence!'

There was no need to escape. Briefly, Violetta caught the whistle of the cane one more time, before she could struggle away from her captors, and then the appalling pain struck her again. This time it came directly across her soft buttocks, where Mandy had pulled down the tight rubber thong to expose her unmarked flesh. Her agonised yelp merely seemed to amuse the chateau owner and his receptionist. Violetta leapt up, rubbing her sore bottom with both hands and staring round at them tearfully, but they made no effort to stop her.

'Why did you do that?' she demanded sulkily.

Mandy shrugged, her smile secretive. 'First the pleasure, then the pain. Later you'll find the pain becomes a pleasure too, Violetta.'

'I doubt it.'

The chateau owner turned away, his dark antlered head swaying as he crossed the stone floor of the cellar. 'How do you feel, *chérie*?' he asked quietly over his shoulder. The voice echoed around the stone walls. 'Now that the shock of the pain is over, do you feel angry or excited?'

Violetta stared after him, surprised both by his question and the answer she knew to be true. 'Excited, I suppose,' she stammered.

The Frenchman reached the door, looking inscrutably back at Violetta before he left the room. His tall antlered figure cast strange shadows over the walls as his head turned slowly towards her. She felt a warm glow of pleasure beginning to spread through her abused bottom, along her inner thighs and towards the soaking mouth of her vagina. His laughter suggested that he knew precisely what she was feeling.

'*Bien fait, ma belle.* You learn quickly.'

Four

Violetta stood on her balcony, staring across at the funereal line of cypress trees which separated the chateau from the outside world. Their sombre green spikes swayed and shone in the sunlit breeze. The skies above the chateau were an intense Mediterranean blue and she could smell the intoxicating scent of eucalyptus again. It was a far cry from her dull London office buildings. Yet in spite of this unfamiliar warmth on her bare shoulders, Violetta could not relax and enjoy her holiday. Her mind was far too preoccupied with the events of the previous day. Things had happened to her yesterday, she thought wryly, which she would never have believed possible before arriving at this unusual chateau. It was almost as if she were discovering another creature beneath this familiar skin, a new and dazzlingly sensual Violetta whom she had never seen before. She was not sure whether to be frightened or excited by this emergence of a different personality, though she was fairly certain who was behind her transformation. For ever since she had set eyes on the Frenchman, with his dark imposing antlers and enigmatic laughter, she had felt desires stirring inside her; strange exotic desires which her film-star mother might have applauded, but which she, Violetta, could not believe were her own.

Turning to get dressed, she found to her surprise that a pale silk dress, embroidered with butterflies, had been laid out for her while she was asleep. She was usually a light sleeper, waking at every small noise in the night, but her exhaustion yesterday must have proved too much for her. Fingering the thin dress, she wondered if Mandy had brought it upstairs for her. Violetta had been planning to wear jeans and a T-shirt today, but the butterfly dress was truly beautiful and, it had to be admitted, the weather was rather too hot for jeans. So, rather than boil herself alive in denim, Violetta rummaged around in her drawers for some light underwear and slipped into the butterfly dress.

The shoulder straps were tiny, barely supporting her full breasts, but after nipping in at her waist the dress flowed gently out over her hips and thighs in a short swathe of silken material which flattered her figure. There were no shoes which could match the dress, so she shrugged and decided to go barefoot, her long shapely legs shown off to advantage by the shortness of the style. In this place, it hardly seemed to matter that she was not wearing any shoes. In fact, the whole outfit made her feel extremely feminine. No doubt that was why it had been deliberately left in her room: to encourage her to behave in a more submissive fashion today. But, looking at herself in the mirror, her head held high, Violetta could not help smiling at such a mistake. If the Frenchman thought that a few strokes of his cane could tame her, he was in for a shock. She was nothing like her mother and she had every intention of proving that to herself, once and for all.

Tiptoeing quietly through the deserted corridors of the chateau, Violetta frequently paused to stare up at modern oil paintings on the walls and at strange ancient artefacts kept under glass. The enigmatic chateau owner appeared to be a keen collector of unusual objects, especially if they related to sexual activities. The oil paintings all seemed to be of nude or semi-naked women, some of them lying alone on ruffled sheets as if they were about to make love, others being whipped by men as they knelt or hung from odd contraptions, their faces always alight with a fierce pleasure. In the glass cases she found collections of possibly Victorian whips and chains, many of them intricately embossed with designs of writhing snakes or naked women. Some of the stranger objects made no sense to her, unless they were metal bits and leather bridles for horses. They seemed far too small for that purpose, yet surely they would be incredibly painful if used on humans rather than on animals?

Violetta shivered, turning away from the case in sudden apprehension. She had seen similar items displayed on the wall racks in the chateau cellars, in apparently perfect condition, ready to be taken down and used. Although she could not imagine ever accepting the use of such terrible implements, Stag had already demonstrated his ability to break down her resistance. For in spite of her fear, she knew that something deep inside her had discovered a secret pleasure in pain. It was humiliating to admit this, even to herself, but Violetta was beginning to suspect that she had inherited more than a little of her mother's submissive streak.

Coming to the end of the corridor which ran past the main staircase, she was about to turn back when she realised there was another door there, hidden behind an elaborate wall-hung tapestry. Pushing the heavy material aside, Violetta found a handle and glanced over her shoulder, concerned that somebody might catch her in the act of spying. She pushed at the ancient tarnished handle, only to find that the door was firmly locked. She ought to have given up at that disappointment, but she guessed there must be something worth seeing behind that door, otherwise it would not be both hidden from sight and locked. Biting her lip with insatiable curiosity, Violetta looked around herself. On the nearest table to the door was a Greek urn, decorated with nude twisting boys. On impulse, she lifted it up as carefully as possible. Her instincts had been right! Beneath the urn lay a large golden key.

But as Violetta's hand reached out for the key, she froze in horror at the sound of approaching footsteps. Somebody was coming up the main stairs and, in less than a minute, would soon see her standing outside this hidden room. From the sound of those heavy footsteps, she guessed it to be a man. Probably Stag himself, who would undoubtedly punish her again for exploring the recesses of his chateau without permission. Her mind reeling at the thought of what might lie in store for her this time, Violetta realised the only way for her to escape further punishment was to hide inside the secret room. There was no time to think. Snatching up the golden key, she inserted it into the lock with hurried fingers, holding aside the heavy embroidered tapestry. And as soon as the key turned, perfectly smoothly, she pushed the door open without any hesitation and slid inside the room to find herself in shuttered darkness.

Her heart thudding crazily, Violetta stood there motionless for a short while, listening for any sound of pursuit from outside. But whoever had come up the stairs did not appear to have seen her enter the hidden room. There was no noise from the corridor and the door remained closed. She would be safe enough in here for a few minutes at least. The room was extremely hot and stuffy without the windows open. She could hardly breathe. Once her eyes had adjusted to the darkness, Violetta was able to make out the shapes of furniture in the room and hurriedly picked her way across the polished wooden floor to where light was streaming in through narrow gaps in the shutters. Opening the smallest window as quietly as possible, Violetta turned to examine this secret room which she had discovered. There was still not much light in the room, so she could not see anything clearly, but it was not immediately obvious why it had been kept locked and why Stag had gone to the additional trouble of concealing the entrance with that heavy tapestry.

A sudden breeze swept into the dimly lit room, blowing a pile of papers across the large mahogany desk against the far wall, and she tiptoed towards them in consternation as the papers began to slip onto the floor. The last thing she wanted was to leave this room in disarray, as it would immediately signal to the chateau owner that somebody had been in here without permission. Crouching to pick them up, Violetta belatedly realised they were photographs. She held one up to the faint daylight, frowning in disbelief as she recognised the semi-naked woman in the centre of the photograph. It was her mother!

To judge by that smooth tanned complexion, the photograph must have been taken at least twenty-five years ago, though Violetta knew her mother had never really looked her age. Embarrassingly, her mother – wearing nothing more than a tiny sequinned thong – had been photographed kneeling beside a swimming pool as she fellated a distinctive silver-haired man in a suit, her scarlet lipsticked mouth stretched around his phallus in an obscene mimicry of a smile. The man in the suit was not smiling, however. His eyes were closed and his hands were clasped on either side of her mother's head, using force to maintain the pace and depth of her sucking. The relationship between them was brutally unambiguous. He was the master and she was his slave. There was no compromise in the arrogant tilt of his silver-haired head. Violetta was left in no doubt, however, that her mother was enjoying this enforced servitude to an older man. There was a hot greedy shine to her eyes and her body language – raising herself eagerly on her knees as if aching to swallow his penis – was that of a woman enjoying herself immensely. The other photographs scattered on the floor contained similar images: her mother posing on the set of an erotic film, swimming nude in a deep azure sea with several other girls, being mounted from behind on a marble floor whilst fellating two men at once.

With a trembling hand, Violetta replaced the photographs on the desk and switched on the small table lamp. The room was illuminated by its soft yellow light and she glanced around at the large photographs covering the walls from floor to ceiling, too shocked to react. Other, more obscene, pictures of her mother had been blown up to ten times their usual size and used to decorate the room. Everywhere she turned there seemed to be images of her mother: down on her hands and knees, hooded and with every orifice filled to capacity, or lying spread-eagled on a bed, accommodating the phallus of some man crouching over her face or thrusting between her legs. In glass cases around the room she could even see costumes which her mother had worn during the filming of some of these scenes, carefully preserved and displayed. Black rubber helmets and leather masks with diamond-studded eyeholes mocked her as Violetta stared back at them, her thoughts whirling in chaos.

Why on earth were these appalling photographs here on the walls of this French chateau? Was that why she had been invited here in the first place, because Stag knew the identity of her mother? Violetta wanted to cry out in fear and disgust at the thought. She wanted to run from the room, pack her suitcase and leave immediately, but she found herself unable even to draw breath properly, lost and bewildered as she stared around at the filthy images of her mother's degrading lifestyle.

Violetta put a hand to her mouth, her legs trembling beneath her in the silken butterfly dress. She ought to have run back to the safety of her own room. But she was so confused by what she had seen, her heart racing with shock, that she did not even hear the door to the hidden room opening nor the soft footsteps of the chateau owner approaching her from behind.

'So you have found my little shrine, *chérie*. I wondered how long it would take you. Are you impressed?'

'She's . . .'

'Your mother.' The masked man nodded, watching her face. 'Yes, I know. That's why I invited you here this summer, Violetta. Because I thought you might be ready to follow in your mother's footsteps at last.'

She felt sick. 'I'll never follow in her footsteps. I'd rather die.'

'Your mother was an extremely talented woman.'

'My mother was a whore!'

Stag laughed out loud at her outrage, coming inexorably closer all the time. She could feel the power his enigmatic presence wielded over her and backed away, horrified to feel her nipples stiffening beneath the silken butterfly dress as she fought not to stare at those muscular thighs or the broad shoulders beneath his antlered mask.

'Candice – your mother – was a passionate and sensual creature, adored by all those lucky enough to enjoy her body. She revelled in her sexual appetite and loved to give men pleasure. Is that your definition of a whore, Violetta?'

'Her idea of sex was perverted!'

'You only say this because you have not yet learnt to appreciate the other face of pain, *ma belle*.'

'What other face?'

He shrugged. '*Du plaisir, naturellement*. Pleasure is the other face of pain. But to understand that you must first experience the purest agony.'

'You mean the cane! My mother may have enjoyed being caned, but I'm nothing like her. I found it abhorrent.'

'Is that why you become so excited?'

Violetta could not answer that question, her face flushing with shame. Abruptly, she turned away, trying not to look at the obscene photographs of her mother covering the walls of his room. But between her pale slim thighs, she had already felt the tell-tale signs of arousal: her clitoris beginning to throb and swell, her outer lips moist with fluid, those inner lips aching to be stretched and filled. It did not seem to matter how much she denied the wilder side of her nature, it always came back to haunt her as soon as this man came anywhere near her. It was like a chemical reaction between them that changed her into some sort of sexual animal, a creature intended for pleasure and pain. At first she had been intrigued and excited by his sexual interest. His intentions were only too plain now, though. Stag wanted her to behave like a whore, to submit herself to the same treatment her mother had received at the hands of many different lovers.

Yet that was a lifestyle Violetta had turned away from in her late teens, refusing to become like her mother as her body gradually matured and men began to look at her with desire. She had not reached her twenties entirely innocent of that erotic underworld, but it was not a place Violetta wanted to inhabit, even though she was not blind to her own sexuality. For instance, she knew it would not take long for the Frenchman's regime of punishment and submission to turn her into the same filthy slut her mother had been, unless she could put up a more strenuous resistance.

'I should leave the chateau straight away,' she managed to say, though her whole body was trembling. 'I thought this was a holiday, but you brought me here under false pretences.'

'You signed an agreement.'

'Which you tricked me into signing!'

'To stay here for the full two weeks,' he continued smoothly. 'And abide by the rules of the chateau, as all our guests do.'

It sounded frightening but it was only a bluff, she was certain of it. She was a guest here and the Frenchman was her host. In reality, there was nothing he could do to hurt her. This talk of contracts and rules was just part of some elaborate game the chateau owner had been playing. But that did not mean she had to join in with the game.

Violetta raised her chin, her reply cool and defiant. 'And if I refuse to abide by those rules?'

'Then you must be punished.'

Standing rigidly beside the deep stream, barefoot and wearing nothing but her thin butterfly silk gown, Violetta stared at the large water-wheel with anticipation. It was a scorchingly hot morning, yet she was shivering. Crossing her arms over her breasts in a defensive posture, she glanced back at the imposing chateau behind her. Most of the great windows were closely shuttered against the sunlight. A few windows on the upper storeys were open, though, and she could see pale gauze curtains blowing outwards in the light summer breeze. But there was nobody in sight.

She glanced again at the wooden contraption above the stream and Stag laughed at her expression. He taunted her mercilessly. 'Does it frighten you, the water-wheel?'

'Of course not. What happens now?'

'Use your imagination.'

He pulled her towards the wheel, stripping the butterfly gown from her body with relentless hands. Violetta gasped and tried to cover her naked breasts but it was useless. The Frenchman was far too strong for her. She felt his hands tugging at her lace thong and then that too had disappeared, her last barrier against indecency tossed aside on the grass. The stiff antlers scratched her cheek as he bent to tie her wrists to the wheel, but he ignored her loud and bitter protests. He kicked her feet into position on the wooden slats, then bound both ankles with rope and she could not help wincing as the ropes bit into her pale skin. Working thoroughly and carefully, Stag tested the strength of her restraints one by one. By the time he finally straightened and stepped back to admire his work, she felt horribly exposed, realising that the cruel chateau owner had spread-eagled her naked body on the wheel for anyone to see.

'How long can you hold your breath?'

With a sudden realisation of what was to come, Violetta stared down at the cool rushing water below her, then began to struggle. 'No ... please ... you can't.'

'*Doucement, chérie.* Don't pull on the ropes like that. You'll only hurt yourself.'

'I'll drown!'

The antlers shook with soft laughter. 'No, you won't. This is simply an exercise to teach you obedience.'

'I'll do whatever you say, honestly.'

'And that's a promise made under duress. You must learn to give your obedience freely, without any co-ercion. That's why you're here. To learn to enjoy your submission.'

Violetta was about to reply when she heard the voices of others coming down towards the stream from the chateau. She tried to turn her head to see who it was behind her, but it was impossible. She was too tightly bound even to look over her shoulder. 'Help me!' she cried, hoping someone would take pity on her. There were several of the newcomers; she could hear them whispering to each other behind her back. Then a face came into view which she had never seen before. It was a crow's head, black and tarry-feathered, its savage beak half-open as if about to eat. The tiny black eye swivelled towards her and Violetta screamed, freezing back against the wooden spokes in fear. The man beneath the mask seemed taller than the others, with a skinny body under the black jeans and T-shirt they all were wore at the chateau. This man had an air of cruelty which frightened her, though she tried to control her desire to shrink away from him, sensing Stag's disapproval at that instinctive scream. At his side stood a man wearing the mask of a fox, its fur wiry and brownish yellow. The large gingerish whiskers brushed against her skin as he leant forward to examine her more closely, laughing at her horrified expression.

Then the others pushed forwards to take his place. Next in line was the man in the horse mask. She instantly recognised him as one of Mandy's tormentors in the bathroom. Thicker-set than the crow, with a glossy chestnut mane and energetic movements, his large firm thighs rippled with muscles under those black jeans. As she stared back at him, Horse stepped towards her and stroked her face. Suddenly frightened, Violetta struggled to pull away from his touch but he did not seem bothered by her reaction, stepping to one side so that the next man could come closer.

This one was the jackal, the second man she had seen punishing Mandy in their bathroom. She remembered that lithe walk, balanced so lightly on his heels like a dancer. His jackal mask moved up and down in an odd motion and Violetta suddenly realised he was admiring her naked body. Then his large hand reached out to cup one of her breasts. She shivered at his touch but said nothing. He weighed her breast in his hand, murmuring his approval, then stepped away.

The Frenchman stepped forwards now that the others had examined her restrained body to their satisfaction. He had seemed civilised enough before, in spite of the three strokes of the cane she had received across her thighs and buttocks, and somehow Violetta could not believe he would go through with this arcane punishment. Being dipped under the water, tied to this wooden wheel like a witch, was almost medieval. Yet she could feel the aching red weals where the cane had marked her skin in the chateau cellars; irrefutable evidence of his innate cruelty, she reminded herself. Now the Frenchman bent to touch those marks with one cool finger, as if admiring a work of art, and laughed as he straightened, seeing that her nipples had become erect. Hating herself for that helpless reaction, Violetta swore at them all and struggled against the ropes which bound her to the wheel.

There was a short, tense silence and she knew that she had seriously offended the chateau owner. Then Stag took a deep breath and stepped back from her tethered body as if he had finally given up trying to convert her. The antlered head turned towards Fox, who was still standing beside her.

'Begin the punishment,' he said, folding his arms across his chest. 'You know the rules. Three times under the water. But if she begs to be forgiven for her breach of contract, the punishment will be terminated.'

She stared around at them all, too horrified to speak. Fox was beginning to turn the wheel now and she could feel her bare feet entering the water. Even in the heat of the sun, it was icy cold.

'Please . . .'

'Beg or suffer, Violetta. That is your only choice.'

The water was up to her calves. She could hear the rushing stream grow louder and louder as the wheel turned, dipping her further into the water. How could they do this to her? But she would not beg them for mercy. The thought was too humiliating.

'You bastards!'

'You still refuse to beg?'

Violetta felt the water pass her thighs. The shock of it against her warm inner lips was terrible. She writhed against the ropes, knowing how they would be enjoying her torment.

'You will be under the water for ten seconds, remember. The water here is deep and extremely cold.'

Violetta. Those ten seconds will feel like an eternity. Simply beg to be forgiven and it will be over.'

Racing across her belly and up towards her breasts, the water was suddenly lapping at her cold erect nipples. Her heart was thudding at her chest like a caged wild beast. The animal heads beside the wheel watched her with their strange dispassionate eyes, but she could not believe they would really go through with it.

'Is it so hard to beg me, Violetta?'

'Damn you to hell!' she gasped as the water reached her throat. Any second now and she would be completely immersed, unable to breathe. Looking up at him through furious eyes, her mouth only inches away from the deep racing stream, Violetta strained at the ropes holding her wrists and ankles, but it was no use. The knots were too tight. She thought wildly about pleading for another chance, but couldn't find the words. The wheel continued to dip her inexorably down, and suddenly she knew it was too late. 'Take a deep breath,' Stag warned her, then his face disappeared and she was under the water.

Those ten seconds were the longest of her life. She had not taken a deep enough breath before going underwater, her head was flailing about helplessly against the wheel, fearing lack of oxygen. She could see bizarre animal shapes glimmering above her through the sunlit stream, but her eyes couldn't focus on them properly. Then the wheel turned and Violetta came up towards the surface again, breaking into hot blinding sunlight, coughing and spluttering as her mouth gasped at the air like a goldfish.

'Are you ready to beg now?' Stag demanded.

Her head was spinning. Part of her wanted to beg and cry weakly for mercy, but the rest of her was still rebelling against his absolute authority. But she had survived his damned test. Why should she crumble now? So she lifted her head and spat water at him. 'Fuck you!'

'Another ten seconds.'

The wheel turned again at his order and she plunged under the water much quicker this time, barely having time to draw breath before she was back in the familiar icy depths of the stream. She fought against losing consciousness, trying not to panic as she had done before. Her body relaxed slightly and she allowed herself to float on the horror of no oxygen, dimly aware that if she could only hold on long enough, it would all be over for a second time. Her thighs and breasts were growing numb with cold by the time the wheel turned again and she was out in the sunlight.

Stag was standing over her exhausted body, his hands on his hips. 'This is a waste of your energy, *chérie*. There's no point in resistance. Now beg to be forgiven and I will release you immediately.'

When she wearily shook her head, he clicked his fingers and Fox began to turn the wheel again, putting her back into the stream inch by painful inch. Her full breasts were stinging now from the immersion, as if they had been punctured by hundreds of tiny burning needles. His voice was so faint as to be unintelligible by the time she felt the approach of that cold rushing water for a third time: 'By the time I've finished with you, Violetta, I promise you will have learnt how to beg.' Her mouth closed tight against the water. She thought, I'll never beg you for anything, but it was becoming harder to keep track of her feelings and thoughts. All Violetta knew was that her last time under the water seemed to last an eternity. Her arms and legs were so numb and weak she could barely feel them any more. Suddenly she was in the sunlight again and there were hands gently untying her from the wheel.

'Spit out the water,' he murmured, close to her ear.

Violetta was lying on her face in the warm grass beside the stream, with the Frenchman kneeling over her, his hands pressing down onto her back. Opening her eyes, she saw the shadow of his huge antlers above her. 'Go to hell!' she tried to say, but the words came out on a bubble of cold water issuing from her lungs. His soft laughter infuriated her and she struggled to sit up, but he wouldn't let her. Instead, his hand trailed slowly down her spine and came to rest just above the curve of her naked buttocks.

'You must learn to obey, Violetta.'

There was a short pause, then his finger moved deeper into the cleft of her buttocks, teasing the tight opening of her anus. Violetta felt herself tense instinctively. She had never had sex there and she was suddenly afraid that he was going to force her. Acutely aware of the other men watching them, Violetta moaned under her breath, hiding her hot face in the grass.

'Please . . .'

'You don't like it there?'

She writhed helplessly as his finger pushed itself relentlessly against the closed ring of her rectal sphincter. The sensation was almost unbearable. She didn't know what she wanted any more, but her nipples were suddenly erect again. Not sure what to say, Violetta rubbed herself against the cool grass, flushed and breathless.

'No . . . I . . .'

But Stag didn't show any signs of stopping. The wet skin of her sphincter gave way under his gentle pressure and his finger penetrated her anus, moving slowly in and out like a tiny penis. The water must have lubricated her, she thought, because there was hardly any pain as she felt him push another finger inside her, stretching the thin walls. A wave of utter burning humiliation swept over Violetta as she realised how she must appear to the watching men. Lying face down on the grass, her wet raised buttocks shining in the hot sunlight, and the Frenchman's fingers working smoothly and tormenting-ly in and out of her anus. This was what he had wanted from her all along. Her complete and utter humiliation and submission to his will. He pushed her damp thighs apart, holding Violetta down with one hand on her spine. His fingers had slipped down between her spread thighs, finding the erect bud of her clitoris and massaging it gently, and Violetta felt an agonising pleasure surge through her at his touch, her whole body jerking with the impact.

Everything inside her had become confused. She wanted to come and come under his clever fingers, writhing and moaning on this damp grass like a sex-hungry slut, yet it was an appalling image. These men were watching her every reaction. What must they think of her now? She had been so brave and determined not to give in when they bound her to the wheel and ducked her under the water, yet here she was, only minutes after being released from that torment, silently begging one of her masked captors to bring her to an explosive and satisfying climax.

Fox had come to kneel in front of her. There was an unmistakable bulge in his jeans as he looked down at her sleek naked body. He raised Violetta to her hands and knees, both hands firmly grasping her shoulders, then reached down and unzipped his jeans in one smooth movement. She was alarmed at her own lack of resistance, knowing perfectly well what was going to happen next and not trying to stop him. His penis was short but thick, with a purplish swollen head, and she gazed at it hungrily. Pre-come was already oozing out as he touched the angry head to her lips, pressing it against her teeth.

'Suck,' he commanded her.

Leaning forwards over her spine as if about to mount her, Stag suddenly slid three fingers up inside her wet vagina. Helplessly caught up in what he was doing down there, Violetta gasped at the pleasure, and as soon as her mouth opened on that soft moan, Fox pushed his prick deeper inside until it was almost knocking the back of her throat.

'Mmmnnn . . .'

She gagged and retched at the intrusion, and Fox withdrew slightly, but then began to thrust gently in and out of her mouth while Stag continued to finger-fuck her. The whole event was obscene, especially with the other men watching from behind in feverish silence. Yet Violetta couldn't deny the exquisitely erotic sensations flooding through her body as she took one man in her throat and allowed another to finger her cunt lewdly. Excited beyond tolerance, she moaned against the thick cock in her mouth, trying to suck it deeper inside. Fox must have sensed her desire because he fixed his hands on both sides of her head like a vice, holding her still as he thrust more urgently between her lips. Her moans seemed to please him, and, as if in encouragement of her new-found acquiescence, Stag manipulated a fourth finger inside her cunt until the thin labia ached deliciously with their fullness.

Stag paused, then slowly withdrew his fingers. Fox stayed in front of her, masturbating furiously as he stared down at her parted lips. Stag was standing out of sight, whispering to one of the others. She couldn't hear what was being said, but knelt there exhausted, barely able to wonder what they would do to her next. Her full breasts hung down, nipples still embarrassingly erect with excitement. Fox groaned at last, several jerks of semen shooting from his penis to land stickily on her throat and exposed breasts. She shuddered at the waves of filthy delight spreading through her body as the semen dripped gradually from her breasts onto the grass below.

Suddenly Stag was in front of her, holding a long whip in his hands. She knelt up at once, covering her breasts fearfully as he tested it against the ground. The loud 'thwack' made her skin tremble with anticipation.

His antlered head swayed gracefully as he bent forwards with the whip for a second time, then leant back like a fisherman, catching the thin tail as it bounced off the ground with another clean 'thwack'.

Stag stared down into her terrified eyes. After his previous gentleness, the command seemed very abrupt. 'Uncover your breasts.'

'No,' she said instantly, horrified. 'Not for that whip.'

'*Merde!*' he swore under his breath. 'I thought we were making progress, Violetta. Why can't you simply obey? Don't make me angry or I shall be forced to punish you more severely.'

But she lifted her chin, still refusing to uncover herself for the whip. He could do whatever he wanted, she was not going to obey his every order like some abject fool. Stag looked down at her from above, his masked head on one side as if thinking about the situation, then he gestured to the others. Crow and Jackal stepped forwards without hesitation, grabbing her hands and pinning them painfully behind her back. As Violetta struggled and swore, one of them tied her wrists together so that she was left kneeling there defenceless, her breasts fully uncovered, the quivering erect nipples thrust out towards Stag as if eager to be punished.

Violetta twisted in fear. 'You can't be serious! I couldn't take the cane. What makes you think I can handle the whip?'

'You disobeyed an order. This is your punishment.'

'All right. I'm sorry.'

'Too late, *chérie*.' Stag shook his antlered head. The voice behind the mask sounded strange and muffled, as though he were struggling to conceal some emotion. 'You must learn to submit immediately. It should come naturally. You must want to obey.'

'But you can't beat me. Not there, not on my breasts,' she whispered, her voice hoarse. 'It would be complete agony.'

'The marks will linger, yes. But do not despair. The marks of the whip can be beautiful.'

She stared up at the long-handled whip, appalled by what she might be about to suffer. Stag lifted his arm, keeping his eyes fixed on those naked white breasts straining beneath him. He seemed so casual at first, as though not about to put too much effort into it, yet when the whip flashed forwards and caught her right across both nipples, she knew that his entire body weight had been behind the blow. Violetta screamed with agony, falling forwards onto the grass in a desperate attempt to stop him beating her. Her nipples burnt and stung terribly. Strong arms pulled her back to a kneeling position, and then the whip caught her again, slightly lower, so that her breasts leapt with the force of it. Violetta found herself screaming again, except this time she was held fast, unable to throw herself down. So she writhed where she knelt, moaning with the pain, no longer caring that they could see her abject behaviour.

'I can't . . .'

'Silence, *ma belle*. You had your chance to obey.'

Stag raised his arm again, and the next few terrible lashes cut across the tops of her breasts in a criss-cross, her body jerking as if electrocuted at each rapid stroke. Her throat hurt with the constant screaming. Lifting her head, Violetta cast her eyes wildly about to see if anyone had heard her, if there was someone in the house or gardens who might rescue her. But the grounds were empty, and her screams merely echoed off the white shuttered windows of the chateau. There was nobody there to help her. Violetta realised then that she would have to get through this ordeal alone, whatever it might cost her.

'Are you sorry for your disobedience, Violetta?' Stag demanded, lifting the whip in his right hand.

'Yes, yes,' she moaned.

'How sorry?'

'I'm very sorry. I won't ever do it again.'

Stag looked down at her prone body, his antlers tilting thoughtfully. 'That's very good. You sound most contrite, *ma belle*. So why don't I believe you?'

The whip sliced across her nipples again, reawakening the pain from last time. She could not stand it a moment longer. Yelping like some wounded dog, Violetta struggled with the men who were holding her down. In spite of their combined strength, they failed to keep her still this time, and Violetta managed to throw herself onto her face again, rubbing her sore breasts against the damp grass.

'Have it your own way,' Stag shrugged.

She did not understand what he meant by that until the whip flashed down again with that terrifying 'thwack', catching her along the tops of her thighs. The agony exploded in her head as she realised he was not planning to spare her. Another whiplash followed swiftly, straight across the full swell of her buttocks. Violetta jerked helpless as a marionette when its strings are pulled, and rolled instinctively onto her back to escape the pain.

'Even better,' he murmured.

She had thought herself safe in this new position until, without any warning, his whip came down like a lightning bolt across the dark triangle of hair between her thighs, slicing into those tender inner lips which only moments before had been moistened with excitement by his fingers. She screamed with the excruciating pain and felt herself lurch upwards, cunt straining wildly for another taste of the whip.

The Frenchman laughed at her reaction. 'You like that, *chérie*?'

Violetta didn't reply, couldn't possibly reply, but simply jolted into an explosive orgasm as the whip fell twice more across her cunt lips. She shuddered with pleasure, hating that mindless reaction to the pain, only to feel the whip slice several times in quick succession across her nipples. Her tormented breasts stiffened ecstatically and firecrackers lit up the inside of her head like a heaven of shooting stars. She moaned in helpless abandon, for she had never experienced such a powerful orgasm before. Nearly passing out with the intensity, she seemed to be coming again and again, her excitement increased by the awareness that all these men were staring at her naked twisting body.

What must they think of her now? She was behaving like nothing better than a cheap whore and the shame of it burnt at her cheeks like a fever. Even after she thought it was finished, another series of climaxes unexpectedly shook her body – like the aftershocks of an earthquake – leaving Violetta exhausted and humiliated on the damp ground at his feet.

Five

Standing alone in the silence of a sunlit afternoon, at the top of a flight of steps which led down into a formal sunken garden, Violetta began to think seriously about leaving the chateau. The sombre row of cypresses which hid the chateau from the outside world was about half a mile away, but it would not take very long to reach them on foot. She had only intended to stretch her legs when the sun beckoned her out of the chateau this morning, but the realisation that she was alone had made her consider the possibility of running away. It was a cowardly thing to do, perhaps, but Violetta was beginning to fear what else might be revealed about her true self if she remained here much longer. The Frenchman had already discovered more of her weaknesses than she felt comfortable with. Biting her lip, she descended the steps into the sunken garden and carefully chose a path which led her away from the chateau. Once she had reached that barrier of cypresses, she ought to be able to find her way out of the grounds. But she had only been walking for a few minutes when she heard a terrible but familiar noise behind her and spun around in sudden trepidation.

She had forgotten the guard dogs!

The three Alsatians came bounding towards her, barking ferociously. She stared at their sharp white teeth, the muscular thighs ready to pounce as she backed away. To the dogs, she must seem like an intruder, waking alone through the grounds at this time of the morning.

Suddenly there was an angry command in French, a piercing whistle, and Violetta realised that Stag himself had appeared at the top of the steps down into the ornamental gardens. The dogs spun back towards him as if on the end of a string, leaving her frozen and terrified on the gravel path. Watching the three guard dogs retreat obediently to their master's feet, she wondered what her punishment might be for leaving the chateau without permission. It must be obvious that she had been trying to escape but she decided to lie, telling the Frenchman she needed a little fresh air, even though she had already guessed from the barely controlled anger in Stag's stance, hands on his hips as he came towards her, that he would never believe such a ludicrous story.

'Where are you going?' he asked silkily.

'Nowhere in particular. The weather's so beautiful this morning, I just felt like stretching my legs . . . that's all.'

'By taking a short stroll back to Nice?' He laughed but there was no humour in the sound. 'Do you think I'm stupid? You're beginning to make me angry, Violetta.'

'It's not like that . . .'

'If you want to leave my chateau, *ma belle*, you are free to do so at any time. No one will try to stop you. The gates are not locked. There's no need to behave as though I'm holding you against your will.'

Pulling her impatiently after him, the Frenchman led her out of the ornamental gardens and down an incline towards a small rustic summer house. Violetta stumbled several times over the rough uneven ground and was forced to clutch at him for balance. He was not wearing a shirt that morning and his muscular back glistened in

91

the sunlight. Her mouth went dry, remembering how he had touched her so intimately the day before. But he did not respond this time, merely bending his head to duck beneath the encroaching trees and gesturing her to stay behind him as the path narrowed to single file. She glanced nervously over her shoulder as they moved further and further away from the familiar walls of the chateau. The three dogs trotted behind them like guardians, tongues lolling over their teeth as they panted in the heat.

'I'm sorry,' she stammered. 'I didn't mean to offend you.'

'Be quiet and keep walking,' was his curt reply.

It was cool and dark inside the summer house. The building itself was almost hidden beneath the surrounding greenery, its walls smothered in a thick tangle of bougainvillea that prevented much light from entering the windows. The Frenchman pushed her down onto hands and knees and lifted her skirt, removing her knickers without preamble.

His fingers explored her inner lips, pushing themselves inside and stretching the muscular walls of her cunt. She gasped but did not dare pull away, her knees hurting on the bare wooden floor. The dogs wagged their tails excitedly, whining and squatting to lick themselves in anticipation. Violetta watched them in fear, wondering what part they might play in the proceedings. Perhaps he had brought his dogs here with other guests and they were remembering those occasions with pleasure. Today though, not even bothering to turn his head, the chateau owner ordered the dogs to be silent and they obeyed instantly. Then he licked his fingers speculatively through the slit in his mask, making an angry noise under his breath.

'You're not ready for me, *ma belle*. That's not acceptable. Don't you realise a slave should always be ready for her master? Perhaps you need to be reminded of your place here.'

That first sharp slap across her buttocks took her by surprise and Violetta stiffened, crying out. She suddenly remembered his warning that she might be spanked if she misbehaved during her time at the chateau, but somehow she had envisaged something a little gentler than this. His pace relentless, Stag barely gave her time to catch her breath before his hand came down again. The next slap was harder and lower down on the fleshy part of her bottom. She shrieked, seeing in her mind's eye the bright scarlet imprint left by his fingers on her white skin. Seconds later, he caught the top of her thighs with a vicious slap that left her gasping. Her pride gone now and her eyes filling with tears, she begged him to stop. But he paid no attention whatsoever. Her bottom was on fire and her body swayed helplessly with the rhythm of his spanking. Stag must have been aware of the pain he was causing her but the enigmatic Frenchman gave no indication that he had heard her cries. But as he continued to spank her, she realised that he was careful to distribute his blows evenly, never striking the same place twice. She could not help wondering though whether that was to save her extra pain or to increase his pleasure by turning her entire bottom a lovely throbbing scarlet.

The Frenchman reached down and released his penis from the tight black jeans he was wearing. Holding it in his fist like a trophy, Stag grasped a handful of her hair and slowly, painstakingly, dragged Violetta's head back until her mouth was level with the thick swollen monster.

Held forcibly in that position, Violetta could smell the musky scent of his pre-come, staring helplessly at the little translucent bead of fluid already bursting from its tip. Clearly he intended to fill her throat with it, and though Violetta was scared of the potential discomfort, she found herself almost eager for the experience. After her convent school upbringing, it was humiliating to admit it but some deviant part of her nature enjoyed gagging on a man's penis. What would the nuns say if they could see her now? But Violetta had no time to dwell on the past. He was already feeding his thick shaft past her lips, one hand gripping the back of her neck to make sure she stayed in the right position for his thrusts. She began to choke as his penis first filled her mouth and then pushed further in, leaving her no room for manoeuvre.

'Hold still and suck,' he said brusquely.

She obeyed, though it would have been hard not to with his hand fixing her so rigidly in place.

'Mmnnn . . .' she groaned, her mouth full of cock.

Tiny electric shocks sparked at the nape of her neck as he tightened his cruel grip on her hair. 'That's it. Take it right in. You like the taste?'

'Mmnnn . . .'

He began to thrust against her tonsils. 'Is this too deep?'

She scrabbled wildly to hold her position as he thrust faster and deeper into her mouth. 'Mmnnn . . .'

'I can't hear you, *chérie*. Speak up.'

'Mmnnn . . .'

'Are you being deliberately insolent?' Her head rang with sudden bells and lights as Stag slapped her face with the flat of his hand. His voice boomed fiercely about the wooden summer house, frightening the dogs who were lying down now, watching their master at work. 'You will obey me when I give you an order, Violetta. I told you to speak up.'

'MMNNN . . .'

He laughed at her struggles. 'Not too deep, then? Good.'

Stag continued to thrust deeply into her mouth, the great antlers high above his head swaying with the motion. Violetta tried hard not to gag, but it was almost impossible in this half-kneeling position. She had deep-throated men before, but never one with such a large penis. Stag seemed oblivious to her discomfort though, watching dispassionately as her eyes filled with tears and she began to choke. Focusing on the cock pushing rhythmically in and out of her mouth, Violetta tried to blot out the pain in order to please him better. Outside in the sun-baked chateau grounds, she could hear birdsong, high and plaintive. It sounded like some restless bird, weeping as it searched those beautiful gardens for its lost mate. Violetta blushed with sudden shame and humiliation to see herself as an observer might, forced down on her knees in this shadowy summer house, sucking the thick shaft which he plunged in and out between her aching lips.

'That's good.' He released her hair. 'Keep sucking.'

Instinctively, she lifted her hands to his hips, tilting her head further back under the onslaught. It was easier to accept his full length this way. Her jaws were sore and tired, but Violetta knew she could not stop sucking until he had finished with her. His masculine smell was almost overwhelming now, and she couldn't help fondling his large balls as she swayed back and forth, feeling her own juices beginning to flow between her legs. Violetta was imagining his massive cock sliding in and out of her cunt instead of her mouth, and the fantasy gave her a terrible secret pleasure. If one of her hands had been free, she knew it would have slipped between her legs to rub the aroused peak of her clitoris to orgasm.

'That's enough,' he said suddenly, easing himself out of her mouth. It was almost as if he had read her thoughts and approved of her desire to masturbate.

He gripped her hair again and pushed her down until her forehead was touching the wooden floor. Frightened, Violetta wondered what he was planning to do next, but as he stepped round behind her and knelt, she moaned softly, sure that he was going to enter her.

'Did you enjoy sucking me?'

'Yes.'

'Yes, what?' he demanded arrogantly.

'Yes, master.'

He spread her cunt lips with his fingers, examining the clear juices running from it. 'You're dripping, little slut. An enjoyable sight. But rather too slippery for my tastes.'

Violetta stiffened with fear as his fingers moved up between her buttocks. The Frenchman had found her anal opening now, sliding his finger lightly around the tightly puckered rim. She felt the pressure increase as his finger pushed inwards, beginning to enter a place no other man had ever explored. Violetta couldn't restrain herself any longer. It was obvious what he intended to do.

'No, please . . . I've never . . .'

Stag slapped her across the buttocks twice, his blows deliberately hard and stinging.

'You must learn not to speak unless spoken to.'

Grimacing from this new taste of fear and humiliation, Violetta felt his hand forcing her back into her original position, forehead touching the wooden floor in a gesture of total submission and her raised buttocks invitingly open to his fingers. The tender skin stung where he had struck her, but that was the least of her worries now. Violetta hissed between tightly clenched teeth as his hands continued their work, dragging her arse cheeks apart to reveal her anal opening and brutally stretching the delicate sphincter muscle with his fingers. Not content with relentlessly fucking her mouth until it ached, the Frenchman was now planning to take her anal virginity. It was a terrible price to pay for her stupid attempt at escape.

Reaching down between her legs, Stag slipped several fingers into her aroused cunt and scooped out some fluid. 'This will do nicely as a lubricant,' he murmured.

Violetta groaned and twitched helplessly as she felt his fingers exploring around her rectal opening. Then two of his fingers pushed against the puckered hole, forcing the muscle to yield. She writhed with shame at her own degradation. This would be the ultimate indignity. She even found herself begging for his mercy without caring how low she had stooped.

'Ugh, no . . .' Violetta yelped at the intense sensations as his fingers drove in and out. 'Please, master . . .'

His unexpectedly violent slap bruised her skin. She could feel the ache beginning even as he pulled away from her buttocks. Then he raised himself and she knew he was poised to penetrate her. Gasping with sudden fear and apprehension, Violetta tried to twist away from his hands, but he caught her by the hips and held her rigidly in place, his sturdy erection nudging between her damp buttocks in search of her anus. She felt the thick cock-head pressing against the puckered opening and cried out. The alert dogs lay there on the wooden floor, panting with what appeared to be genuine enjoyment as they watched their master push his penis against the tight ring of her anal muscles. Screaming aloud with the sudden pain, Violetta closed her eyes and gritted her teeth as she felt him force himself slowly, inch by terrible inch, into her unused rectal channel.

'That's good,' he muttered. 'Nice and tight.'

Her distended anus stung and burnt with the unaccustomed sensation of being stretched. Stag was holding her bottom cheeks apart now as he forced his full length into her rectum. They both gasped at the same time as he pushed right up to the hilt, and she felt his hairy balls pressing against her buttocks and thighs.

Violetta couldn't help letting a moaning sob escape her lips as he began to withdraw his shaft.

'Shhh. Enjoy the pain, *chérie*.' He was breathing more heavily now, the wooden floorboards creaking under his knees. The pain was less intense now that he was inside

97

her and Violetta relaxed a little, even beginning to enjoy the sensation of having something so large and smooth working its way in and out of her anus. 'You should not hide this prize away from men. You should be proud of such a magnificent arse.'

'Yes . . . master . . .' she managed to whisper.

'Put your hand between your legs, like you do when you are alone. I want to watch you play with yourself.'

Automatically, Violetta obeyed his command. Her hand reached swiftly between her legs and found her slick sex. Aching with unreleased tension, the erect bud of her clitoris responded instantly to her fingers, swelling even more. Within seconds, she felt the old familiar heat begin to creep into her cheeks and Violetta leant her face against the cool floorboards, moaning softly under her breath. She did not want this man to realise she was growing excited. His amusement would be too humiliating.

'You enjoy my cock in your arse?'

'Yes,' she whispered.

His slap stung her raised bottom. 'Yes, what?'

'Yes, master.'

'Good girl. You want it deep?'

'Ahh . . .' Violetta squirmed helplessly, her buttocks slickening with sticky heat as his hands gripped them. She wanted him deeper, yes, but she didn't want to beg for it.

'Say it!' Stag commanded her sternly. 'Do you want my cock deep inside your arse, Violetta?'

'Yes,' she hissed at last, writhing in humiliation. A rain of vicious stinging slaps along her buttocks and upper thighs reminded her of her subservient position here. Gasping with shock, Violetta stammered in her hurry to get the words right, raising her buttocks even higher to show her subservience. Her face burnt scarlet at the rude language. 'I want your cock deep inside my arse, master.'

'And so you shall have it,' he warned her softly, quickening his pace. 'But keep playing with yourself. I want to hear you come first.'

Her fingers feverishly manipulated her erect clitoris as she felt his cock push as deep as possible into her rectum. There was suddenly more pain and she had to arch her spine, groaning as his cock-head made contact with the soft muscular back of her channel. Yet the pain seemed right somehow, even more exciting than before. Her fingers worked faster. The pleasure was building to an intolerable crescendo as each thrust bruised and tore at her hidden flesh and at last Violetta felt herself spasm into an intense climax. It seemed the most all-consuming orgasm of her life. Her body pulsed with electricity as she gasped and moaned, pushing her hips back against him in an attempt to take all of his shaft inside her anus, every inch of his thick flesh.

'Ahhhh . . . I'm coming . . . I'm *coming* . . .'

Fluid gushed freely from her sex as she climaxed and Violetta caught it on her fingers, bringing her hand automatically up to her lips and tasting the sweet-sour liquid of her own pleasure. Still plunged deep inside her anal cavity, his penis twitched and leapt as though it had a mind of its own. Violetta's tongue licked eagerly around each crevice of her fingernails and along the knuckle joints, lapping up every trace of the heady-scented juice. But the man behind her continued to thrust hard as her climax faded away, pushing her face right down onto the wooden floor.

'Who is your master?' he grunted.

'You are, Stag.'

He tensed at her submissive answer and drove his cock to the furthest limits of her rectal passage, then she felt the throbbing and pulsating against the thin-stretched walls which meant that he was coming. And as the man shot his semen deep inside her rectum, his muffled groan of pleasure reminded her of the mask he wore and the animal he represented: the virile stag chasing the deer through the forest in search of a mating. She raised her buttocks to capture every last drop and felt his hands gripping her hips to maintain that position for as long as possible. Her bowels were now full to the brim with his hot thick sperm and Violetta couldn't help masturbating herself again at the filthy thought, mouth wide open as she gasped into another orgasm under the manipulation of her fingers. When Stag eventually withdrew, the spunk was already beginning to dribble out around the sides of his shrinking cock, loosing warm splashes of come onto her inner thighs. Violetta instinctively shifted position, trying to press her legs together as her sex ached deliciously in the aftermath of orgasm, and her anus let out a long slippery fart.

Stag heard her sharp gasp and laughed. 'Don't be embarrassed, *chérie*. Those are the noises of love.'

'Yes, master,' Violetta whispered, collapsing thankfully onto the wooden floorboards and hugging her throbbing buttocks with both hands as she stared up at him. His spunk oozed out onto her fingers as a tangible reminder of what she had just taken up there. Her spine and neck were aching with the effort of holding that position for so long, yet for some reason Violetta didn't seem to care about the discomfort. All that mattered now was the sense of physical release running like soothing water over her body. Her limbs were heavy and liquid, and she couldn't hold a single thought in her head.

'So now you have taken a cock in your arse, Violetta, and it will never hurt that much again.' The strange antlered head swayed as he looked down into her languid face. For once, she found those husky foreign tones reassuring instead of frightening. 'Today's lesson is at an end.'

* * *

100

'I can't seem to make a decision any more. Should I stay or go home? Being here at the chateau has really confused me, everything's mixed up in my mind. I feel as though I'm going mad.'

While Violetta was speaking, Mandy rolled onto her belly and cupped her chin in her hands, her chestnut hair curled prettily around her face. She had removed her pig mask because of the heat, though she knew she would get into trouble if any of the others caught her talking to a guest without it. But there was something so easy and casual about Violetta, it was hard to think of her as a bona fide guest of the chateau. To her mind, they were already more like best friends.

There was hardly any breeze coming through the windows today, so her bedroom was even sultrier than usual, but since it was far too hot during the siesta hour to wear any clothes, both of them had stripped right down to bra and panties. Personally, Mandy felt much happier now that she had shed the stern black skirt Stag always insisted she should wear as chateau receptionist. It might show off her legs to advantage, but a short black skirt was not sexy enough for her. She much preferred the less formal outfits he expected her to wear *outside* her hours at the reception desk.

'It's the same problem with pleasure and pain, isn't it?' she murmured, giving Violetta a knowing smile. 'I mean, where does one end and the other begin? Or are they actually the same thing?'

'Exactly.'

'But nobody can tell you the answer to that, sweetie. You have to find it out for yourself.'

'But why?' Violetta wailed.

'Well . . . because everyone's answer would be different, I suppose.' Mandy shrugged. 'We all have our personal limits, don't we? Different pain thresholds. Some of us are just designed to take more punishment than others.'

101

Violetta nodded. She understood that concept without needing it explained any further. Her brief time here had taught her that much already. Closing her eyes for a moment, she tried to relax and sort out the chaotic thoughts in her head. She was sitting right on the end of Mandy's bed, high up in the attics of the chateau. It had been a secret relief to escape from the confines of her bedroom and sneak up the narrow back staircase, knocking discreetly at each door until she found the right one. Following her encounter with Stag in the summer house, Violetta had desperately needed to talk to another woman about her doubts and fears. This holiday was proving more of a challenge than she had expected and she was not sure how much more she could handle without falling apart.

She kicked off her heels, drawing her bare feet up and curling her arms around her knees in a childish gesture of self-protection. Her body still ached from the various whippings and punishments she had taken over the past forty-eight hours, and her bottom had been embarrassingly sore ever since Stag had decided to initiate her into the joys of anal sex. But at least here she felt safe, chatting quietly with the English receptionist. The staff quarters might not be as luxurious as her own suite of rooms on the first floor, but the low ceilings lent them an air of cosy intimacy and the views across the hot sun-drenched valley were superb.

Mandy watched the other girl in a sympathetic silence, remembering her own confusion when she had first arrived here. She too had come to the chateau not realising what lay in store for her behind its impressive walls, answering an innocent-sounding advertisement for a receptionist and finding herself flung into a spiral of pain and ecstasy within a few days of accepting the post. It had taken several weeks to adjust to her dual position. For she had agreed not merely to act as chateau receptionist during her time here, but also to perform the duties of a sex slave for staff and guests alike. The split personality that occasionally demanded had felt almost impossible to perfect in those early days, but eventually she had realised that the boundaries between her two roles were fairly clear-cut. It was simply a question of learning when to stop being a receptionist and accept whatever commands Stag threw at her, however much they humiliated or pained her.

In the end, Mandy had found a certain satisfaction in her ability to perform both jobs without becoming muddled or making any embarrassing mistakes. There had been awkward times when, being sodomised on her hands and knees or bent over the desk for a caning, she had been expected to answer the telephone to potential clients and handle their enquiries with an air of consummate professionalism. It had been a point of pride to her that no one had ever complained at such times. Indeed, some clients had been more eager to book a holiday at the chateau after hearing the unmistakable sound of a cane being applied to the backs of her thighs and waiting for the break in her voice which never came. That deliberate lack of reaction had taken months of training at the hands of a master.

Though she could appreciate how difficult it must be for a girl like Violetta, trying to reach that level of subservience without anyone to guide her through the initially bewildering maze of rules and conventions. Most guests and staff arrived at the chateau with open eyes, entirely aware of how the system operated and more than willing to join in with the elaborate role-play and physically demanding games. Violetta, however, appeared to have been invited here without being given any idea of what would be expected of her. It was an odd situation, though Mandy knew better than to interfere or question her master's plans. No doubt Stag had his reasons for bringing this young innocent to the chateau and she had no intention of risking severe punishment by speaking out of turn.

Violetta moaned suddenly, covering her face for a moment, then looked up at her. 'Can you keep a secret?'

'That depends on the secret.'

'Please!'

Mandy sighed, wriggling her bare stomach against the sheets. 'Go on then, what's your secret? I won't tell a soul, I swear it.'

'I'm going to run away.'

'Don't be stupid! Stag and his men would run you to ground within minutes and beat you silly. Why not just relax and enjoy yourself for a few weeks? Stop getting so wound up about the punishments. They can be very pleasurable if you know how to accept the pain.'

'But I don't think I could ever get used to being a slave,' Violetta whispered hoarsely, glancing over her shoulder at the door. She paused and bit her lip, clearly nervous of being overheard. Mandy was relieved to see her caution. At least the risk of angering her masters did not seem to have escaped the girl. 'I don't understand how you can stay so calm. Don't you find the way they treat you humiliating and degrading?'

'Of course.'

'Then how can you bear it?'

Mandy laughed at her inexperience. 'Are you saying you felt no pleasure at all in the way Stag took you this morning?'

'You mean . . .?'

'In the arse, yes. Didn't you climax?'

Violetta reddened at her crudity and dropped her gaze, struggling with her immediate feelings of shame. But she knew there was no point pretending that it had not excited her. 'In the end, yes,' she admitted. 'Though it was agony at first.'

Standing up and stretching luxuriously, Mandy went to her wardrobe and began looking through her favourite outfits, though she kept talking to Violetta over her shoulder. 'Of course it was agony. You told me it was your first time. But losing your anal virginity can be magical as well as painful.' She paused, pulling out a rubber catsuit and mentally measuring it to see if it would fit Violetta. 'And for the master, too, not merely the slave. Did you offer your body to him? I mean, did you raise your bottom and beg him to take you there?'

'Yes.'

'Good. That will have pleased him.'

'Do you really think so? I find it so difficult to work out what Stag is thinking, with that mask completely hiding his face.' Violetta hesitated, a slight tremble entering her voice. 'Mandy, what does Stag look like without the mask? Have you ever seen his face? He sounds so . . .'

'Attractive? Exciting?'

'*Yes*!'

'I've never seen him without the mask, unfortunately, so I can't help you.' Mandy threw the rubber catsuit down onto the bed, a rueful smile on her face. 'But you're right. His voice gets me wet within seconds, especially when he's angry.'

'Do you think I should stay or go?'

'That depends on you. To be honest, I think you want permission to become his slave. But only you can give yourself that permission.'

Violetta nodded slowly as she digested the truth of that remark, leaning forward to stroke the rubber catsuit with curious fingers. 'This is amazing. But what is it for?'

'It's a sort of performance outfit. Stag likes me to wear it sometimes. When there are special guests or he wants to make an impression on someone by handing me over for punishment.' She caught Violetta's astonished expression and shrugged. 'You learn to accept that sort of arrangement. Honestly, it's not as difficult as it sounds. When Stag orders you to please somebody, you obey. Without argument or question.'

'And if you refuse?'

'*Refuse?*' Mandy echoed, laughing at her naivety. 'Baby, that word doesn't even feature in a slave's vocabulary.'

The girl was turning the blue catsuit over in her hands now, gasping in shock as she discovered some of the concealed flaps and openings which left the wearer open to both punishment and reward whilst remaining fully dressed. The crotch folded back and could be fastened in position with a metal stud while the bodice, by means of a discreet zipper, came away almost in its entirety so that both breasts could be whipped or uncovered at will. It was deliberately a little too small for Mandy so that when she wore it, the material clung to her as though she had been poured into it, her bottom protruding invitingly at the back and her breasts, always too full for her bras, straining at the rubber until it was ready to split. Stag had chosen it for her to amuse himself, he had said when she first put it on for his guests. He apparently enjoyed the way she could barely walk about the room, the act of bending over the table almost an impossibility for her ... though one hard stroke of the cane was usually enough to force her into the most agonising contortions at his command. And if she was honest with herself, Mandy quite enjoyed being ordered to bend and expose her voluptuous curves for his guests to abuse. Each client who spattered her catsuit with semen or cut aching red weals on the soft flesh of her inner thighs was a personal triumph. To her mind, Stag's approval was worth any amount of painful humiliation.

Violetta was shaking her head in wonder. 'This outfit is utterly indecent. Yet it makes me excited, just touching it. How does it actually feel to wear something like this in front of other people?'

Mandy drew a deep breath. 'Are you sure you want to know?'

'Yes.'

'OK.' She smiled at the other girl's insatiable thirst for information. 'They make me feel incredible. Completely available. As though I'm no longer a free individual but belong to my master, body and soul.'

'May I try it on?' Violetta asked shyly, holding it up against her body as if to check the fit. 'I enjoyed wearing that girdle and thong he gave me before. I mean, I was scared too, but if I'm going to stay here, I want to learn how to please him. Do you understand?'

'Of course. That's how I felt when I first came to the chateau. Stag was my master and I needed his approval.'

Violetta stood up from the bed, removing her lacy white bra and panties without any sign of embarrassment. The reddish triangle of hair between her legs shone like fire in the sunlight. Mandy could not help admiring the other girl's slim waist, tucked in below the full swing of her breasts, and the feminine curve of her hips which dropped into such long pale legs that she could see why Stag had spent so much time punishing her over the past couple of days. He must find it hard to keep his hands off that white skin of hers, with only three striped bruises from the cane already fading at the tops of her thighs and a few harsh weals from the whip across her breasts and belly. Such pure skin would always show the marks of whip and cane perfectly. She was no longer surprised by Stag's interest in this girl. Her whole body could be a showcase for the most exquisitely painful punishments and no doubt he had plans to fully exploit it as such during her stay with them.

Mandy watched the other girl pulling on the rubber catsuit and licked her lips with sudden lascivious greed. She ought to be ashamed of herself, wanting to corrupt

107

that shining innocence. But the situation was just too tempting, finding herself alone with the soft-skinned redhead and knowing how little experience she had of their world. She could teach her so much with just a few well-placed slaps. As Violetta struggled into the tight-fitting rubber, the firm white bottom bounced, mere inches above those fading purplish marks of the cane. Mandy fixed her gaze on those smooth curving cheeks as if mesmerised. She imagined how the girl would squeal – first in pain and then in delight – as Mandy held her down over one knee and spanked her bottom, slowly at first, then speeding up and covering every inch until all that white skin was warmed and flushed with the force of her hand. She knew how it felt to be spanked. Now Mandy wanted to know how it felt to watch the skin redden and hear the girl cry out beneath her. It was a wicked but exciting realisation, discovering a desire to turn from tormented to tormentor, for she had never before relished the idea of inflicting the punishment rather than passively receiving it.

'You look odd,' Violetta said, hesitating as she dragged the blue catsuit snug against her breasts. 'What's on earth's the matter?'

'I want to spank you.'

There was a brief silence as Violetta stared back at her across the bed, uncomprehending. 'What?'

'Haven't you ever been spanked?'

'No.'

'My God, you're such an innocent! What am I going to do with you? Hang on ... don't move, I've got a brilliant idea.'

Mandy spun to the chest of drawers and rummaged for one of her favourite outfits, a black leather bra top and thong, slipping hurriedly into them before the mood passed. Their precious siesta time would soon be at an end and she would have to return to the office downstairs. She admired herself in the mirror for a moment before turning back to Violetta. The leather thong cut pleasurably into the fleshy pouting lips of her sex, reminding her that she had not yet enjoyed an orgasm today. Her breasts, which poured over the tight edges of the bra top in a delicious manner, were much larger and softer than Violetta's. But they lacked the other girl's marbled white perfection, slightly tanned by the sun so that freckles nestled prettily in the shadow of her cleavage. She tried to imagine their two naked bodies together, touching and fondling, rolling decadently under the sheets, and felt that honeyed warmth begin to stain the leather between her thighs.

There was such a hungry eagerness in her face today, Mandy thought, pushing back her hair with an impatient hand. Her lips were swollen and bruised where she had been biting them and her cheeks delicately flushed with excitement. In fact, she looked less like the pig she was meant to be and more like a little tigress. The thought aroused her even more.

'Did I ever tell you how I won my pig mask?' Mandy said, crossing to Violetta and stroking the other girl's fine red hair.

Breathless and apprehensive, Violetta met her eyes. 'Did they hurt you, Mandy? Like he hurt me?'

'Girl, you don't even understand what pain is!'

'You mean it gets worse?'

'No.' Mandy smiled. 'It only gets better. So come here, and don't worry, I'm not going to make you cry.'

Violetta moaned quietly as the other girl pulled her down across her knee and ran an experimental hand over the blue rubber catsuit. She was clearly scared of what lay ahead, though she made no attempt to escape. Mandy slipped one hand between Violetta's thighs, unfastening the crotch flap and expertly fastening it in place. She guessed that her pale-skinned captive was eager to discover what it felt like to be spanked, especially by another girl, but did not relish admitting that aloud. There was a series of low moans as Mandy explored her soft inner thighs and brushed against the fine reddish hairs clustering about her love lips, and then a sharp cry of alarm as the tight rubber was peeled further back to reveal that superb white bottom and the tops of those slim thighs. She could not resist fingering the three fading weals left by the cane, their purplish bruises tapering to a daffodil yellow as the skin healed. It would hurt more to strike the girl on the same site, which was a terrible temptation, but for her first time it might be a better idea to start with a considerate approach and build gradually to a higher level.

'Coping with pain is all about acceptance. That's what submission is, in a way. Accepting your place as a slave and never fighting against your domination.' Mandy laughed. 'Not that I always appreciated that. Before I could explain the benefits of submission to potential playmates, I had to learn how to submit myself. It was so hard at first, I nearly ran away on several occasions. But in the end, I came to see how easy it is.'

'Easy?' Violetta repeated in a shocked tone.

'Yes, easy.' Mandy looked down at her prone body with a mocking smile. Her hands played between the other girl's splayed thighs, stroking that sensitive area just below her first red wisps of hair. She enjoyed the way Violetta jerked under her touch and considered how it would feel to hear her cry out, this perfect bottom writhing beneath a rain of sharp slaps. 'Learning to submit yourself can be simplicity itself once you pass beyond this tiresome early stage of resistance. Stag taught me exactly as he is teaching you now, sweetie, through a traditional system of punishments and rewards. Some days he would order me to strip in front of the other members of staff, strapping me down to a table or desk and leaving me to be mauled and abused by them however they wished. Other times he would

110

take me down to the cellars for a session in the punishment room. After I had been thoroughly caned and fucked, usually both anally and in the throat, he often amused himself by lashing my hands behind my back and hanging me from the ceiling overnight. Once there was a really disgusting friend of his that he wanted me to ... service ... and I annoyed Stag by refusing point blank. So he handed me over to the chateau gardeners. They flayed me with their leather belts until my skin was black and blue, then entered me from behind and used me as a human wheelbarrow, fucking me while I was forced to run on my hands up and down the steps and through the ornamental gardens. It took weeks for the skin on my palms to heal but I learnt a valuable lesson that day.'

Violetta turned her head to stare, wide-eyed, her body trembling in the rubber catsuit. 'Never to refuse his orders again?'

'No, baby. I learnt that Stag is my master because he always knows what's best for me.'

'I don't understand.'

'It's so simple.' Mandy closed her eyes, remembering. 'I enjoyed that obscene brutality, the way those men treated me. Their abuse didn't frighten me ... it excited and aroused me. And do you know what I did afterwards? Once the gardeners had finished with me, I crawled on my hands and knees to the guy's room and begged him to hurt me too.'

Violetta shook her head in disbelief.

'And that's why I'm still here, sweetie. Because this is where I belong, in my rightful place under his feet. I know you find that hard to understand but you will eventually learn to feel the same.'

Letting her hand trail across the quivering buttocks towards the tell-tale marks of the cane, Mandy lingered over those tempting raised weals, torn between a desire to kiss this soft flesh and the urge to redden it with a stinging slap. She could tell by the girl's breathing that Violetta was aroused by her stories of punishment and submission, and indeed her own sex had moistened with excitement as she recalled her first heady days at the chateau, imagining how it must feel to be a novice again, trembling on her knees in the face of pain and unprepared for the intensity of her body's reactions.

'Stag has a heavy hand, Violetta, but you need to let the pain he gives you flow through your body like a river, to accept his punishment and not flinch. Only then can he can take you to a different place inside, to a person you did not even know existed. That's what Sophie told me.'

'Sophie?' the other girl whispered.

'She was the receptionist before I came here. One of Stag's friends took a fancy to her and offered her a job in New York. That's why the job fell vacant. But before she left, Sophie showed me the basics and explained the rules of submission to me. In fact, it was Sophie who suggested that I should wear the mask of a pig. She herself was a weasel, a natural blonde, very smart and incredibly sexy.'

Mandy ran a slow finger between Violetta's thighs and was amused to realise how damp the other girl's sex had become during their conversation. It was clear the effect her words were having on Violetta's fertile imagination. She once again felt the urge to slap the immaculate bottom below her hands but suppressed it. There was no point leaping ahead to the moment of greatest pleasure before the less experienced girl was ready to appreciate it. So instead, Mandy contented herself with nipping and rubbing her swollen labia, listening to those soft little noises Violetta made in response to her stimulation. Her plan was working. The juices began to trickle down over her fingers. Soon the slender redhead would be ripe for a lesson in pain management. Locating the hidden bud of her clitoris, she teased it gently until it grew swollen and erect. Violetta twisted slightly on her knee and moaned, laying what was obviously a hot face against the bedsheets.

'They staged a mud wrestling contest between us on Sophie's last day and invited all the chateau guests to watch. Sophie was such a petite little blonde, even slimmer than you. It wasn't hard to force her down and keep her there. You should have seen us, we were absolutely plastered from head to foot in the thick gooey mess by the end, but it was great fun. When the wrestling-match was over, Stag gave us both a good hard caning in front of his guests and then ordered us to kneel in the mud and raise our backsides to be fucked. I was incredibly sore after taking the cane but I wanted to please my new master. So I copied Sophie and did what I was told. I knelt down beside her in the mud and pulled open my bottom cheeks for the watching men.' Mandy smiled to herself. 'I can't remember the number of times they buggered me that night. I wasn't a virgin there but it still hurt like crazy. The men said I looked like such a filthy slut, rolling about in the mud and begging to be fucked in the arse, that I should wear the mask of a pig. And that's the story of how I won my mask.'

'Hurt me,' Violetta whimpered suddenly.

There was a tense breathless silence in the attic bedroom. Mandy stared down at the rubber-clad body on her knee, her hands stilled on the warm flesh. *Hurt me*. Had she heard those words correctly? Her mouth turned dry as she registered the note of acute need in Violetta's voice. There was no doubt in her own mind that she wanted to oblige the other girl with a spanking – badly needed to, in fact – but she did not want to frighten her by misreading the invitation or moving up a gear too fast.

'Are you sure this is what you want?'

'Yes.'

113

'OK.' Mandy licked her lips, her heart beginning to race. 'But before I start, baby, there are a few rules you should –'

'Just hit me!'

Her jaw hardening angrily at the unwarranted note of command, Mandy raised her hand and brought it down without warning on the exposed buttocks below. There was a sharp intake of breath from Violetta which she ignored. If the girl really wanted to be hurt, she was not going to refuse her. Mandy might take orders from Stag or the other men at the chateau, but she would not take them from this girl. Speaking like that showed a lack of understanding of the basic rules by which they had chosen to live here. Violetta needed to be taught a lesson in the respecting of status, she thought furiously. Her second slap was even harder than the first, leaving a flushed look to the skin as her hand came away. This time she heard Violetta give a high involuntary cry, her face driven deeper against the sheets as though to muffle the sound. She ought to have paused there to check how the first two blows had been taken but she did not bother. Instead she continued to slap the other girl relentlessly, making that firm rounded bottom jerk and quiver. It was what she had wanted to do as soon as she saw the girl pouring herself into the blue rubber catsuit, yet for some reason her breathing was almost as anguished as Violetta's.

Many times her hand rose and fell, though she took care not to strike the same place too often. She knew her master would not want one of his guests marked without permission. Violetta began to struggle and cry out, begging her tormenter to stop. It was obvious that she could not take much more. Yet still Mandy refused to halt, her arm trembling with the effort and her own sex lips aching for release as they pressed against the soaking leather thong. Her anger had disappeared and been replaced by a strange sense of exhilaration. It was

114

like being caught in the middle of a violent storm. Everything inside was fluctuating wildly and she could not seem to stabilise her emotions. Soon she found herself on the verge of tears, as though she were the one being punished, and yet her body was alive with such an electrifying excitement that she yearned to bring both herself and Violetta to orgasm.

Afterwards, she was never really sure which of them had come first. It had probably been Violetta, buttocks raised in violent ecstasy, skin bright scarlet from a spanking which had taken her beyond speech or reason. But Mandy's own climax had followed so swiftly they might as well have been simultaneous, her fingers scrabbling for that tiny tortured peak of flesh and rubbing against it only once before she orgasmed, releasing the scream which had been building up inside her for what felt like years.

Six

Towelling herself dry after a long relaxing shower, Violetta tensed nervously as the door to her bedroom opened. But it was only Mandy, wearing her pig mask. The pink snout came sniffing round the door first, then the girl followed it into the room, dressed in a black PVC skirt and tight-fitting top. 'I've brought your outfit for tonight.'

Violetta stared apprehensively at the tiny strapless dress over Mandy's arm. It was made of glittering fake snakeskin. Nothing more elaborate than a rectangle of material designed to skim breasts and crotch, the dress would leave little to the imagination once Violetta was wearing it. The narrow silver zip running down the front of the dress glinted in the light as Mandy came forward.

'Is that it?'

'And these.' Mandy held up a pair of high heels in the same snakeskin design.

'How about some panties? Or a bra perhaps?'

'Sorry.' Mandy shrugged, laying the dress over the bed for her. Her eyes travelled up and down Violetta's freshly showered body, barely covered by her white towel. 'But I shouldn't worry about it. That dress won't be on you for long anyway.'

'What do they have planned for me?'

'Not my place to say, is it?'

'But you know what it is?' Violetta stared into the secretive blue eyes behind the pig mask. The girl seemed

116

to be her only ally in this place. But if Mandy was going to become close-mouthed about what was happening, Violetta didn't know how she could possibly go on coping with this most unusual of holidays. 'Mandy, please give me a clue. Just a little one.'

'Only a little one?' the pig girl asked, teasingly.

Violetta felt her eyes on the smooth skin of her breasts, and raised the towel slightly, only to realise that her bottom half had now been uncovered. She felt herself flush, remembering the girl's mouth moving so skilfully between her legs. But she did not think she could cope with Mandy one-to-one tonight, even though the idea made her moisten embarrassingly. 'Please, Mandy. I need to know what I'm facing.'

Mandy's blue eyes flickered, but she didn't refuse. 'Think of big tops,' she giggled at last.

'What?'

'Work it out for yourself . . . you'll see.' The pig girl came closer, hooking a finger around the edge of the protective bath towel. There was a suggestive note in her voice. 'Do you need any help getting ready, Violetta? I could brush your hair for you. Or dry any bits you might have missed.'

'No thanks,' Violetta said huskily, then decided to go for the direct approach. She dropped the towel altogether and reached for the snakeskin dress, aware of the other girl's eyes travelling over her nude gleaming body. But she didn't want to be tempted into another lesbian encounter, however much she had enjoyed herself before. 'Look, I'll be late if I don't hurry. They said nine o'clock sharp and it's already a quarter to. You'd better get back downstairs before they miss you. You wouldn't want to risk another punishment, would you?'

'No,' Mandy said uncertainly, then shrugged and turned away. But there was a malicious gleam in the pig girl's eyes as she left the bedroom, closing the door softly behind her. 'I've been given the night off, by the way. So you'll be on your own with them, darling.'

Disturbed by that revelation, Violetta frowned. She wasn't keen on the idea of coping alone with those masked men downstairs, but there wasn't much time to ponder her situation. Thoughtfully, she stroked the strange glittering fabric of the dress. It was covered in thousands of tiny iridescent sequins, shining like real snakeskin as she shook it out and the light caught it. Violetta felt an odd sense of *déjà vu*, but couldn't pinpoint the source. Where had she seen a dress like this before? It seemed so achingly familiar, as though she were reliving some long-forgotten dream of her past. But the memories it had aroused were so hazy and disconnected, she couldn't be sure whether or not she was imagining that reaction.

'Big tops,' Mandy had said. But did she mean clothes for large-breasted women or tents of the circus variety? It was a fairly meaningless clue and Violetta tried to forget it. Mandy was probably just being spiteful, winding her up to get a reaction. After all, the receptionist was jealous as hell of the Frenchman's special interest in Violetta. That stood out a mile.

She slipped the dress over her shoulders and breathed in, drawing up the long silver zip which ran from hem to cleavage. She smoothed it down, but still felt half-naked. For a moment, Violetta was tempted to rebel. Go downstairs dressed skimpily in her bath towel and leave the dress on the bed. Except that she would probably be punished again if she refused to wear it, a painful outcome which didn't bear thinking about. No, the dress was intended for her and she had better put it on. Besides, Violetta thought drily, catching her reflection in the mirror, the dress looked pretty stunning on her. Its smooth skin-tight material displayed her curves and narrow waist to perfection. If Stag had intended Violetta to play the part of a femme fatale tonight, he should be well satisfied by her appearance . . . even if her behaviour failed to match the dress.

Violetta perched on the edge of the bed and slid her feet into the matching stilettos. The dainty criss-crossed straps fitted snugly about her ankles, and she lifted one foot in admiration. The heels were made of exactly the same iridescent snakeskin as the dress, and made her feet look achingly delicate. Like the other clothes she had received from them, everything fitted her perfectly. It was as though these men must have known her dress and shoe size before she even set foot in the place. She shivered at the thought, realising that they could have been watching her for weeks, maybe even months, before deciding to send her that bogus holiday invitation. She had been lured here deliberately by Stag, he had admitted that himself. But there was no way Violetta was going to turn out like her mother, begging for punishment and loving every minute of it. That thought alone was enough to horrify her.

Trying to ignore her own appalling excitement as nine o'clock grew closer, Violetta concentrated on brushing her long coppery hair until it shone. Stag had insisted she should wear it loose tonight. He was planning something special, she was certain of it. But after what had happened to her since her arrival at the chateau, Violetta barely dared guess what torments might lie in store for her tonight. Mandy had certainly been determined to keep her mouth shut. But that silence had come from her fear of reprisals, most likely. The receptionist might be well used to receiving the whip, but that didn't mean she enjoyed the prospect of another thrashing for talking to Violetta without permission.

Dressed and gently perfumed, Violetta wandered down the broad staircase, once again admiring the beautiful hallway with its huge gilt-edged mirrors. Her heels clicked emptily on the red and gold tiled floor as she crossed to the central table to admire the flowers there. Its polished mahogany surface reflected her face and the hanging chandeliers above her head. In that elegant cut glass vase, the white lilies of yesterday had been replaced by long-stemmed roses, their lush red petals unfolding like the curves of a woman's inner lips.

'How beautiful,' she murmured appreciatively. Violetta stooped to smell the heady fragrance, trailing her finger across one velvety petal. Stag was no mere thug, she reminded herself. This man had taste and style in abundance. In fact, the more time she spent here in his chateau, the more she began to admire him.

Violetta hated herself for that instinctive admiration, attempting to repress it even as she acknowledged its presence in her heart. The Frenchman was a cruel and vicious jailer, she told herself sternly, and such a man didn't deserve to enjoy her body. Violetta closed her eyes, turning away from the luscious temptation of the roses. She betrayed her inner weakness every time she thought of the enigmatic Frenchman without hating him.

'You like the flowers I chose?'

With a shock, Violetta opened her eyes to see Stag standing before her. Below the magnificent stag mask, he was in his habitual black jeans, those muscular thighs as powerful-looking as ever. Yet this evening he was also wearing an impressive red and gold-trimmed coat with black tails, like something a circus ring-master or lion tamer might wear. 'Big tops.' That was what Mandy had said. So it was definitely circuses then. But meaning precisely what? She already felt as though she were balancing precariously along a high wire in this place. All Violetta needed for disaster was one injudicious step and she would be free-falling through space.

Stag was still watching her silently, waiting for an answer. His chest was bare under the unbuttoned jacket and, although she tried not to stare, Violetta couldn't help noticing the broad strength of his chest, the wiry black hairs curling over his rib-cage. She felt her legs weaken slightly and despised herself for such a reaction.

'S-sorry?' she stammered. What had he just asked her? Oh yes. The long-stemmed roses. 'They're lovely.'

'I'm glad you approve, Violetta. I had you in mind when choosing them. Sharp little thorns along their stems ... but those buds open out into such sensuous flowers. It makes the irritation and effort of arranging them worthwhile.'

Violetta glanced away as he came closer, suddenly too nervous to meet that hypnotic gaze. 'Thank you for the dress and shoes,' she said huskily.

The antlered head moved from side to side as Stag walked around her in a leisurely fashion, admiring the snakeskin dress which fitted so snugly about her breasts and hips. Then his strange dark eyes dropped to her legs, their white slimness accentuated by the thrust of such high heels. Violetta knew that her pale shoulders were sensuously brushed by her long red hair, the snakeskin dress and shoes glistening superbly under the chandeliers, and felt a warm glow of pride at her own attractiveness.

As if he had sensed her thoughts, the Frenchman's voice was deep and approving.

'They suit you perfectly. I knew they would.'

'They fit me perfectly too,' she couldn't help pointing out.

'Yes, they do.' The dark stag eyes lifted to her face. There was soft laughter from under the mask. 'And you are wondering how?'

'It does seem strange.'

Stag hesitated for a moment, then stepped even closer. 'No, not strange at all. I've been watching you for years, *chérie*. I know everything about you.'

'Everything?'

The laugh came again, slightly muffled this time. His hand reached out and stroked her pale cheek. 'Almost everything. The rest you can tell me yourself, if you like. Spare no details of your past. You will find me an avid listener, *chérie*.'

'I have no past to speak of.'

The fingers caressed her parted lips. 'Yes, you were sheltered in that convent school. You never learnt what it means to give yourself freely to a man, to surrender yourself to his every command.'

She was trembling. 'How do you . . .?'

'Know about your childhood?' He laughed again, slipping one finger lovingly inside her mouth and then slowly withdrawing it, his gaze admiring the way her body swayed towards his instinctively as if she wished that contact could have lasted longer. 'I told you, I have been watching you for years. Ever since I was a teenager myself, watching your mother's films in darkened cinemas and wondering how it would feel to be inside such a woman myself. Then I heard that Candice had a daughter . . .'

'You seem to think we're alike,' she said suddenly. 'But that's not true. I barely even know my mother.'

'She was very careful not to draw you into that world, wasn't she? It must have been a terrible shock for you,' he murmured, watching her face closely. 'To leave the safety of that convent school and discover what your mother did for a living. To hear about her secret life in those erotic films. Did your mother tell you the truth herself?'

Violetta shook her head slowly, remembering. 'I was nineteen. One night, my boyfriend put a film on for us to watch together and . . .'

'And you recognised your mother?'

'Yes,' she said huskily.

'Poor Violetta.' He stroked her cheek achingly. 'You are so like your mother. So beautiful, so responsive. Look at yourself now. Your body begs for my touch with its every gesture. If I didn't know better, I would say it was Candice herself standing in front of me.'

'I'm nothing like my mother,' she repeated mechanically, pulling away and turning her back on him. The long-stemmed roses in the vase mocked her with their lush red petals.

'You've tried hard not to be, *chérie*. But you can't run forever, not from yourself. Sooner or later, you'll have to acknowledge what fear and guilt have repressed in your nature. You'll have to accept that part of yourself which is so clearly your mother's daughter.'

'You're wrong. We're two completely different people."

'You can believe whatever you wish, Violetta.' Taking her abruptly by the wrist, Stag pulled her across the hallway towards one of the closed doors. The voice beneath the mask was terse, but she couldn't be sure whether it was with anger or disappointment. 'But I know the truth about your sexuality. You may push me away and deny it, but you secretly yearn for my touch. You want to be punished and fucked. I've seen it in your face, and felt it in the heat of your body beneath me.'

'No,' she moaned in humiliation, but felt a betraying red flush begin to creep across her cheeks. Violetta knew he was speaking the truth. She had enjoyed what they had done together, she couldn't deny it to herself. But she must continue to lie to him, if only to preserve her own dignity. She couldn't bear to let him see how eager she was to experience that sexual torment, to twist agonisingly under the lash while his men held her legs spread for their thrusts.

Unaffected by her breathless protests, the Frenchman led her into a darkened room off the hallway, and Violetta saw with anguish that the other masked men were already there, waiting for her. 'We have a special treat in store for you tonight, *chérie*.'

Violetta struggled uselessly against him, drawn without option into the flickering darkness of that room. A special treat? That could only mean more pain and humiliation at their hands. She knew then that this evening would bring a even greater test of her integrity than she had faced so far. But whatever Stag believed, Violetta was nothing like her porn-star mother. She refused that possibility entirely. The only problem was, could Violetta bear their hands on her body again without betraying at least some of her delight at such abuse?

'Are you comfortable there, *chérie?*'

Speechless with indignation, Violetta stared up at the antlered man as he towered above her. She was lying on her back, tethered to a narrow bed in the centre of the room. It was padded and fitted with adjustable stirrups like a gynaecological examination table. Heavy steel manacles had been used to restrain her wrists to a rail running along each side of the bed, and the metal was chafing painfully at her skin.

Her eyes still adjusting to the candlelit darkness, Violetta thought the Frenchman seemed more than ever like a real stag instead of a man: that powerful chest and shoulders beneath the antlered mask, the lithe and graceful movement of his thighs as he circled the bed, looking down on her helpless body with neither pity nor remorse.

Flickering eerily around the edges of the room, seven enormous black candles mounted on iron candlesticks cast great dancing shadows across the walls. By their light, she could see the cruel beak of Crow, and the leering dog-eared head of Jackal. Fox was there too, stooping at Stag's command to check that her wrists were firmly secured to the examination table. Whatever dire punishments they intended to inflict on her tonight, they were obviously keen to make sure she could not escape before they were satisfied.

'I hate you,' she stuttered at last.

'You hate me?' Behind his stag mask, the Frenchman's deep voice sounded amused for once. 'That's a compliment. Hate is the flipside to love. You will understand your misapprehension soon enough.'

'Never.'

For one tense moment, Stag stared down at her without responding. She sensed a frightening stillness about him, but his voice was as controlled as ever when he finally spoke. 'That is a hard word from such a beautiful woman . . . *never*.'

In spite of risking certain punishment for her behaviour, Violetta repeated the word deliberately, pleased to see his body instantly betray his anger. The massive chest muscles under his open ring-master's coat flexed and tightened at the repetition of those two rebellious syllables. Violetta might not be able to see the man's face under the antlered stag mask, but she was learning to gauge his moods quite accurately from his voice and physical reactions alone. It gave Violetta a stab of triumphant satisfaction to know that she could be tethered like a beast for slaughter, open to any abuse he and his men cared to throw at her, and yet somehow remain inviolate in herself.

'As you wish.' Stag took a step backwards, allowing Fox to move to the other side of the examination table. He folded his arms across his chest as he watched her, those dark eyes glinting with some concealed emotion. But when he spoke again, the order he gave was flat and impassive. 'Open her dress.'

Fox leant over her prone body, his furry mask close to her face. Without a word, he slowly unzipped the snakeskin dress from cleavage to hem, and peeled back the material on either side to reveal her naked body beneath. There was a murmur of appreciation as the other men crowded closer, staring down at the pale skin of her breasts, her flat belly, the slim curves of her thighs. A sudden air of lust filled the room, and Violetta shivered. She was helpless to hide herself, though she did manage to clench her thighs together under their hungry eyes. She would resist them for as long as possible.

Showing absolutely no reaction to her naked body, Stag kept his arms folded across the ring-master's coat. But he had spotted her quick defensive movement and obviously took great pleasure in his next command. 'I think Violetta needs to understand her place. Spread her legs wide and make sure they're well secured.'

Fox grabbed each of her legs in turn and forced them into position in the high padded stirrups. There was a click as some metal ring locked into place around each ankle, so that it was impossible for Violetta to move. From the sharp tugging sensation between her legs, she knew that her vaginal lips must be gaping open, her most intimate inner depths exposed for them all to see and gloat over. Flushed with humiliation, nevertheless she felt herself moistening as their hungry male eyes turned to examine her. The snakeskin heels were jammed irretrievably into the stirrups and her thighs had already started to ache with their unnatural position, lifted so high and wide.

Violetta shrank inwardly at the knowledge that she would probably enjoy whatever torments they were about to inflict on her. She hated herself for being so affected by the crudity of her exposure, aware that they would take great pleasure in her shamelessness. But her cunt was moist and her nipples were already stiffening in anticipation. There was no way to hide such an obvious physical reaction from them, and she knew it.

'Is the camera ready?'

'Nearly.' Horse moved forward from the outer darkness, a video camera raised to his shoulder. A brilliant flashlight mounted on the camera body was swivelled rapidly into position. The lens clicked and zoomed in on Violetta, presumably capturing her nude well-spread body on film. Behind the video camera, Horse could barely contain his enthusiasm. 'Oh, yeah, that's the perfect angle . . . the cunt's so wide open, I can see right up inside her.'

'Good, keep the camera rolling.' Stag was still cool and aloof as he stood above her. 'Now run the projector.'

Jackal moved to flick some hidden switch on the floor, and Violetta stared up at the ceiling, completely astonished to see a film projection appear immediately above the examination table. As the all-too-familiar soundtrack began and the film titles flickered up with scarlet lettering on a black background, she read the words *The Animal House* with a sinking heart. It was one of her mother's most infamous erotic films. They were going to force her to watch it with them, secured to this table so that she could not escape the experience.

'You know this film?' Stag asked softly.

'Yes,' Violetta whispered.

'Then you know what's coming next, *chérie*.'

'Yes . . .' she managed to say before her voice broke. Twisting against her bonds hopelessly, Violetta simply could not tear her eyes away from the opening scene. She knew the film well. It was the same one she had seen on that first occasion with her boyfriend. A special treat, he had said, and Violetta suddenly understood what he meant by that. No doubt each of the men here would have hungrily pumped himself into every orifice in her body by the end of the film. That was why he had chosen this snakeskin dress and heels. Because that was the outfit her mother had worn during the filming of *The Animal House*. Violetta had realised the dress was familiar, but somehow her memory had blocked out the truth. Now, watching the screen action beginning above her, her past rushed back to haunt her.

'One of her best films,' Stag murmured, watching her face as she stared up at the ceiling with wide frightened eyes. 'Candice was a perfectionist. Every detail had to be right. And she never faked any of her orgasms for the camera. They were all real.'

That was true enough, Violetta thought wretchedly, remembering scenes which had shocked and horrified her. After watching that film with her boyfriend, she had gradually discovered the truth. Her mother possessed a voracious sexual appetite, never tiring of opening herself to the men in her films and her personal life. But Violetta could never bring herself to follow in her mother's footsteps, to debase herself in such a similarly relentless pursuit of pleasure.

As if sensing her instinctive denial, Stag looked down from the film and straight into Violetta's eyes. 'Horse is filming your ordeal on the video camera. Soon you will be able to watch yourself perform and then perhaps you will understand your true nature.' His breathing quickened as he watched her body twist helplessly against her bonds. 'It's such an arousing sight. Nipples taut and begging for attention. Cunt glistening with juice. Your body was made for this pleasure . . . just like your mother's before you.'

Shuddering with humiliated fear and excitement, Violetta fixed her eyes on the film above her. She did not want to look, but the picture held her as forcibly as if she had been hypnotised. There was a hum of excitement from the other men in the room as the camera zoomed in on her mother's agonised face, then panned down to show her slim body in the snakeskin dress as she was secured by ropes to a long table in the centre of a circus ring. As the ring-master unzipped the glittering material, a circle of men crowded close about her naked body, erect and eager to take their turn inside her.

'See how your mother enjoys her debasement. Listen to how she begs her masters for more,' Stag said in a hoarse voice. Violetta realised that he had released his erect penis from his jeans and was now masturbating openly as he stared up at the ceiling projection. 'Watch your mother come again and again as she suffers. Learn from her example. Soon it will be your turn, *chérie*.'

Above, the broad-shouldered ring-master in his red and gold coat bent to pick up a handful of sawdust, rubbing it brutally across her mother's navel and between her legs. Then he bent his head and the camera focused on his long tongue, lapping between Candice's spread legs. Another man, stripped to the waist and gleaming with sweat, beat her rhythmically across the breasts with a thin cane. Violetta's naked mother began panting and screaming with delight as her breasts turned from milky white to a series of vicious red stripes, her open mouth stretched in a tormented exhalation of pleasure.

The ring-master rose from between her mother's spread thighs and turned to the half-naked young woman standing behind them, her breasts painted with gorgeous green swirling patterns, nipples topped with little silver tassels. She was holding a large snake in her outstretched hands, the heavy greenish coils draped about her shoulders like a living necklace. The ring-master took the snake from her hands and laid it carefully on Candice's throat and cleavage, encouraging the scaly reptile to slither across her weal-covered breasts and down along the pale heaving belly.

Staring down at the writhing snake, Violetta's mother screamed on a high note of fear. But she was helpless to escape as the great wedge-shaped head slithered nearer and nearer to her gaping sex as if it knew what it was looking for. The gleaming bare-chested male recommenced his caning of Candice's breasts, panting with effort now as he brought the thin cane repeatedly down across her nipples. Her body jerked painfully with each blow, but when the camera lifted to reveal her face, her expression was one of agonised pleasure, eyes rolling and mouth wide open as she neared her climax.

'Turn the film off,' Violetta begged. 'I can't watch any more.'

'It doesn't excite you?' Stag demanded.

'No,' she lied desperately.

As if by way of a reply, Stag reached down and put his free hand between her legs. Violetta jerked in shock, then began to groan as his fingers rapidly manipulated her clitoris. His voice held amusement as well as excitement. 'Then why is your cunt soaking? Why are your sex lips hanging apart as if ready for penetration?'

Violetta groaned in wordless denial, twisting her head from side to side. Her long red hair was splayed out over her naked shoulders, and she could feel her nipples tautening unbearably as she listened to the hoarse grunts and moans on the film still showing above her on the ceiling. The ring-master had removed the snake and was plunging in and out of her mother's cunt, his firm hairy buttocks clenching on each forward thrust and relaxing as he withdrew. Her mother was bucking with excitement, trying to raise her hips from the table as if unable to get enough of the man's penis inside her.

Stag continued to work his fingers between Violetta's cunt lips, his eyes fixed on the flickering film projection.

'You see how she loves the pain, how she can't get enough of it? Look at her nipples, they're practically weeping from the cane. Isn't that what you crave, *chérie*? The agonising lash of a cane across your breasts and belly?'

Violetta moaned helplessly.

'Your cunt is so wet and open. Doesn't it need to be properly stretched and used?'

When she didn't reply, the Frenchman leant further forwards and inserted one long finger inside her. She moaned at the unexpectedly pleasurable sensation, and then twisted uncomfortably as he squeezed a second finger in beside the first.

'Relax.'

'I can't take any more . . .'

'Yes, you can.'

Another finger slipped inexorably inside, followed by another, and then finally his thumb, until his entire fist had entered her vaginal orifice. His knuckles ground

130

against her fleshy lips as he slowly rotated his wrist and pushed further inside, appearing to take pleasure in her cries of humiliated agony. She gasped at the shock of such a massive intrusion, her cunt now stuffed to capacity as though it had swallowed a watermelon. Even though he had reached his goal, she could still feel his fingers moving inside her, exploring and probing at the tortured walls. Standing behind him, Horse was breathless with excitement as he zoomed in on her writhing body with the video camera lens, no doubt capturing the tortured lips of her cunt straining to accommodate Stag's entire hand: fingers, knuckles and thumb.

'You like that? You want it deeper?'

'Ahhh ... no ... yes ... please.'

But Stag withdrew his fist, laughing at her howl of agonised frustration. 'You see, *chérie*? What did I tell you? I know you better than you know yourself.'

She whimpered, closing her eyes on a dizzying wave of desire. It was true. She could not escape her own sexuality. Above her head, her mother was moaning now in the aftermath of some tremendous climax, the ring-master grunting between her spread thighs as he pumped his load into that spunk-hungry cunt. And Violetta knew she wanted the same things to be happening to her. For years, she had been hiding her true self behind a façade of frigidity. Triggered by this strange masked man and his obsession with her mother, Violetta's frustrated sexuality suddenly rose to the surface in a great flood tide of need. She strained at her bonds, thrusting her breasts into the air and raising her hips off the padded table, moaning for the same physical satisfaction her mother had so repeatedly experienced. All shame was forgotten as that repressed hunger finally took control of her body.

'Take me and fuck me, then,' she hissed at the surrounding men, almost daring them to try. 'Hurt me, make me scream.'

Stag was still standing between her spread legs. He was massaging his swollen penis with his fist. Although clearly excited by her demands, his voice was angry and inflexible. 'That's no way to ask your masters for pleasure.' The Frenchman jerked his head at Crow, who stepped forwards out of the darkness with a cane in his hand. 'You must be punished for your insolence.'

The cruel beaked bird mask turned sharply as Crow looked down at her naked writhing body, then he raised his arm without saying a word and she watched the cane descend in a flash of pain and excitement. It landed straight across her nipples, winding her for a second of numbed shock. Belatedly, agony shot through her breasts as though they had come into contact with a live electric current.

Her entire torso tried to leap off the padded table in reaction, but the bonds held her fast and she sagged again immediately, screaming at the unexpected intensity of that pain. The pale tender skin of her breasts and nipples was unprepared for such physical torment. She tried to keep control of her reactions, but the agony she was suffering was almost beyond human tolerance. As the cane burnt across her breasts for the second, third and fourth rapid strokes, Violetta felt her head spin into darkness and knew that she was about to faint.

'Not so proud now, *ma belle*?'

Through the spinning darkness, Violetta hung onto the sound of the Frenchman's voice and tried to stay conscious. She couldn't speak though, because she had no breath left for anything but gasping and whimpering with pain. A fifth stroke, even more powerful than the others, landed in a straight line just beneath her nipples, sending her entire body into convulsive shock. Yet even as her breath was sucked away by the powerful aftershock, Violetta felt her exposed cunt begin to swell and ache with desire. It was an appalling sensation, for Violetta knew what it indicated. The pain itself had sexually excited her, just as it had excited her mother in *The Animal House*.

'Beg for mercy, *chérie*, and it will finish.'

Violetta wept and twisted against the examination table, desperate not to lower herself to begging. But she had no choice. Her body simply couldn't take the cane for much longer without blacking out. And to lose consciousness at their hands would be the final indignity.

As she fought to catch her breath, finally ready to humble herself and beg for mercy, the cane flashed viciously through the air once more. She had been too slow. This time the cane sliced into the tender white flesh of her belly. It was sheer agony, as though a knife blade had slashed her. Violetta let out a yelp and strained uselessly to be free of her bonds. Her sex leapt and twitched with ecstasy as the pain spread across her belly, the tortured flesh between her legs unbearably hot and succulent. It was a bizarre combination of heaven and hell, her breasts shrinking from the agonising cane even as the pain excited and stimulated her sex into wanting more.

Stag tipped his antlered head to one side, carefully considering the extent of her suffering. The tone of his voice seemed balanced enough, but his breathing was ragged and she realised he must be on the verge of orgasm, one fist rhythmically wanking his swollen penis. 'Should Fox continue your punishment? Or do you agree to be my slave?'

'I'm your slave, master,' she gasped.

'And you'll obey every order I give, without question?'

'Yes, master.'

He stepped closer. 'Open your mouth.'

She obeyed instantly, her body still arched with the excitement of that final stroke. Then she realised that his iron control over his own orgasm must have been

133

phenomenal. Within a matter of seconds, she could feel the hot splash of his come splattering over her face. One long thick jet of spunk hit her in the back of the throat as the Frenchman stood between her spread thighs, directing his erupting shaft straight into her face.

Violetta choked, spluttering as she tried to swallow before the next spurt hit her.

But even as he finished pumping his load, she saw Fox and Crow stepping closer, their own cocks being wanked furiously to orgasm, and knew that more humiliation was to come. Moments later, the combined splashes of their spunk were spurting repeatedly over her face, pouring down her stretched throat and between her aching breasts. The thin red stripes of the cane stung terribly as the spunk reached them, and she screamed with pain again, wrenching at her bonds. Several last spurts landed on her belly and ran between her spread thighs. Yet she found herself moaning with fearful excitement, aware that there would be more degradation to come that night. Gobbets of spunk began to dribble obscenely down her hair and her wide parted lips were coated in the salty white fluid.

'Do you understand now what it means, *chérie*?' Stag's voice was fierce and exultant with release. 'To enjoy pain like your mother, to give yourself freely into the hands of your masters?'

Violetta couldn't manage a verbal reply, though she understood that the Frenchman didn't really need one. He only had to use his eyes to see her excitement. Her entire body was covered with spunk, yet she was still hungry for more. She had become nothing but a filthy slut, moaning at her own debasement as Jackal stepped closer to her face and pushed his massive penis down her throat.

Gagging at the sheer size of that vein-swollen monster, her throat contracted automatically around his penis. Jackal groaned loudly as he felt her helpless reaction. He thrust even further in, wedged deep in her throat as he grasped her sperm-coated hair for balance. He was rigid with excitement and it was clear his orgasm could not be held back for long. Almost immediately, his shaft began to throb, pumping what felt like gallons of creamy spunk past her tonsils. Jackal's hips jerked feverishly with each spurt, humping her face like a dog. Violetta had no choice if she wanted to avoid the indignity of choking on his sperm. Convulsively, she gulped most of it down her throat. But some of his salty fluid still pooled at the back of her mouth for a few breathless seconds, only sliding down her throat as she choked and tried to swallow at the same time.

Aroused by her own humiliating act of submission, and acutely aware that the other men were watching her retch and twist under yet another torrent of spunk, Violetta gasped for control. But Stag's fingers were still hard at work between her spread thighs, torturing the excited flesh until it could take no more. No longer able to hold back, Violetta felt herself explode into a cataclysmic orgasm. Burning as if she had been covered in sulphur, her entire body convulsed. Her legs shook and her stiff nipples engorged with blood, tautening to puckered red buds. Clenching her fists inside the restraining manacles, she experienced wave after wave of furious heat rolling across her body. Violetta wanted to scream with the sheer release, but Jackal's penis was still buried deep in her throat. Far from spoiling the experience, though, that restraint only seemed to add to the intensity of her orgasm.

When Violetta recovered, she found that somebody had switched off the film projector and the room was silent and dark. Jackal's flaccid cock slipped easily from her mouth, and she looked up in a daze to see Stag still standing between her spread legs. His penis was semi-erect, as if the sight of her orgasmic pleasure had aroused him again, and he was wanking it now like a man possessed. Violetta licked the spunk off her lips, staring mesmerised at his cock. The livid red helmet was glistening with come as his hand jerked up and down over the slippery shaft.

But instead of filling her mouth with spunk once again as she hoped, the Frenchman gestured to Fox, who went to the darkest corner of the room and carried back a large glass tank. Inside the tank, coiled up asleep, Violetta could see the thick menacing body of a reptile. Stag's voice was uneven as he watched her expression change from sleepy pleasure to horror. 'This is for you, *ma belle*. A little present to remind you of your mother's artistry.'

'No!' Violetta screamed, straining her wrists against the manacles but unable to break free. 'I can't stand snakes.'

'You are my slave now, Violetta. Your likes and dislikes are irrelevant,' he said flatly. She shrank as the Frenchman lifted the glass lid and put his hands under the scaly coils of the snake. It stirred drowsily at his touch, but allowed itself to be brought out of the box. 'But you needn't be so afraid. He's not poisonous.'

'Don't let it touch me!'

Stag's voice grew stern under the antlered mask. 'Do you want to feel the cane again?'

'No ... no ...' she sobbed helplessly. 'But I can't stand snakes, please don't bring it any nearer. I'll do anything you want, but not that.'

'You are being foolish now, *ma belle*. I told you, the snake is harmless. You will enjoy his attentions. He's been well trained, he knows what to do.'

'No,' she repeated in a shaking voice.

'A refusal so early in the game? I'm disappointed to discover how quickly my new slave forgets her lessons in obedience.' Stag stared down at her exposed body, the coiled reptile supported across his hands and wrists. She met his eyes stubbornly, but with a certain fear for what the reprisal might be. The tension between them was tangible. 'This is not the reaction I expect from a submissive, Violetta. Your mother welcomed this particular pleasure, as you have just witnessed.'

'I told you, I'm not my mother!'

'Then you must learn to be.' Ignoring her frantic screams, Stag placed the snake on her belly and stepped back.

Almost immediately, its long flickering tongue came searching out of the reptile's mouth as it lifted its head to stare at her, and Violetta shrieked in sheer terror. The beat of her heart was staccato, tripping over itself under her ribcage as she suddenly realised what horrors lay ahead for her.

'No . . .' Violetta screamed, shaking uncontrollably, closing her eyes to blot out the terrible sight of its slithering greenish coils. Strangely though, the reptile's body didn't feel slimy as she had expected. In fact, its scaly coils were quite dry and cool against her tortured skin. But it was still a repellent sensation, and Violetta couldn't bear the feeling of that long scaly body on hers, and her whole body tensed in simultaneous excitement and panic. When she opened her eyes to look down, she saw the men crowding close about the table, watching the reptile with silent fascination. In spite of her fear, Violetta felt the familiar heat begin to trickle down her spine like sweat. Her sex felt unbearably hot and wet, the juices seeping out in an embarrassingly visible indication of her arousal. Even her buttocks were flexing and tensing now against the examination table, reacting instinctively to her arousal.

The Frenchman began to massage his shaft again. 'Does the snake's presence excite you, *chérie*?'

'Mmnnn . . .'

'Close your eyes,' he whispered, encouraging her with his voice. 'Give in to the sensations. Let them overwhelm you.'

Automatically, Violetta obeyed his command, closing her eyes and trying to persuade her body to relax. Behind the darkness of closed lids, Violetta could hear the breathless wanking of the masked men around her, and the knowledge that her terrible ordeal had aroused them was almost too much to bear. The snake continued to tickle and torment her erect clitoris as she fought against the insidious pleasure. Finally, its dry coils slipped into a clamping position across her thighs and began to tighten, increasing the mounting tension in her body. As if in response to her panic, the heavy body slithered sideways across her navel and began to slip down towards the damp triangle of hair between her thighs.

The Frenchman sounded pleased. 'Look how he knows where your heart is, *ma belle*!'

The last thing Violetta remembered was the snake being removed and Stag positioning himself between her spread-eagled thighs, his massive penis pushing into her sex. Full penetration was what she had desperately required, and her body accepted him gratefully. Violetta had been longing for him to fuck her ever since she arrived at the chateau, and at last he was inside her. Her sex lips screamed silently as that enormous purple-headed cock forced them aside and drove deep into her tortured flesh. Violetta wanted to wrap her legs around his back as he bucked himself into her, but they were held fast in the stirrups. Tethered securely to the examination table, all she could do was accept his swollen penis and let it fill her.

The Frenchman's swift urgent fucking didn't last long. Within minutes, his penis was pumping a stream of hot spunk into her belly. But the muffled grunts from inside his antlered mask seemed to indicate immense pleasure and satisfaction at his new slave's performance. Pulling his cock almost immediately from her sex, he slipped his hand down between their sweating bodies to manipulate her clitoris. Exhausted as she was, Violetta couldn't prevent herself from groaning into one final devastating climax, head spinning in bewildered delight as she arched and orgasmed under his skilful fingers.

Violetta awoke with a sudden jerk, sitting up in bed. She was alone. Her bedroom was in darkness. The shutters across her balcony door had been pulled shut, and a heavy iron bar lowered to secure them. Outside, she could hear water beating against the roof and walls of the chateau. It was raining steadily. There had been that prickling feeling all day, Violetta reminded herself, of being on edge, of the tension that often precedes a downpour in hot climates. Now the storm was here at last, drumming insistently against her shutters.

She slipped out of bed, nude and aching. Her body still hurt from the caning she had received. Padding silently across polished floorboards, Violetta lifted the iron bar away from the balcony door as quietly as she could, not wishing to draw attention to herself in case any of the men were still awake and heard her. At last, the shutters creaked open on the black rainy gardens. But although Violetta paused for a few moments in trepidation, listening for footsteps along the landing or lights under the door, nobody came.

She had been dreaming of her mother, that pale body writhing pleasurably under the cane. Now she stared blindly out of the balcony door into the blackness, remembering her dream, its fierce unforgettable clarity. Violetta had not dreamt about her mother for years. She must have woken herself deliberately, not wishing to remain in the past any longer. But the memory was still here, trembling at the very tips of her fingers as Violetta pushed the hair back from her face and walked out onto the gleaming balcony.

Her nude body stung with the rain, though it was surprisingly warm on her skin. Her bare feet trod gingerly through the puddles on the balcony. It seemed like a crazy idea but she wanted to see the storm at close quarters, let it fill her with wildness and release.

For a moment, Violetta had the sensation that she was being watched, but when she glanced nervously at the windows above and around her, they were all in darkness. There was no sound to be heard from the sleeping chateau. She must have been wrong. It was only the moon who was watching her tonight. Clouds had been covering that stormy face, but now they passed on, leaving the clear light free. Staring up at the moon in silence, Violetta gripped the wet stone rail with both hands and let her mind drift back into the dream.

She knew what it signified. Her mother was resurfacing in her life after years of being consistently denied and repressed, pushed to the back of her mind so that Violetta could forget her past and get on with her future. But the Frenchman had deliberately dragged those memories back into her present. Now she couldn't get rid of his voice in her head, insisting that blood was thicker than water, that it was *like mother, like daughter*. For how could it not be true, having witnessed her own physical reactions over the past few days? Images of herself responding to his savage thrusts, squealing with delight under those terrible punishments his men had inflicted, burnt before her eyes like the ghosts of flame left behind by a child's sparkler. She could not deny her own inheritance. The Frenchman had demonstrated that tonight, and the proof was her bruised but sated body. It was in her blood to submit to such treatment, to expose herself, to be utterly abused . . . and to love every second of it.

Sinking nude to her knees, accepting the wet stone floor of the balcony and how it grazed her skin, Violetta wept silently for her lost innocence. Rain beat down on her head and the bowed curve of her spine. It slid between the secret crease of her buttocks and washed away the sperm that had collected there. Yet the memory of what she had done with those men could not be washed away.

Recalling their brutal hands on her body, and her own lascivious reactions to their demands, Violetta again felt that strong and inescapable heat begin to burn between her legs. It was no use trying to pretend that she was repelled by what had been done to her. Somehow those men had unlocked a secret desire in her heart, to submit herself to such tortures and serve her masters well.

Violetta glanced around herself furtively, but the chateau was still dark and silent. With a quiet moan, she slipped her fingers through the damp wiry triangle of hair, finding the aroused peak of her clitoris and massaging it slowly. The rain soaked relentlessly through her hair until it clung sleekly to her head. Her sex lips grew heavy and warm under her fingers, parting achingly as if they needed to be filled again ... and again ... and again. Her hunger was all-consuming. It drove tiny whimpers of desire from her parted lips, making her forget everything, every last barrier of shame, in her need to climax.

Violetta lifted her eyes again to the moon in a spasm of sheer pleasure. Arching her back, she felt the stinging kiss of rain against her erect nipples and that tortured furnace between her legs. Leaning backwards to open her thighs as she imagined a whore might do when offering herself submissively for penetration, Violetta used her fingers to spread her sex wide open to the rain, experiencing a fierce elation as the water cascaded down through the hot secret channels of her flesh.

A long howl of desire rose uncontrollably from the pit of her stomach. It was as if she wanted the storm itself to fuck her, to take her back into the dark, into that maelstrom of twisting pleasure. Then her fingers began to work feverishly in and out of her sex, remembering how Stag had penetrated her there so forcefully, leaving behind this sticky deposit still lodged between her thighs. Every muscle and nerve in her body strained itself to the limit of physical response as Violetta trembled into an intense orgasm that left her breathless and shaking, prostrate now on the stone balcony.

Opening her eyes in the aftermath, Violetta stared about herself. Her body was aching with pleasure, yet her mind seemed strangely disorientated. Where were the brutal hands she had imagined roving all over her body, squeezing her breasts and parting her thighs? Where was the man who she had fantasised was thrusting deeper and deeper into her belly?

But the rain had stopped falling and the night air was quiet. The moon gleamed impassively along her nude breasts and belly, silvering the pale curves of her thighs. Violetta was alone and aching.

Seven

'I'll see your cards,' Fox said briefly, tossing another marshmallow into the kitty on the green baize.

Her lashes lowered to conceal the expression in her eyes, Violetta glanced down at the playing cards in her hand. The king of spades and a pair of sevens. It was not a great hand for three-card brag, but it might be enough to keep her tormentors at bay for another few minutes. She had the strong impression that losing might mean having to submit to more punishment at their hands. She laid them out on the green baize one by one, enjoying the crisp sound of each card as it bent to reveal itself.

'What have you got, Fox?' Violetta asked nervously.

If he had beaten her pair of sevens, she hardly dared to imagine what forfeits lay in store for her. Violetta had still not been allowed any underwear, and she knew what that signified. Under the demure white shift dress she had been given to wear that day, her bare thighs pressed stickily together with anticipation. There was a tense moment of silence, then Fox sighed and shook his head. The furry gingerish whiskers seemed to be quivering as he tossed his cards down on the baize.

'Jack high.'

Smiling again, Violetta dragged the small pile of pink and white marshmallows towards her, popping one into her mouth and enjoying the sweet sensation as it melted against her tongue. They had been playing for half an hour, yet still neither Fox nor Crow had beaten her. She was not entirely sure what would happen when they did, but at the moment, her belly was comfortingly full of these deliciously soft marshmallows they were using as money. From the look of disappointment on both their faces, she was sure that some dire punishment was to be meted out to her when she did eventually lose a hand. Until then, though, she was enjoying herself immensely.

'Why has Stag left the chateau? When will he be back?' she asked again, not wishing to seem too eager but unable to resist another attempt at prying the truth out of them.

'Just shuffle the pack and deal us another hand,' Crow said sternly, the cruel beak turned sideways as he watched her across the table with one glinting eye. 'He'll be back soon enough.'

Obediently, Violetta bent her head to her task, her long fingers flicking rapidly through the pack of cards, splitting and shuffling them for another game. At least by playing cards she was able to occupy her mind, instead of pointlessly pondering the Frenchman's absence.

Violetta stared down apprehensively at the cards she had just dealt herself. Three of spades. Two of diamonds. Eight of clubs. It looked like her run of luck had come to an end at last. Her cunt twitched with nerves as she considered what might happen next if either of the other two players had better cards. There was only one thing she could do in this situation. Bluff frantically and hope it worked.

'Good hand?' Fox asked slyly.

'Uh-huh,' she said, pushing a marshmallow into the centre of the table. 'How about you?'

Unnervingly cool, Fox picked up a marshmallow and chucked it down next to hers in the kitty. 'We'll see.'

Looking less sure of himself, Crow hesitated for a moment, examining his cards. Then he shrugged and placed another marshmallow in the centre of the table, as if deciding to take a chance on his cards. He twisted the savage beak to one side and glanced beadily at Fox. 'It's about time we had some better luck with these cards.'

'The bitch can't win forever.'

'Who says?' she replied tartly, putting her next marshmallow into the pile without any indication of fear.

Fox slid another marshmallow into the centre. 'I do.'

'You'd be wrong.'

The gingerish whiskers quivered as if the man was laughing silently beneath his mask. 'I doubt it.'

Violetta felt a sudden stab of trepidation. Fox was far too cocky, too sure of his hand. From beneath discreetly lowered eyelids, she stared nervously across at the cards in his hand. The backs were decorated with wrestling tigers, bold and and striking and colourful. But she didn't have X-ray vision. She had no idea whether Fox truly had a winning hand there, or if he was bluffing too. Still, it wouldn't take much to beat her at the moment. Eight high was not exactly an earth-shattering hand for a game of three-card brag. But that was why it was called 'brag', Violetta reminded herself sharply. The players were meant to bluff it out with each other like this when the cards were low. That was the name of the game.

Crow was shaking his head. 'I'm out.'

With a triumphant laugh, Violetta glanced across at Fox, knowing that the odds against her losing had narrowed considerably. One on one. Now it was a question of holding her nerve steady and hoping that he didn't pay to see her before jacking his hand in himself. She raised her chin, pushing her own marshmallow into the kitty.

'Looks like it's just you and me, Fox. How cosy.'

Fox obviously disliked her arrogant tone. He hesitated before placing his bet, those calloused fingers hovering above his three remaining marshmallows as if he was dying to pay to see her, but not sure if he should take the chance of losing again. Another bad strike like the last one and he would probably be out of the game altogether. This was all about bluff and counter-bluff, she thought. It was simply a matter of waiting to see which way Fox decided to swing.

'I'll see you,' he said at last.

Her colour fading, Violetta stared at him. 'What?'

Tersely, Fox repeated his request, throwing two marshmallows into the centre of the table to make sure she understood. He watched her face for a moment, his fingers tapping restlessly against the green baize cloth. Then, as the seconds ticked by without Violetta responding, his shoulders began to shake with laughter as her expression changed from triumph to growing consternation. He had won this particular hand, and he knew it. 'Come on, show us your cards.'

'But . . .'

'Lay your cards on the table.'

Violetta was trembling. 'Can't we play on a little longer?'

'I've paid to see you. Drop the cards.'

Her body jerked at his commanding tone. Glancing at both masked men with a gathering sense of dread, Violetta laid her playing cards face up on the green baize one by one. Two of diamonds. Three of spades. Eight of clubs. There was a long silence. Violetta took hope from that, assuming that Fox too had been bluffing and that his own hand was no better than hers. But her optimism was short-lived.

'I knew you were bluffing!' Fox laughed again suddenly, throwing his own cards down on the table. Ten of spades and a pair of kings. She had lost the hand. Getting swiftly to his feet, Fox grabbed her wrist and pulled Violetta towards him around the card table.

'Let me go!'

Terrified of the consequences of losing, Violetta felt his stiff ginger whiskers brushing her face and tried to break free of his grasp. But he was far too strong for her, and within seconds, Crow had stepped behind her and blocked her escape route.

Fox stared down at her body, laughing hungrily. 'You lose, I win. Those are the rules.'

His hand tightened on her wrist, moving her to one side so that her bottom was thrust painfully against the baize-topped card table. Fox was leaning on her now, and through the thin white shift dress she could feel his growing erection pushing into her belly. On her other side, Violetta realised that Crow must have unzipped his black jeans and removed his penis, because she could hear the rhythmic sound of wanking. The punishment for losing was to have sex with them, she knew that for sure. But what kind of sex? And without Stag's protective presence, what new torments might these men have in mind for her?

Crow was breathing heavily as the birdman pressed closer. 'I liked what you did last night at the film show,' he muttered. His hand was jerking feverishly now up and down his exposed shaft. He was so close, she could practically smell the pre-come oozing out of its narrow slit. 'You're just like your mother. Same hair, same breasts, same hot little cunt.'

Violetta shook her head vehemently. 'I'm nothing like her!'

'Don't bother to deny it,' Fox insisted hungrily, running his hands over her body in the thin shift dress. 'We all saw you. Panting for it, begging for our spunk, loving every minute of what was happening to you.'

'I hated it,' she lied quickly. 'I only did it because I had no choice. You tied me down, remember?'

'But you loved being tied down, you slut!'

'No.' Violetta shook her head, tears springing helplessly into her eyes. 'And I didn't beg for your spunk. I begged you to stop.'

But she knew he was right. She had actually begged for sex in the end, desperately aroused by the way they had tethered her like a mare in heat, ready for mounting. Now she could see from their excitement that her humiliating ordeal was far from over.

'What are you going to do?' she whispered.

Fox hesitated, as if unsure himself, then gave her a gentle shove so that she fell backwards. The card table collapsed, its heap of pink and white marshmallows rolling across the polished floor. Whimpering with fear, she tried to scrabble away from her tormentors on her hands and knees, but Crow caught her, dragging her into a kneeling position by her long red hair. Fox was two steps behind him, and she soon felt his hands reach under the thin white shift dress to locate her warm cunt, playing it like an instrument with his coarse fingers.

'The whore's good and wet for us,' he muttered to Crow.

'Push her down! Spread her legs!'

'No,' Fox said, still dragging his rough fingers back and forth over the nub of her quivering clitoris. 'I've got a better idea. Grab some of those marshmallows.'

Speechless, Violetta stared up into his masked face. What on earth did he have planned for her? She moaned with horrified excitement as two, three, four of his fingers spread themselves painfully inside her sex, stretching the damp muscular walls.

'Here you are.' Crow had gathered a handful of pink and white marshmallows from the floor. He passed them to Fox with a curious laugh. 'What are you going to do with them?'

Ignoring his question, Fox barked at her abruptly. 'Bend over and touch your forehead to the floor!'

Obediently, not wishing to anger either of these men, Violetta bent her face to the floorboards and raised her buttocks towards their faces. She felt somebody push the thin shift dress up to her waist and suddenly there was cool air on her exposed sex and thighs. Trembling with apprehension, Violetta waited for their next onslaught, wishing that Stag was here to keep his men under control. Whatever the Frenchman might do to her himself, whatever orders he might give the others so that she could be humiliated and tortured, there was always a sense that he was in control. That nothing would ever really harm her while his watchful presence was in the room.

But here she was alone with his men, and Fox was already reaching between her spread legs, several marshmallows in his hand. Pushing open her outer lips without preamble, he began to stuff the soft marshmallows up into her sex, one by one, the squidgy sweets bulging inside her belly as he crammed each one of them carelessly up between her spread thighs as though stuffing a turkey. Violetta groaned, trying to hold onto the unusual load with her internal muscles, but the marshmallows were becoming sticky with the heat and moisture of her sex. In the end, she felt one or two slip out without warning, slithering to the floorboards in a mess of white or pink goo.

'Oh dear, I think you dropped something there,' Fox laughed, scraping the goo off the floor. Then his voice changed, hardening into a command. 'Raise your arse higher, slut.'

She obeyed instantly, but found herself struggling to keep control of that warm marshmallow goo inside her sex as her muscles automatically shifted position. Sore and humiliated, she raised her buttocks even further towards the masked men. Fingers ruthlessly probed her anal opening. She hissed with disgust as the soft mess pushed against her tightly puckered outer sphincter, then felt it slide inside with a sticky plop. Not content with this bizarre torment he had dreamt up for her, Fox scooped some more sweet goo out of her bulging sex and smeared it between her buttocks before also pushing that firmly home inside her rectum. His long thick finger followed it for a few moments, exploring lewdly inside her bottom until she moaned at the sheer degradation of her position.

Crow was wanking more energetically now. He grabbed her by the scruff of her neck and raised her head. Directly in front of her eyes, she could see the narrow slit of his bulbous cock-head. The one red eye of his shaft glared back at her, obviously poised to spurt hot spunk into her face – given the right trigger. Which she guessed was going to be her mouth. Crow yanked savagely at her hair again, prodding his long cock closer to her face.

'Suck it, whore.'

Violetta parted her lips and let the swollen penis fill her. She was in no position to argue. But as she sucked and massaged him with her lips, his sweat-slick shaft thrusting heatedly in and out of her mouth, she felt her own arousal steadily growing. At each withdrawal, she let her tongue drag along the shiny underside and its blood-filled vein, and as he plunged back down her throat, she tried to relax her muscles so that she wouldn't gag at his length, voluntarily tilting her head to allow him greater depth of penetration. But at least Crow seemed to be following a regular rhythm, which gave her some sense of relief. His penis was so long that any sudden violent thrusts might have hurt her badly.

Grabbing quick swallows of her saliva whenever she could, Violetta took pride in the sound of his satisfied groans above her. She was gradually learning to accommodate a larger penis in her mouth now, after years of only being able to lick gently at a man's bell-end. It seemed amazing to her what was physically possible once she had no choice in the matter. Without their coercion, she would never have dreamt she could have managed to take a cock this size in her mouth without retching. Somehow it made Violetta feel immensely

150

feminine to be in this position, down on her hands and knees, getting her throat forcefully shafted by this stranger.

With lewd muttered comments under his breath, Fox continued to finger her tight anal opening. He pushed his thick finger into her bottom. And dragged it out again. In deeper. Out again. The sticky marshmallow gunk seemed to be providing a generously slick lubricant for his work. Her sphincter flexed involuntarily as he abruptly withdrew and let fly a pungent dribbling marshmallow fart into his face.

Crow groaned and she felt his penis begin to throb between her lips. Thrusting his hips forwards, Crow seized her head with both hands and impaled her throat on his enormous weapon. He shouted his relief as he came, thrusting in up to the hilt. It was like trying to accommodate a scaffolding pole in her mouth.

Violetta gagged helplessly as thick creamy spurts of come shot down the back of her throat, bathing her mouth in so much of his hot salty liquid that she could neither breathe nor swallow for a few terrible seconds. She thought for a moment that she was going to come again with the sheer excitement of experiencing such brutality, then Crow released her without warning. Choking and gulping oxygen frantically into her lungs, Violetta collapsed onto the floorboards at his feet, remnants of his spunk that she hadn't been able to swallow dripping like white sauce down her chin.

But Fox had not finished with her yet. With one brutal hand, he shoved her dress further up her back and kicked her legs wider apart. Then he straddled her prone body. His knees came down to clamp her firmly into position on the floor. There was a pause, and Violetta secretly hoped that he was going to bugger her at last. Then she felt his penis teasing her buttocks apart but still he didn't enter her. Instead, he leant further forwards, wanking himself energetically. After only a few seconds, Violetta felt a thick wad of his come shooting up at her anal crack and along the exposed curve of her spine. Grunting with the force of his orgasm, Fox continued to rub his spurting cock along the marshmallowed crack and around the puckered entrance to her rectum.

Violetta howled with delight, raising her sticky buttocks towards him. Heat suddenly filled her face and she knew her own orgasm must be close. In spite of the fact that both men were watching her, Violetta slipped one hand between her spread thighs and massaged her aching sex to an instantaneous and unforgettably lush orgasm. Her nipples were still weeping fluid from the vicious caning they had received only the night before, but they stiffened inexorably as her cunt lips swelled with blood and exploded into a starburst of pure heat. In the final throes of orgasm, Fox pressed down on her body, crushing her against the polished floorboards and pumping the last few spurts of his come between her buttocks.

Their breathless bodies lay tangled together on the floor for a few moments, then Fox stood up. The masked man towered above her, placing his boot on her neck and pinning her down in a humiliating position. 'You really enjoyed that, didn't you? You dirty little slut. You can't get enough cock to satisfy your lust, can you?'

Violetta whimpered in pain and excitement, feeling his heavy black boot press harder against her neck. 'No, master.'

'Spread her legs for me, Crow. Nice and wide, so we can see where the slut took my spunk.'

Crow knelt in an unhurried fashion behind her body and pushed her soaking thighs even wider apart, exposing the swollen-lipped cunt and the small dark hole of her anus. Its abused crease opened stickily with its gunk of pink marshmallow and the rivulets of trickling spunk.

She knew what they must be seeing as they looked down on her naked body, and writhed in horrified humiliation at their feet. Nothing could be hidden from these men. Nothing. She was utterly helpless in the face of their power, and they knew it. Yet something warm and erotic stirred in her belly at the thought of her ordeal, to be used repeatedly in whatever manner they desired.

'Look at that mess between your legs, you dirty whore. Your spunk-holes need to be swilled out before Stag gets back.'

Violetta groaned at the sound of Fox's derisive laughter, his boot still punishing the fragile bones in her neck.

'Please . . . master . . .'

'Silence.'

There was a momentary hesitation, then she felt hot fluid cascading over the weals on her thighs and buttocks, and spattering freely between her legs. Shock flashed through her body as she realised what was happening. Fox was urinating onto her. The golden liquid began to burn into the lash marks still criss-crossing her buttocks and Violetta jerked in pain. He ignored her, his boot exerting a little more pressure to keep her in place. Wholly unable to escape her punishment, Violetta lay there with her face pressed hard against the floor, flailing hysterically as the urine splashed over her most intimate parts. Then, just as the stream began to slow and trickle to a halt, she felt the boot ease gradually off her neck. Violetta sobbed with relief, trying to sit up and put her hands to her stinging buttocks.

'No more, please . . .' she sobbed in desperation.

But Crow clearly had his own plans. He seized her by the hair again and dragged her weeping to her knees. 'Shut up, slave. Your shower's not over yet. Your cunt and arse may be clean now, but you took spunk somewhere else too, didn't you?'

Too late, she realised his meaning and cried out in horror. His large semi-erect cock was being held directly in front of her face again, but this time the masked man grunted and let the urine spurt from his cock instead of sperm. At such close range, the amber fluid sprayed violently into her eyes, nose and mouth, blinding her and leaving her gasping for air. As Violetta tried desperately to jerk away, she felt his hand grip her hair tighter so that she couldn't move. She was being utterly degraded, but her belly was coiling with heat and she almost wished she could see herself, held down while this man sluiced the spunk off her face with his urine.

Then Crow shifted his position slightly, so that the hot stream was pouring straight down her throat. Violetta tried obediently to swallow the sour liquid, but within seconds she was retching and scrabbling about frantically to be free.

'Come on, swallow it down.' Crow was laughing now as he shoved himself deeper. 'You need your throat swilled out too.'

When he had finished at last, and she was lying in a warm puddle of piss on the floor, Violetta moaned with misery and excitement as Fox dragged her once more to her feet. Bruising her arms, he ripped the sodden white dress from her body and threw it down onto the soaked floorboards.

'You won't need that dress. We're finished with you now, but the others may want their turn later.'

Fox tangled his fingers in her long piss-soaked red hair and dragged her out of the games room into the mirrored hallway. Under his mask, Fox seemed to find her shrieks of pain amusing.

'Does that hurt? Excellent. You must learn not to answer your master back.'

'I'm sorry . . .'

'That's not good enough. You've done it once, you may do it again. You must be taught a proper lesson for your disobedience,' Fox snapped in reply. He gestured to Crow who removed the vase of luscious red roses from the centre table in the hallway, and lifted up the spare table leaves into position, revealing chains and metal clips attached to the wood. Violetta stared at them in horror, having always associated this place with peace and beauty. Now she could see herself reflected in the huge gilt-edged mirrors lining the hallway, her nude piss-slick body still covered in yesterday's red weals and darkening bruises. She had changed and so had the beautiful hallway, suddenly a place of torture and punishment for her aching body.

Fox dragged her forward to the edge of the table. 'Climb up there and spread your legs, slave.'

Violetta lay on her back as she was commanded, trembling and sobbing. The heavy chains and manacles were fastened into place around her wrists, stretched above her head like a sacrificial victim. Fox grabbed hold of her spread thighs and lifted them back up against her chest. He pressed down so hard that Violetta screamed in panic, thinking he was about to fuck her again. But Fox merely laughed at her expression of fear, manacling each ankle in place on the polished table top. When he had finished, she was positioned with her knees squashed against her breasts, arms stretched above her head, her cunt and anal orifice utterly exposed to whoever might be passing and in need of relief.

'Perfect.' With a grunt of satisfaction, Fox stepped back and dried his hands on his jeans. The whiskered gingerish mask moved from side to side, admiring his handiwork. Then he turned to Crow, shrugging his shoulders with a barbaric laugh. 'Stag should be back soon. He may want to use his slave before dinner.'

Hours passed like centuries as Violetta's body throbbed helplessly with the pain of restraint. Every muscle was screaming for release, but she knew it could not come until they were satisfied with her suffering. Humiliating as it was, Violetta could not help feeling a burning pleasure between her raised open thighs, and wished there was some way she could touch herself, relieve that incredible pressure of desire. But her wrists and ankles were manacled to the table so fast that she abandoned all hope of relief or escape, closing her eyes and groaning with a mixture of pain and exhilaration at her own helplessness.

Violetta felt she had been bound there for ever by the time the great entrance door to the chateau opened with a click. There was a brief hesitation as whoever it was took in the sight of her glistening body bound helpless to the table, then the door clicked shut again without emphasis.

Firm masculine footsteps approached the central table. Violetta opened her eyes and stared dizzily up at the red and gold patterns on the ceiling. She could not lift her neck more than a few inches to see who it was, but her instincts told her that Stag had finally returned to the chateau. The trembling in her limbs started again, shaking her entire body as he came closer.

With a deep sense of humiliation, Violetta tried to imagine what the Frenchman must be seeing before him. Her white pearl-slick thighs clasped tight to her chest and spread wide for his convenience. The glistening piss-damp triangle of her pubes. Her swollen cunt lips, gaping where she had been repeatedly filled over the past few days. And the dark puckered hole of her anus, surrounded by tiny coarse hairs. No doubt the skin there was a little reddened and stretched from the bout of sodomy she had endured, and still coated with the pinkish gunk of melted marshmallow and spunk.

Violetta knew she must look like some submissive whore, and that was precisely what Fox had intended when he tied her down to this table, her most intimate parts abused and exposed for her master's examination.

Flushed and aroused by that realisation, she knew it was no mere illusion. Over the past few days, she had indeed shifted from being an appalled innocent to a willing slave.

'Good evening, *chérie*.' The voice inside the mask was slightly muffled as always, but he sounded amused. 'How thoughtful of somebody to leave me such a beautiful present.'

She whimpered with excited fear as his fingers reached out and stroked between her damp sex lips. Manacled to the table, with her thighs pressed painfully against her chest, she was powerless to resist him. But a terrible illicit pleasure began to coil in the pit of her stomach as she considered the possible torments he was about to inflict on her. The searching fingers moved lower, sliding into the sticky crevice of her anus and casually fingering the tiny puckered hole there. Violetta writhed and moaned without being able to stop herself, her sweat-soaked back and buttocks squeaking against the polished wood.

Violetta heard the sound of his jeans being slowly lowered. It was appalling to think that she could enjoy such a degrading situation, but her mouth was already salivating with desire at the knowledge that her master was planning to take her, right there in the hallway, still tied down to the table like some obscene pornographic exhibit.

She felt him move even closer between her legs, fingering her anus again in a puzzled fashion. 'But what have we here?' The Frenchman straightened for a second, licking his finger through the mouth slit in his stag mask. His voice registered surprise and delight. 'Marshmallow?'

'It was Fox and Crow, master. They put it inside me.'

'I'm glad to see you have not been idle today, *chérie*. Did you enjoy your time alone with my men?'

Violetta blushed with pure shame, closing her eyes at the memory of her ordeal that afternoon. But she

couldn't try to deny her feelings to him, it was impossible. Stag was too perceptive for that. He would see
through any subterfuge and punish her severely for
having the temerity to lie.

'Yes, master,' she whispered truthfully at last. 'I did
enjoy it.'

He watched her face. 'Did they fuck you?'

'Yes, master.'

'Where? In your cunt?'

She would have remembered that. 'No, master.'

'In your arse, then?'

'Yes, master.'

Experimentally, the Frenchman stroked his finger in
and out of her dilating anal orifice. 'I can still feel spunk
lodged there.'

'Yes, master.'

'Good, *chérie*. I'm pleased with your obedience.
Where else?'

'In my mouth, master.'

'Mmm . . .' He paused. 'Which of my men took you
there?'

'Crow, master.'

Stag made an appreciative noise under his breath,
watching her face. 'Crow has a large prick. Did he hurt
you, *chérie*?'

Violetta opened her eyes once more and gazed up at
the beautiful hallway. Behind the hanging chandeliers
the red and gold patterns on the ceiling seemed to be
spinning, like some brilliant merry-go-round. Relaying
that sordid activity had made her breathless and dizzy.
She was suddenly glad of her cruel restraints, sure that
she would have fallen from the table without them. 'Yes,
master.'

'Badly?'

'Yes, master. My throat is still sore.'

He stared directly down into her eyes. 'But did you
enjoy the pain he inflicted?'

158

'Yes, master,' she whispered.

'Bravo, *ma belle*. I only wish I could have witnessed that myself, but I felt it was better to ...' Then he hesitated and lowered his head in the heavy stag mask, as if searching for something between her thighs. The sharp antlers grazed her belly for a second and she cried out involuntarily, sure from the pain that he had drawn blood. The Frenchman straightened at last, his voice husky and uneven. 'Your cunt and arse smell of piss. Did my men baptise you there, *chérie*?'

'Yes, master.'

'And did you enjoy your baptism?'

'Yes, master.'

There was a long powerful silence. Violetta could not begin to guess what the Frenchman was thinking, but she could hear that his breathing had quickened at her submissive replies. Swelling with blood, her cunt lips and clitoris began to sting with pleasure at the mere thought that her master might be tempted to enter her. Closing her eyes again, Violetta gave in to the sensations, acutely aware of her humiliating position and how much pleasure it gave her to be helplessly spread open like this for her master's penetration. Only a few days ago, Violetta would surely rather have died than submit to such debasing treatment as she had suffered that afternoon – and might still suffer tonight – but now her belly felt warm and heavy with desire. Desire for her master. Desire for pain. Desire for degradation. Desire for more.

From the jerking sounds she could hear, Violetta suspected that her master was standing between her legs, masturbating. She tried to raise her head to see his hands at work, but it was no use. Her neck was too stiff and heavy to lift off the table, and the way she was manacled permitted little movement of any other part of her body. Resigning herself to her fate, Violetta tried to relax her straining muscles in preparation for what might come next. Perhaps her master would choose to enter her piss-soaked cunt. Or force himself into her exposed anal orifice for his own pleasure. Maybe Stag was tired and would simply wish to shoot his load across her sex lips and belly, leaving her aching and unsatisfied on the table. Violetta realised once again that she had absolutely no choice in the matter, and the thought made the bruised flesh between her legs gush with pleasure.

'Who do you serve?'

'You, master.'

His voice was brutally casual. 'I'm going to fuck you now.'

'Yes, master.'

His massive penis pressed against her outer lips and forced them apart. He had decided to take her sex. Violetta moaned with wild pleasure, hoping that her vagina was well enough lubricated for his penetration. It was true, she had not lied to him or to herself. Stag was her master now, and Violetta wanted to obey him. She wanted to please and satisfy him in every way she could. In a flush of heated ecstasy, she strained to raise herself for his cock. His grunt of satisfaction made her insides clench with delighted excitement. She was pleasing him with her abject submission, and that was all she needed or wanted to do now. To please her master and feel his pleasure.

Stag placed his hands on either side of her head, leaning forward until the antlers were swaying right above her eyes, those cruel bestial tines blotting out the red and gold ceiling and the glitter of the hanging chandeliers. Staring down into her face, he ploughed her sex with deliberate and controlled strength. Each forward thrust right up to the hilt told her she was his slave and must submit to his every demand. Each slow withdrawal told her he was her master and could prevent her from experiencing pleasure whenever he pleased. Licking her lips and watching those powerful shoulders moving rhythmically back and forth above her, Violetta moaned quietly as a token of her complete submission. Her master responded by lengthening his thrust, his balls slapping repeatedly against her buttocks as he drove deeper and deeper inside her.

Violetta allowed her eyes to close briefly and felt her skin begin to stir with an electrical excitement. Never before had she understood her own nature so accurately as she did at this moment. She realised that she would do anything in the world, pass any boundary he cared to select for her, emotional, mental or physical, in order to serve her master to the utmost of her ability . . . and beyond. Whatever he might ask of her in the future, however painful or barbaric, she would respond with his unquestioning obedience. That was the way it must be for her now.

Violetta suddenly understood that she had finished with that childish dream of love she had once longed to feel for other men. This was a true love which she felt for her master, an adult love. It accepted and received pain as an integral part of pleasure, obedience as an integral part of trust. His men could enjoy her body at their wills, but she knew it was always only at *his* will that they used her. She belonged to her master because he desired her to belong to him, because she knew it was the only true path she could have taken after their first meeting. The path of submission.

Watching in mesmerised heat as her master fucked her, Violetta could see thick blue veins standing out on his neck as Stag neared his climax. He gave a quick muffled grunt of satisfaction each time his penis drove against the neck of her womb, his whole body focused on their union. Her own body responded to his concentrated pleasure by swelling and opening up like one of those lax petalled roses in the vase, inviting more and more of his power inside her. It was a dance they were performing together: away and towards each other back and forth, the rhythm forever changing even as it neared its end. But Violetta knew that she didn't need to move in order to perform this dance with her master. Her restraints were teaching her how to join and pleasure him without physical movement. It was a matter of complete acceptance. He gave, she received. Pain or pleasure, pleasure or pain, there was no difference in the dance.

Groaning and clenching his fists on the table beside her head, Stag drove up to the hilt in her belly and ejaculated. Although that sudden fierce penetration was painful, Violetta took his spillage of warm semen and accepted it. Felt it seep into her flesh and even the bone beneath. Joyfully, Violetta imagined it as little droplets of mercury, running down into her veins and bubbling under her skin. All day long she had been craving his sperm as a baby craves the taste of its mother's milk, wondering when her master would return to fill her. But now he was here at last, brutally pumping his climax inside her, and she was secure in his presence.

Now that he had finished with her, Violetta longed to stroke his body, run her hands over his powerful spine and shoulders, but she was restrained by the manacles. Such contact was forbidden. Because her master did not desire her touch. He desired her merely to be still and receive him. And she ached to obey him.

The Frenchman pulled out of her at last and straightened. The antlered mask inclined as he watched his spunk trickling gently from her exposed cunt. When at last he spoke, his voice was husky. 'That was well done. You have learnt more than I expected, *chérie*.'

It was genuine praise, and Violetta blushed.

'Today was hard for you, *ma belle*. But tomorrow will be harder,' he added, zipping up his jeans. 'Try to rest.'

He left her without another word, still bound helpless on that polished table, staring up at the chandeliers as

162

his cooling sperm continued to ooze from her sex. It dribbled down between her buttocks and pooled on the mahogany surface below. Violetta tried to obey her master and get some rest, but the glittering lights directly above her head burnt into her eyes and made sleep impossible. It must have been several hours later when Fox finally came to release her stiff aching limbs from the manacles, carrying Violetta upstairs in silence and laying her down to sleep between clean white sheets.

Eight

'That's far enough. Now clasp your hands behind you head and hold that position.'

Completely naked, her mouth ball-gagged and he unruly chestnut hair blinding her eyes, Mandy felt he feet being kicked wider apart as she bent face down ove a padded bench in the punishment block. For an instan she nearly lost her balance, her cry muffled behind th ball-gag, but then managed to steady herself in time t stop herself falling. She listened to the slight scuffin sound of Stag's bare feet against the stone floor, hi movements almost inaudible as he turned away from th bench towards the wall. Her bottom stinging and sor from a comprehensive spanking, Mandy feared wha this latest command might mean. Was there going to b worse pain ahead?

In spite of her apprehension, she obeyed Stag withou delay, struggling to clasp her hands behind her hea while the muscles in her upper arms ached from th awkward posture. Her stomach rumbled and sh blushed with embarrassment, hoping he had not hear the tell-tale sounds of her hunger. Normally she woul have been eating lunch by now and looking forward t another lazy siesta. But it had been a long mornin Mandy thought irritably, made even longer by a fe stupid administrative mistakes which had earned he this punishment session, not that she disagreed with he

164

treatment. This way she should remember not to hurry over her calculations in future, even though she might not be able to sit comfortably for the next week or so. Now she tensed, aware of Stag walking about behind her. From the occasional rattle of metal against stone and the smell of oiled leather, she guessed he must be searching through the assembled implements on the wall rack for something to prolong her suffering. Closing her eyes tightly, Mandy hoped that he would not choose the cane. He rarely used it on members of staff, preferring to reserve that particular torture for his guests, but Stag seemed in a rather prickly mood this morning and her punishment might be correspondingly more painful than usual.

'Did I say you could move?'

She stiffened with fear at his angry question. Those observant eyes must have spotted her quick, almost imperceptible shake of the head. He took two steps towards her and Mandy felt his fingers bite cruelly into the back of her neck, stilling and controlling her.

'Do you need a retraining session, Amanda?' Stag sounded weary now, as though she had disappointed him. 'When I order you to hold a position, I don't expect you to move. Not even a single muscle. Now open your eyes. You will not close them again without permission.'

He moved to a control panel on the wall and she waited, her upper body stretched tautly backwards as instructed, trying hard to control her breathing so that her body would remain as motionless as possible.

'Stretch your head further back. No, further than that. *Merde*, what's the matter with you today?'

Impatiently, his hands helped to adjust her position, tilting her chin backwards until her pale throat was completely exposed and she was staring upwards at the ceiling. There was a film screen fixed across the beamed cellar floor in this part of the punishment room. She had often watched Stag's films like this before, though more usually lying on her back whilst being penetrated or performing fellatio, the erotic movie playing above her as inspiration. This would be more like punishment than inspiration. Her muscles were already protesting, unused to maintaining such an unnatural position, but she tried to ignore that nagging discomfort and concentrate on what was required of her. Mandy had long since realised there was nothing worse than disappointing her master, even if her body had to suffer for such painstaking obedience.

'That's better. Now stay perfectly still and watch the film.' Stag stood behind her, his hands toying with her buttocks in an almost absent-minded fashion. 'And don't be afraid to tell me what you think. You know I always welcome your opinion.'

Her body trembling with the effort of holding this gymnastic position, Mandy stared rigidly up at the screen on the ceiling. The film began with an opening shot of Violetta's naked body, lying on her back on what appeared to be this same bench, with a snake coiled across her belly. The girl's pale skin shone with a mixture of sweat and oil, her nipples darkening and swelling as the masked men on either side of her manipulated them cruelly. It did not take long for her mouth to be entered and used, the thick shaft of a penis stretching those innocent lips to their limit.

In complete obedience, Mandy watched the film without any change of expression, her torso arched painfully backwards and her throat muscles screaming in silent agony. It was difficult but not impossible, she thought at first, not realising how slowly the minutes would drag by as the lurid scene above them unfolded. But by the time the other girl's face and breasts had been covered in semen, that antlered mask poised between her spread thighs for the final act of penetration, Mandy suddenly disgraced herself by being unable

166

o hold the position any longer. Her raised arms faltered and dropped, her body slumped forward onto the padded bench, and she groaned her despair behind the restrictive ball-gag.

'Is that your idea of obedience? *Dieu*, have I just been wasting my time with you?'

The deep note of anger in Stag's voice was terrifying. She shook her head in mute protest, struggling to regain the position, but it was too late. His hand grasped her hair, yanking her to her knees on the stone floor. Although she could not cry out, her eyes began to water as he dragged her towards him by her hair, swearing incoherently in French. It was well known amongst the chateau staff that Stag had a violent temper when roused, but Mandy had never experienced it at first hand before. It was not something she ever wished to repeat. His slaps knocked her from side to side, again and again. Hurting herself on the cold stone, she tried to shuffle her knees further apart for balance. As she did so Stag wrenched at her hair again, jerking her up and bringing her sideways motion to a halt, strands of her shiny chestnut hair pulling free under his rough fingers. Tiny electric shocks tore at each root on her scalp and Mandy screamed behind the gag. Her sex, which must have been so visible to him, moistened with instant need. Even on her knees, she attempted to rub her damp thighs together. His cruelty always made her want to come. Stag had spun away to find the implement he had selected earlier, an elaborately decorated leather tawse he had recently acquired for his collection and which she herself had unwrapped a few days before. But when he saw what she was doing, Stag dragged her back to her feet, snarling like a wild animal inside the antlered mask. He was too angry to allow her that gratification yet.

'Spread your legs, slave, and keep them apart. You have not been given permission to pleasure yourself.'

167

He hesitated, still holding her naked body close against his. She was so petite, less than five foot to his six foot three, and felt completely vulnerable faced with those dark eyes glittering beneath his mask. Stag was only wearing a pair of black denim shorts, broad tanned chest curling with short dark hairs, and his masculine scent was a powerful aphrodisiac. Lifted almost on tiptoe by the overwhelming strength of his grip, her breasts brushed against the flat upper abdomen, nipples stiffening and swelling in automatic response.

'I don't understand your behaviour this morning. There's never been a problem with discipline before. What's the matter?' He was silent for a moment, watching the confused expressions chasing across her face. His voice became sharper. 'Is it because we filmed Violetta's initiation? Don't tell me you're jealous of that little innocent?'

Unable to reply because of the ball-gag in her mouth, Mandy could only shake her head in quick denial but she knew he was right and her cheeks coloured guiltily. She had disliked viewing Violetta's performance. The other girl was a natural subject for punishment and it showed on the screen. But her obvious aptitude – and the way Stag had marked her breasts so deliberately with the whip – had only served to infuriate Mandy. It was as though he had been branding Violetta as his own possession. Which was so bloody unfair, Mandy thought bitterly. She had been Stag's favourite for the past season and proud of the fact. It was nothing short of humiliating to watch this fresh-faced English rival waltz into the chateau and steal her master's attention without even trying.

'You know jealousy is forbidden here,' he continued grimly. 'And what the punishment is for displaying it.'

She stared at the far wall, her eyes bulging with terror as Stag forced her face down across the bench once again. This time though, her hands moved instinctively to cover her naked bottom, only too aware of the pain that could be inflicted by a tawse. Much to her chagrin, however, her master caught and manacled her hands behind her back with the deftness of long experience. He must have had the restraints ready before they began, she thought, trying not to panic. The cold metal snapped shut around each wrist; secured with a key, its design based on an antique original, a short chain linked the two cuffs and prevented any movement. Mandy remembered their use from previous sessions and shivered, realising that her suffering was to be comprehensive today. Whatever punishment was about to be inflicted on her, Stag had ensured she could not disobey him by shifting position again. Not that she would have dared to move anyway. His anger had taken her too much by surprise.

Her arms ached terribly, forced high up behind her back, but Mandy held the position as perfectly as she could. Fighting to keep her breathing steady, air dragging in and out through her nostrils as the ball-gag blocked her mouth, she pressed her face into the padded surface of the bench and waited for the inevitable. Her sex ran with sudden warm fluids, excitement growing at the same pace as fear. She heard Stag take up position behind her. The silence between them was so intense that she began to think he had changed his mind.

Then the tawse exploded across her buttocks like white lightning. Her entire body jerked into the air as though she had been electrocuted, her scream muffled against the ball-gag.

Stag waited for a few moments for that wave of agony to pass through her, deliberately allowing her numbed skin to recover some feeling before he raised the tawse again. Then he grunted with effort as it tore into her softness for a second time, only lower, just catching the tops of her thighs with its three vicious leather strips. Unable to make a single sound in protest, Mandy experienced that pain in every fibre of her body, from her outstretched toes to the very roots of her hair. The world gradually blurred to a sort of nightmarish darkness, her sex moist and hot with need. She sensed rather than heard the tawse being lifted above her again but was no longer capable of fear. Everything within her body was being driven towards release, her leg muscles tensed and her hips pumping against the padded bench. By the third stroke, falling much higher on her buttocks, Mandy writhed in agonised pleasure and thought at last that she was about to come.

His hands pitiless, Stag turned her over on the bench and examined her tear-soaked face. She lay with her legs sprawled wide apart as she had been told, her manacled hands pressing uncomfortably into her back, and waited for the next stage of her punishment. She knew Stag too well not to realise there was more to come. The only thing she did not know was how much it would it hurt. Although she could not see the marks left by the tawse, Mandy was well aware that her bottom and thighs must look like a battlefield. The throbbing agony had began to die away now, replaced by a heated desire to be fingered and fucked, though she appreciated that her satisfaction was not to be part of this punishment. She could see from the cruel bulge in his shorts that her master was aroused, yet he had made no attempt to relieve himself.

Instead, with one long thoughtful finger, Stag stroked her cheek and played across the straining scarlet of her lips, stretched in a lipsticked grimace around the ball. Then without warning he released the straps and removed the gag from her mouth. Groaning at the almost intolerable ache as her jaw was at last allowed to close, Mandy felt a long dribble of saliva escape from her numb lips onto her chin. Her hands still cuffed, she was helpless to move and could only try to ignore the humiliating fluid.

Watching her struggle to retain some semblance of dignity, Stag reached for a cloth from the table and cleaned her face with a gentle dabbing motion. She could sense the excitement behind his voice even though he still did not seem interested in taking her.

'I'm pleased with the way you accepted the tawse, Amanda. You've done well.'

'Thank you, master,' she managed to whisper.

'Now just relax, and let me guide you.' His hands slipped down to cup her breasts, those clever fingers manipulating her flesh until both nipples tautened into dusky peaks and she felt the hot seam between her legs pulsing in response. His tone was deceptively casual. 'I need your nipples erect before I can apply the clamps.'

Nipple clamps! A memory of intense pain flooded her mind and she was suddenly lost to coherent thought. Beginning to stutter a refusal, Mandy saw his eyes darken behind the mask, her voice dying away into silence as she realised that once again she had disappointed her master. She fought with a childish desire to protect herself from further pain, knowing how imperative it was to sort out her priorities before her position was jeopardised. Stag demanded complete capitulation from his slaves, but that unquestioning obedience had to be given freely. His eyes swept down over her nude body and her face flushed. In spite of his determination to use the clamps, or perhaps because of it, her physical arousal must be clearly visible to him, her outer labia soaked and her nipples erect. It was pointless trying to refuse him when her own physical excitement at this punishment could not be hidden.

It took less than ten seconds for Mandy to reach the correct decision and raise her breasts towards him in a suitably submissive manner, muttering an apology for that moment of rebellion.

He said nothing in response, but his fingers pinched and squeezed her nipples before reaching for the first

171

clamp, increasing the pressure until she gasped. To her shame, though, his cruelty only seemed to make the puckered skin around the nipple tighten and draw up even further. She had expected Stag to reach immediately for the tawse again, but his mood must have been softened by her abrupt return to obedience. Now he seemed merely curious to see her reaction to the pain. Gripping her left breast with one hand, he leant forwards and pressed the clamp open so that its vicious metal teeth were poised over the very back of the nipple.

His eyes moved upwards to her face, noting her pale apprehension. His voice was solicitous. 'Are you afraid, *ma petite*?'

She nodded, biting her lip hard.

'I told you, just relax,' he murmured. 'The pain will soon pass.'

Stag fixed the metal clamp over her nipple and released it. She cried out and her entire torso jerked up off the padded bench as a bolt of agony shot instantly through her skin. The pain was centred first in the tortured areola, then spread like a bush fire across her chest, arms, throat and abdomen until it hit the sticky heat of her sex and burnt inwards, leaving her flushed and trembling as though from a fever. For those first few minutes, Mandy thought she had never experienced such terrible and all-consuming pain. It was all she could do not to throw herself down from the padded bench and run back to the safety of her own bedroom like a terrified schoolgirl. But as that initial shock began to fade, it was gradually replaced by a squirming warmth between her thighs and the desire to rub herself against her master like an animal on heat. It frightened her, this unexpected sensation of pleasure. Her left nipple throbbed dully under the cold teeth of the clamp. But her sex ached to be touched, the outer lips protruding as her thighs drew closer together.

He laughed and kicked her feet apart again, the dark antlers swaying as he looked down at her prone body. 'I told you the pain would pass. Now keep your legs spread. You English are so greedy.'

The second clamp was delivered to her nipple in as cold and callous a manner as the first. Yet this time Mandy helplessly arched her spine towards his hand as the metal bit into her tender flesh and her head spun in a burst of pleasurable explosions. Unlike other types she had seen displayed on the walls racks, there was no little chain to link these two clamps. Instead, a tiny silver bell dangled from the back of each clamp, so that when he finally lifted Mandy to her feet and her breasts danced in that ecstasy of suffering, the unexpected sound of ringing accompanied every gasp. Yet she was beginning to welcome the pain, as though she had realised how much she learnt when she had to go through it and emerge at the other end, breathless and shaken, but somehow triumphant. Her master had administered this kind of punishment to her before, of course, but never before had she felt such an overwhelming sense of belonging. For a hazy moment Mandy wondered how far she would allow him to go, but that tentative thought was swept away by a certainty that Stag was to be trusted. However cruel her master seemed at times, he would never take a woman beyond her own limits.

Stag led her aching body, hands still manacled behind her back and her nipples firmly clamped, out of the cellar and up the steps to the ground floor. It was hot and still in the entrance hall. Everybody else appeared to be asleep for the siesta time, guests and staff alike. His hand propelled her across the red and gold tiled hallway and pushed her out through the kitchens onto the back patio where Violetta was lying on a lounger, apparently asleep. Her face burnt with embarrassment at this uncaring treatment – being dragged naked about the house, manacled and tortured like a common slave

173

– her shame mounting as she felt the tell-tale slide of juices beginning to trickle down her inner thighs. Mandy, the efficient receptionist and chateau whore! She hung her head, not sure which was worse, having Violetta witness her degradation or her obvious arousal.

Their English guest had been sunbathing naked, her high breasts white as milk and her pale legs shimmering in the sunlight. But the tinkling little bells on the nipple clamps must have alerted her to their approach for she turned her head at the sound and leapt up from the sun lounger, rather pointlessly grabbing at a robe to cover her nudity. She looked astonished to see her friend in such a terrible condition, though it was clear she would not risk punishment herself by saying anything in front of Stag.

Stag forced Mandy down onto the baking slabs of the patio, ignoring the yelp as her knees met the hot stone. He stared across at Violetta, the husky French accent more pronounced than ever. 'It's time for you to learn how to administer a punishment, *ma belle*.'

'Turn round,' Violetta whispered sympathetically in her new friend's ear. She undid the metal clasps of the ball-gag with unsteady fingers. 'I've got to do your front now. But it shouldn't take long.'

The sun was beating down on her naked bottom and legs but Violetta obediently held her position, kneeling beside Mandy's manacled body. Stag had ordered her to coat the receptionist in honey, telling them she was to be staked out on an ant hill not far from the swimming pool as a punishment for her jealousy. In this blinding heat and with thick golden honey covering her breasts, back and belly, he had said with amusement, the ants would love to sample her sweet-tasting skin. It seemed an appalling punishment and Violetta ought to have protested, but at least it was not happening to her. Her fingers had become incredibly sticky, she realised. She hesitated then furtively licked them, glancing over her shoulder at their master.

Stag was still crouching beside the pool, scooping out handfuls of water to splash his hot chest. The heat that afternoon was intense and even his tanned shoulders were looking uncomfortable in the sun. Above them, his dark antlers moved as he looked up and saw her watching him.

'Keep working, *chérie*,' he said softly. 'You do not want to make me angry. Not like Mandy did.'

Biting her lip, Violetta shook her head and continued with her task. Her fingers slipped several times on the honey brush and her concentration was easily distracted. Mandy's full breasts shone in the sun, the nipples reddened under those metal clamps with their little silver bells, and it was difficult not to stare as she tried to cover every inch of her skin with the honey. Her eyelids lifted slightly and the receptionist glanced at her from under them, her face clearly hot with embarrassment and desire.

Her hands trembling, Violetta brushed inadvertently against one of the cruel metal clamps. Mandy's eyes opened wide and she cried aloud, though the cry sounded more like lust than pain. Her spine arched and the large honeyed breasts bounced invitingly to the music of the bells. Violetta could not help feeling a thrill of envious excitement as she bent to brush honey over the other girl's belly. Mandy seemed so much more experienced than she was at this business. Stag had spent most of the morning down in the punishment block with the pretty receptionist while Violetta had lingered up here by the pool, occasionally servicing the chateau men as they passed, obediently sucking Crow to orgasm after breakfast and later bending to receive Fox's penis in her already sore back passage. She had made a real effort to remain silent unless given permission to speak and to obey their every command without hesitation, precisely as she had been taught over the past few days, yet somehow she always seemed to fall short of their high standards. There seemed little difference between the two girls, except that Violetta was slimmer than Mandy and had rather smaller breasts. So why could she not be more like the receptionist when it came to pleasing her new masters? Kneeling naked in the scorching heat, hands manacled behind her back and her full breasts jutting forwards, Mandy looked every inch the submissive slave and Violetta found herself wishing she could achieve the same perfection of attitude: part obedient availability, part unconscious provocation.

Once Mandy's body was entirely coated in the sweet sticky honey, Stag supervised the staking out of her body on a nearby ant hill under the burning sun. His punishment was deliberately cruel. Hundreds of tiny red ants appeared almost as soon as the soil was disturbed, at first only a few of them wandering curiously over her wrists and ankles. Then more began to emerge from the dry soil, until a steady stream of red ants were pouring out of the nest and heading en masse towards her naked honey-covered body.

The receptionist screamed and writhed against her bonds as she realised what was about to happen. But Violetta sank to her knees beside the terrified girl and whispered in her ear, pointing out the beauty of this punishment; how she could not only enjoy the intimate tickle of hundreds of tiny feet across her breasts and along her inner thighs, but also take delight in the knowledge that she had pleased her masters with such an act of complete submission. Then, her fingers sticky with honey, she forced herself to clasp Mandy's hand and endure this punishment with her friend, watching the red ants crawl drunkenly over her own knuckles and wrist before beginning to advance up her arm. That was when Violetta lost her courage and abruptly cried out.

shaking off the ants as she leapt to her feet and ran back towards the chateau.

Standing beside the rippling sunlit water of the pool, Stag threw back his head and bellowed with laughter under the antlered mask. There was sweat on his bare chest as he beckoned her towards him. She had expected him to be angry after her attempt at solidarity, but he merely seemed amused by the way she had abandoned her friend.

'Down on your knees,' he said and she obeyed instantly, dropping to the hot hard stone under the pressure of his hand. 'Suck.'

He did not move to assist her, so with rather unsteady fingers, Violetta unzipped the black denim shorts and tipped back her head to take his penis into her mouth. It was already semi-erect, swelling to full hardness almost as soon as her lips closed around the thick purple head. Over the past few days she had grown to love the shape and taste of his penis, its masculine scent filling her nostrils and its swollen length pressing firmly against the back of her throat. It seemed odd to her now that she had often refused to fellate her lovers in the past when the act held so much hedonistic pleasure. But her mind had been opened to these joys and could never be closed again. The Frenchman was owed a great debt of gratitude for educating her in the ways of submission, she thought dreamily. Without his severity and experienced guidance she would still be confused about her own sexuality, lost in a world where she did not know her place. She could hear Mandy's high-pitched cries in the distance, calling to her with a mixture of fear and excitement as the red ants crawled between her sticky thighs and over her sex. Unable to close her ears to those cries from across the dancing surface of the swimming pool, Violetta began to feel a similar uncontrollable heat rising within herself and sucked more vigorously, pulling the bevel-tipped head even deeper into her throat, her eyes closing on a long wave of heat.

Her hands slipped behind her back as she worked, remembering a little late to adopt a submissive stance whilst serving him, but for once Stag did not appear to have noticed her lapse. His rigid penis filled her mouth, one hand gripping Violetta's loose red hair to jerk her closer against his groin. With his other hand, he yanked his shorts further down and freed his scrotum without breaking rhythm. Feeling herself sway backwards, she was forced to widen her kneeling stance as the heavy balls slapped against the underside of her tilted chin, almost knocking her off balance. Though it was a matter of some pride to Violetta that, in spite of this rigorous mouth-fucking, her hands remained obediently behind her back. Mandy, still helplessly spread-eagled on the ant hill, suddenly screamed and cried out his name, though it was not clear whether she was writhing in the throes of an unexpected orgasm or begging to be released. Not that it made any difference to their master. His only response was to thrust deeper into Violetta's throat, his hands tightening on her hair and his breathing becoming ragged as he neared his climax.

Lost in a maelstrom of incoherent desire, Violetta no longer knew which she preferred: this thick penis gagging her throat or the anticipation of those hot pulsing jets of semen. The dignity in which she had once taken so much pride now fell completely away from her and her face burnt, driven almost insane by her own need for release. Between her thighs she could feel her sex oiling itself with excitement and knew how slippery it must be down there, throbbing like an engine and eager to be touched. She did not dare to unclasp her hands though, however urgent this need for orgasm. Violetta might not be as afraid of punishment as she had been on her first day here, but his disapproval was something she refused to risk. Her master's satisfaction was sacrosanct. That was the most important lesson for the submissive to learn, she thought fervently, if not the only lesson. So her skin flamed in the sunlight and her throat laboured hard against his penis, sucking and squeezing and manipulating, her own needs pushed aside until he had taken his full pleasure in her mouth.

He rode her face right up to the last second, still pumping in and out as his semen began to discharge. When it burst against the back of her throat Stag cried out in French, his exact words muffled beneath the dark antlered mask, but he did not slow his pace. His hands clutched painfully at her hair instead. The warm invisible fluid began to slip past the root of her tongue like a spillage of mercury. Her muscles convulsed around his seed and she swallowed, his penis still wedged thickly in her throat.

Her knees stung as he took a step backwards and dragged her with him. The patio stones were like an oven under her bare skin and yet still he did not release her. Instead, Stag drew her higher and pinned her mouth against his sex like a butterfly mounted in a display case. Her eyes watering in acute discomfort, Violetta began to choke on his penis and fought the instinct to break away, to drag oxygen into her tortured lungs. She tried to look up but there was nothing to see but darkness, his hard flesh blinding her. Panic set in and her fingers momentarily unclasped, ready to push her torturer away. Then she stopped herself, deliberately slowing her thought processes as she had been taught.

This was another one of his tests, she reminded herself, an exploration of her capacity for submission. *Obedience has no significance if never put to the test.* The hands which held her might be cruel but the man behind them remained unemotional. It was Violetta who seemed unable to contain her emotions. Stag was in full control of this situation and his decision was law. All she had to do was trust him and allow the experience to lift her onto a higher plane. The Frenchman seemed able to read her thoughts, muttering words of approval as he watched his slave struggle against years of social conditioning. But for another few agonising seconds, he continued to hold her in this servile position, the iron grip of his hands almost a caress. It was as though he wished Violetta to understand the essential purity of her humiliation: his discharge lingering saltily on her tongue; her throat still brutalised by his thrusts; the blood throbbing at her temples as she strained to accept his penis completely inside her body. That was when she realised it was not his hands at all, but his penis, the absolute lynchpin, which held them together. Between her thighs, the slippery heated flesh burnt with a desire to be taken, penetrated, used.

Her mouth locked on again, sucking at his shaft until it was clean, and there was an involuntary groan from somewhere far above her head. Violetta began dimly to perceive how the balance of power could shift during these exchanges. How she, the dominated, might be given an opportunity to become the dominator. Then his hands opened and she fell backwards onto stone, her cry almost one of bereavement as her mouth was abruptly released.

'*C'est toi*, Heidi?' he said in a surprised tone, pulling on his denim shorts again and turning away at the sound of high heels on the patio. 'I wasn't expecting you until this evening, *mon ange*, but you are still welcome.'

Down on her hands and knees, her throat aching and her sex still bitterly unused, Violetta raised her head and saw a beautiful teenage girl walking towards them from the car park. Though *walking* was the wrong term, she thought with instant jealousy. With one hand on her hip, the other holding a jacket she had flung ever so casually over her shoulder, this blonde *sauntered* across the patio with the self-assurance of a film star. Her silver metallic boots came up to the mid-thigh, followed by the briefest shorts and bandeau-style top that Violetta had ever seen. She might as well have been wearing nothing. The two curved cheeks of her bottom protruded from the shorts and her small high nipples were accentuated by the tightness of the bandeau. From the perfect tanned skin, she was probably about nineteen years old.

The new girl ignored Violetta and stopped at the far edge of the pool, shooting Stag a dazzling smile across the water.

'Munich can be so boring in the summer. Everyone leaves the city for their holidays. There was no one left to fuck, so I took an earlier flight.' The accent sounded German, her voice high and deliberately girlish. 'You don't mind, *liebling*?'

'How could I? Your master has told me so much about you. Hans has often exaggerated about his girls in the past, but not you.' There was an indulgence in Stag's voice that made Violetta's cheeks burn with humiliation as he moved away and inspected the new girl's body, walking around her like a car he had thinking of purchasing. 'That mouth, that tight little arse . . . I'm certainly looking forward to your training.'

He had not ordered her to stay where she was, so Violetta struggled to her feet and reached for the robe she had abandoned earlier, keeping one wary eye on the antlered mask ahead of her. It was likely that Stag would prefer her to remain naked. But that particular humiliation would be too much to bear in front of this *child*, she thought, tying the front of her robe with fierce angry movements. Only too aware of the curious blue eyes turned in her direction, Violetta bent her head and wiped away the traces of semen from around her chin and lips. Though it was hardly worth the effort. The younger girl must surely have seen them from a distance, locked together like two combatants, her kneeling excitedly while he rammed her throat.

'But you should be introduced to one of my other guests this week, Heidi. This is Violetta.' The dark antlers swayed as he turned and surveyed her robed body. She thought he would be angry that she had dared to cover herself without permission. But there was only a brief hesitation before her master shrugged and continued, his French accent huskier than ever. 'Her mother was a great erotic film star and Violetta shares many of her talents, I'm happy to say. She came here all the way from England.'

'To learn about making films?'

He laughed then, shaking his head at the blonde. 'Not this time. But why do you say that? You think Violetta is photogenic?'

Heidi was pouting now. It made her beautiful face rather ugly. She turned her head like a spoilt kid, eyes flashing angrily in Violetta's direction and then back at Stag. It was obvious she had not come here to talk about another girl. Those red painted nails looked as though they were designed to be raked down a man's back during intercourse.

Violetta sat down on the sun lounger and took a careful sip of her iced tea. The taste was extremely refreshing. It seemed strange to her that she could remain so calm and unflustered after that brutal session with Stag. She must have learnt more than she realised over the past incredible week. Certainly she understood more about the dynamics of submission than this long-legged German teenager. Yet was that something she ought to applaud or deplore in herself? Her jaw still ached from holding him so deep in her throat. With an uncertain smile, Violetta put down the glass and watched Heidi from under lowered eyelids.

'No,' the girl was saying sulkily.

'You don't think she would work in front of a camera?' Stag seemed determined to press the point. 'But you find her attractive?'

'No.'

'Yes, you do. Would you like to fuck her, Heidi?'

Heidi looked a little shocked. But she did not say anything. Her cheeks held a slight flush as she glanced at Violetta again and shook her head.

'Of course you would,' he insisted. 'All women want to fuck other women. They just don't like to admit it.'

Stag turned to Violetta, no hint of amusement in his voice as he folded his arms across the bare chest and watched her dispassionately.

'Uncover yourself, Violetta. Let the girl see what you have. Hurry up, that's too slow. Now open your legs and show her your cunt. No, no. Do it properly. Use your fingers to spread the lips. Good . . . that's much better. Now turn around and bend down. Lower than that, please. Hold your buttocks apart.' He glanced at the young blonde's shocked face. 'Have you ever licked another woman there, Heidi?'

'No,' she repeated, stammering.

Bent over in silence, Violetta waited patiently for his next command, her mind closed to the flagrant exhibitionism of her behaviour. This was what her master had ordered her to do. That was all she needed to concentrate on. It had only been a handful of days since she came here, yet she was already beginning to forget the realities she had known in the world outside the chateau. They had been false realities, anyway. She was a different person now and could never return to that old style of living. Even her pale skin seemed to have taken on a strange blueish hue, her ankles almost translucent as Violetta listened to his murmured order and obediently reached down to grasp them. The chateau owner's reason for shifting her position then became obvious as she felt her inner lips turn slowly outwards, displaying their moist fullness.

It was as though Stag had flicked some internal switch on the day they met, electrifying her and bringing her back to life after years of numbness and sleep. She knew the tiny puckered star of her anus must be opening too, the sun hot on her raised buttocks as his voice ordered her to place her hands flat on the patio and Violetta obeyed, unthinking. Her thighs hurt in this position but she controlled her breathing and allowed the pain to pass over and through her. Then his fingers were between her spread buttocks, feeling for the once tight sphincter he and his staff had already stretched. Even though she had been used there over the past few days, Violetta could still not prevent a gasp as the masked man pushed one finger inside the wrinkled opening and rotated it. It took only a few seconds of this contemptuously casual treatment for her cheeks to flush with shame and her nipples to stiffen into taut peaks. That was a sensation she would never adjust to, she thought hazily, however many times she experienced it.

She heard him call Heidi to his side and recognised, with a sinking heart, that faint note of cruelty in his voice. 'Kiss it,' he said softly.

'I can't,' the German girl whispered.

'Of course you can. Your master spoke highly of your skills. Now place your lips there and let me see how well you perform.'

'But I've never . . . not with a woman . . .'

There was a brief violent movement, barely perceptible, and Violetta heard the young blonde cry out in pain. She guessed that the Frenchman must have gripped Heidi by the neck and dragged her forwards, feeling warm skin and the hint of tears suddenly pressed against her buttocks. Normally Violetta would have felt sympathy for the plight of this new girl. But the urgency of her own desire was growing every second she stood bent over, her private parts so brazenly displayed, listening to those low moans from beyond the swimming pool where her friend still lay staked out on the baking earth. To be so exiled from the chateau, that was true suffering. This young German girl had not even learnt the meaning of the word punishment yet.

'You have come here to learn obedience, Heidi,' the chateau owner said bluntly. 'This is lesson one. Now kiss her arsehole.'

Widening her legs even further, Violetta felt the breath catch like a hook in her throat as she waited for the touch of another woman's lips against that dark secret opening. She did not have long to wait. Those trembling lips found the tiny hole and kissed it, straightening and trying to pull away as soon as the task was completed. But Stag had other plans. With a muffled sob, the young German girl was forced back between the silken curves of Violetta's cheeks. This time she was ordered to lick it, and it was clear that there would be no chance for a second refusal. Tentatively, the girl's tongue narrowed itself to the space and poked forward until it met the puckered star of her anus. Violetta groaned at the unexpected sensations and let her head hang down between her legs, dishevelled red hair shining in the sun. Her nipples were painfully stiff now and her belly hurt as though it had been punched.

Heidi's tongue felt like a paintbrush stroking against each tiny wrinkled fold of skin. Violetta began to pant softly as its wetness explored her even further, nuzzling between the lightly furred skin of her buttocks. She wanted to exhale and push back, unfolding that closed star so the clever little tongue could dig deeper, lick her out properly. But her master had not given either of them permission for such wanton behaviour.

'That's enough.' As though he sensed her temptation, Stag released his grip and allowed the German girl to collapse onto her knees behind Violetta's spread legs. 'Violetta, take Heidi her across to the punishment zone immediately. I would like her to meet our receptionist.'

'Yes, master.'

'There will be a dinner party tonight in the great hall to honour our new guest. But you are required to work in the kitchens tonight, *ma belle*. Is that understood?'

Violetta stared at him, scared but excited. It was clear that her own training was far from over. 'Yes, master.'

'*Parfait.*' The muscular chest rippled as Stag stretched lazily in the sun, those dark antlers swaying. 'Now, I have a few phone calls to make before dinner so I leave Mandy's punishment in your hands, *chérie*. I have always considered her an exemplary submissive, but recently her obedience seems to be slipping. Bring her back to the path for me.'

'Yes, master.'

Nine

Mandy woke to feel cool hands sponging her forehead. For a moment she could not quite place where she was, her mouth dry and her head dizzy with the heat, then she jerked at her bonds and stared wildly up into Violetta's face. Where had Stag gone? His cruelty was so implacable. He had left her staked out in the nude, arms and legs dragged far apart, with no protection from the intense Mediterranean sun. She felt an intense itchiness between her thighs and strained upwards in anguish, suddenly remembering the red ants crawling across her honey-slick skin.

'Shhh . . .' Violetta was stroking her cheek soothingly. 'You'll only make it worse if you struggle.'

'Please help me. Undo these ropes first.'

'I can't.'

Mandy stared at her, her eyes wide with disbelief. 'But you're not going to leave me like this? Look at me. There are ants all over my body, on my breasts, between my legs . . .'

'I know,' Violetta whispered. 'Doesn't it make you hot to feel their little bodies crawling all over your body?'

'No, it's really awful.' She had already come several times, in fact, but Mandy did not want to share that sort of embarrassing information with the other girl. 'Please untie me. I can't bear it any longer.'

But her pleas were completely ignored. Violetta was too busy stroking the curve of Mandy's honeyed belly, her face lit up with excitement. Mandy cried aloud in despair as the other girl's hand slipped lower until it lay between her spread thighs, then closed her eyes. She could feel that intense pleasure beginning to build inside her body again and knew she was not far away from another orgasm. Yet she could hardly believe the change which had come over Violetta. She had never expected to witness such filthy behaviour from the strait-laced young English girl.

Then her eyes flew open in astonishment as she realised a second pair of hands was fondling her breasts. There was a blonde stranger kneeling beside her naked body, flicking at the nipple clamps with a cruel finger until their tiny bells rang merrily. Mandy gave an agonised cry and tried to twist away even though she knew it was impossible.

'Do not waste so much energy struggling,' the blonde girl told her in a thick German accent. She was clearly excited by what she saw, judging by the stiffened nipples beneath her bandeau top. 'You cannot escape, so why not lie still and enjoy yourself?'

'Who are you?' Mandy gasped.

'Don't worry, she's just a new guest at the chateau,' Violetta said quickly. 'Her name's Heidi. She only arrived today but she's already started her training.'

'And you're the naughty receptionist who needs to be punished,' the blonde remarked coyly, leaning further over her tortured prostrate body and licking a long trail of honey from around her navel. The slow sensuous movements of that tongue woke a flickering heat in Mandy's sex and she moaned, trying to lift herself closer.

It did not seem to her that this new girl would need much training. Heidi was already experienced with her tongue, and her hands apparently knew their business too, pinching and squeezing the swollen outer lips of Mandy's sex until she was rewarded with a high-pitched cry of desire. Now she made a satisfied noise under her breath, still on her knees, glancing up at her victim's flushed face.

'So tell me, naughty girl, what is your name?'

'Amanda . . . Mandy . . . oh, please . . .'

Heidi bent closer, that blonde hair brushing against her sensitive sun-burnt skin. 'Yes, *liebling*? What is it you want?'

'Touch me . . . lick me . . .'

The slap that followed was a hard and uncompromising crack across the face. Even her breasts bounced under the impact, the tiny bells tinkling again. Mandy gasped in shock, her right cheek throbbing with pain and stars bursting behind her eyelids. Instinctively she wanted to raise her hands to her face but, tied up like this, there was no way to defend herself. This little blonde has a heavy hand, she thought tearfully, and reminded herself to speak more cautiously in future. It had only hurt so much because it was unexpected, but she did not relish receiving any more slaps like that. Her punishment session with Stag that morning had already left her body sore and aching. This girl could break her spirit if she was not careful.

'That is not how you speak to your mistress, is it?'

'I'm sorry,' Mandy whispered submissively.

'You are forgiven.' The hand that had slapped her became gentle again, tracing the dry outline of her mouth. 'But you're so thirsty, poor Mandy. Would you like me to wet your lips for you?'

'Yes, please.'

The kiss was so soft at first that Mandy longed to have her hands free, to pull the tantalising blonde closer. But then Heidi pressed harder against her body, her tongue exploring Mandy's mouth and moistening those dry lips as she had promised. She had been kissed by

189

another woman before, of course, but never so seductively. There was an intense eroticism about it which she had not expected from such a young girl. Over the blonde's shoulder, she could see Violetta on her knees, pleasuring herself with one hand and stroking Mandy's sex with the other, her breathing growing laboured as she watched the two girls locked together in such a passionate embrace.

Mandy closed her eyes and felt the tortured lips of her sex respond to Violetta's insistent fingers, swelling with an even greater arousal. No doubt sensing an approaching climax, the other English girl did not hesitate any longer but dipped between her wide-spread thighs and began to lick her out. Mandy gasped as Violetta's lips lapped and sucked at her fleshy erect clitoris, tentatively at first and then with greater confidence, barely able to believe the changes in the girl since she had arrived at the chateau. Many untrained young women had been through this place over the summer yet none of them had learnt this quickly or this eagerly. She certainly would never have guessed that Violetta was a natural submissive.

The little blonde sat back on her heels and smiled, her pink lips moist and shining after their kiss. There was something spiteful about that smile. Slowly and deliberately, Heidi released the metal clamps on each nipple and watched shock accumulating in her victim's eyes as initial numbness gave way to excruciating agony. The clamps jingled for the last time as she tossed them aside. Then she dug her nails into Mandy's right breast and laughed at her cry of pain. Mandy could hold it back no longer. The unexpected cruelty had triggered a series of explosions in her sex and she found herself on the verge of coming. Her spine arched upwards and her legs began to tremble, a slow wave of heat spreading across Mandy's body as the muscles inside her slick channel finally spasmed and sent her spinning into an intense orgasm. The little blonde sat watching her, hissing with satisfaction.

Still down between her thighs, Violetta took Mandy's engorged clitoris between her teeth, biting down hard until the pain forced Mandy into another orgasm. Her throat stretched back in a long scream of release and she howled out her master's name, knowing that wherever he was in the chateau, Stag would hear and approve.

Examining her reflection critically in the mirror, Violetta wondered again whether she had ceased to exist and someone new had taken her place. In this provocatively dressed creature there was little trace of the inexperienced young English girl who had arrived here ... what, less than a week ago? Or maybe it was longer than that? She could not be sure; she had lost track of the days. Time seemed to have no meaning here.

Her eyes flickered over her slim figure and down over the expanse of legs under the high hem of her dress, if it could be called a dress. The outfit was all straps and metal studs, long thin strips of some stretchy fabric that wound around her breasts and hips rather like the bindings of an Egyptian mummy. Her pale flesh shone through the black material, tantalisingly hidden as she stretched to fasten her matching high heels. She was uncertain what would be expected of her tonight. All Violetta knew was that she must honour her promise to work in the kitchens and serve dinner to the other guests. Anything less would result in Stag's disapproval and some dire punishment such as the one he had meted out to Mandy this afternoon. She shivered delicately at the thought, brushing her fine red hair until it lay flat against her shoulders. It was better to obey and face whatever tests he had prepared for her.

There was a sudden knock at her bedroom door and Violetta turned, a little apprehensive. 'Come in.'

But it was only Mandy, wearing her velvety pig mask, who poked her head round the door to check the room. 'No Heidi?'

'She's resting after her trip. I think she wants to be fresh for this special dinner party tonight. Are you going too?'

Mandy nodded, coming into the room and closing the door behind her. Dressed more conventionally now in a short black skirt and see-through blouse, the receptionist climbed onto the bed, catching her breath in pain as she tried to curl up on the sheets.

'I have to, it's part of my job. Though I can't see myself enjoying it. I'm exhausted after this morning and my bum stings from taking that bloody tawse. I don't know how you manage to stay on your feet.'

Violetta smiled at her. 'Sheer stamina.'

'Crow told me you're working down in the kitchen tonight.' When Violetta nodded, the receptionist's voice rose. 'But that's awful. It's a really terrible ordeal.'

'Come on, it can't be that bad.'

'It's worse than you could possibly imagine. Stag made me work in the kitchen once too, just to see what it was like. Trust me, it's a complete hell.' She shrugged. 'You may not want my advice, but if I were you, I wouldn't make Badger angry.'

'Badger?'

'He's the chef. He doesn't come out of the kitchen very often. That's why they gave him the Badger mask, I suppose. Because he's a bit of a loner. Crazy too, if you ask me.' Mandy hesitated, watching her fixedly through the pink-rimmed eyeslots in her mask. 'Promise me you'll look out for him, Violetta. He loves inflicting pain, especially if you're new here. Badger can be a vicious bastard when he's in the mood.'

Shrugging, Violetta fixed her earrings in place. These warnings about Badger did not bother her too much. She was becoming used to handling the cruelty of men, and even, as Stag had promised, finding pleasure in the way they treated her. Still, there was no point upsetting her friend by making it obvious she was going to ignore her advice.

'All right. I'll be careful.'

'Good.' Mandy sounded satisfied, sitting up again. 'Now, there's just time for some quick gossip before I have to go and change for dinner. I wanted to ask what you thought of Heidi.'

'Heidi?'

'I don't know why the men seem so pleased with her. She's so skinny, she's hardly got any tits at all.'

Violetta laughed at the malicious tone in her voice, her hand steady as she applied a second layer of mascara to her eyelashes. She had guessed early on that Mandy was not keen on the young blonde. There had been fury as well as excitement in her gasps when Heidi had clawed at her breasts and unclasped those ringing nipple clamps. It was obvious that the receptionist preferred men to administer her punishments, though she would never have admitted such a preference aloud. Stag had made his rules on the matter clear cut. Any slave undergoing punishment at the chateau was common property, to be used by anyone who passed, regardless of gender. Mandy might have taken an instant dislike to the blonde teenager but she knew better than to go against Stag's wishes.

'She's very young.'

'Barely nineteen, I'd say.' Mandy's eyes had narrowed to two angry slits, her tone disapproving. 'Or less.'

'Does that bother you? She seems very experienced for her age.'

'She's a slut!'

'Is that a compliment or an accusation?' Raising her eyebrows, Violetta glanced round at her friend, amused by the unnecessary vehemence of her tone. 'She wants to be a film star, you know. That's why she's here. To learn how to perform.'

193

'I hope we're allowed to mark her,' Mandy said spitefully.

'Ouch.'

'Stag seems very impressed, though I don't know why. She's just a kid. He wants to be first with her at the party tonight.'

'To be honest, I was quite impressed by Heidi too.' Violetta smiled and straightened her skin-tight dress, looking at herself in the mirror to check that all the strips of black material were in the right place. 'When I was her age, I'd never even seen a penis. She may be young but she already knows what goes where.'

In actual fact, Violetta had seen a penis by the time she was nineteen. That had been her first real taste of sex, straight out of school and only too eager to find out what the other girls had been whispering about for years. But she was not going to admit that to Mandy, in case she demanded to hear the whole sordid tale and was shocked to discover that her friend was not as innocent as she looked. It was not much to be proud of anyway, losing her virginity to the man who ran a corner shop near her home. Not that Violetta had wanted or expected anything more memorable for her initiation into the world of sexual intercourse. Anything had been better than fumbling around with those clumsy young boys who had shown an interest when she was at school. No, the shopkeeper had been a perfect choice: a stout man in his late forties, he had turned the shop sign to 'Closed', shown her through a bead curtain into a dingy back room with the radio playing, and taken her right there on his grime-encrusted sofa.

She could still remember the garlic on his breath, and the way he had given her breasts a perfunctory squeeze before pushing her skirt up to her waist. She had not been wearing any knickers that afternoon; it had been a premeditated act, the discarding of her virginity, something Violetta had been planning for months before it actually happened. His eyes glazed with lust, the shop-keeper had reached down impatiently to part her outer labia, hurting her with those rough fingers. Not wanting to embarrass herself by crying out at the moment of penetration, Violetta bit down on her lip as his rigid shaft stretched and broke the fragile membrane of her hymen. He fucked her rapidly and in engrossed silence. The only noise he made was when he came, a short series of satisfied grunts, pulling out and leaving a sticky white mess on the sofa.

Afterwards, the magazines and chocolate bars had not been enough to stop the trembling in her legs, though the blood wiped away easily enough. She left the shop some hours later, her knees sore from the wooden floor and semen salting her throat. Part of her had expected to break down and cry, to despair at her own wantonness and promiscuity. But when she looked in the mirror, Violetta had felt nothing but an odd numbness inside. She had offered her innocence and the shopkeeper had taken it without hesitation. How simple it had been in the end, after all her childish fears and imaginings, to spread her legs and allow herself to be used as a whore. For it was over now. The deed was finally done.

Violetta had never gone back to the corner shop after that afternoon, too horrified by her behaviour to face the shopkeeper again, always taking the longer route home instead. Though she never blamed him for taking her the way he did. Violetta had been flaunting herself in front of him most of that last year before she left school, excited by the way his bloodshot eyes lingered over her short-skirted school uniform and white socks. Once she had left school, it had not been difficult to make him see how willing she was. Strangers ask no questions, she had told herself at the time, and they don't expect to see you again. The shopkeeper had misinterpreted her lack of emotion for sexual experience and taken her without any preliminaries.

Yet somehow it seemed to be his roughness which had excited her most, just as the Frenchman's had done since her arrival at the chateau. She had relived that first experience many times in the privacy of her bedroom, fingers working at her sex until her limbs stiffened in a breathless climax. Sometimes she would lovingly embellish the memory, adding a few hard slaps or being forced onto hands and knees so the man could enter her anus. It seemed to be the anonymity which excited her most. But a dark tide of shame always rose in her afterwards and Violetta would punish herself with an ice-cold shower, as if those stinging jets of water could wash away her guilt.

Now as she sat down to watch Mandy trying on her collection of shoes, mincing around the bedroom floor in ridiculously high stilettos, Violetta could not help wondering why there had to be so much shame attached to what happened in the privacy of one's own imagination.

'What do you think?' her friend asked, slipping into a pair with slim red blade-like heels and leather thongs lacing across her foot and up her ankle.

'They suit you.'

'Really?' The soft pink pig mask tilted thoughtfully to one side, admiring herself in the mirror. 'Could I borrow them for tonight's dinner party, then? I'm going to wear red and these would match perfectly.'

'Of course.'

'Thanks. You're a star.'

Violetta took a deep breath, lying back on the sheets and staring at the ceiling. It was becoming so hard to focus in this place. She could no longer be sure that she understood who she was. Even her body felt odd in this dress of black fabric strips, as though it belonged to somebody else. Her exposed skin shone through the gaps, shimmering white as a pearl at her breasts, belly and hips, and so incredibly sensitive that she did not think she could bear to have anyone touch her there.

'Mandy, do you think . . .?' She stopped and flushed scarlet, looking away in sudden embarrassment. 'I mean, you've seen the sort of things I've done this week . . . the way I've changed since I arrived. Do you think I could ever please Stag enough to stay here after my holiday has finished?'

'*Stay here*?'

'OK, work here.' Violetta shrugged. 'Just like you do. Give in my notice at home and become a member of the chateau staff.'

'I don't know. To be honest, sweetie, I doubt that he would take you on. Complete obedience pleases Stag more than anything else. But that's always going to be a problem for you, isn't it?'

'What do you mean?'

'Oh, for God's sake. You're naturally disobedient. You can't deny that.' Mandy looked at her seriously, shaking her head. 'It's a challenge for him and Stag enjoys forcing you to submit. But he'll soon grow tired of your refusals. This dinner party's another one of his tests and it's going to be tough. *Really tough*. So unless you can prove yourself tonight, Violetta, you might as well give up the idea of staying on at the chateau.'

The kitchen ceiling was high, at least fifteen foot high, and festooned with a selection of wooden and metal racks secured to the walls with ropes. There was a vast ancient fireplace at the far end, with a roaring fire and a spit standing directly in front of the chimney piece, half a dozen whole chickens skewered on its slim metal and already roasting noisily. The exposed brickwork had been darkened by centuries of smoke while the terracotta floor tiles surrounding the hearth were cracked and sometimes missing. Strange unearthly shadows – presumably cast by these enormous brass pots and pans hanging from the ceiling racks – flickered constantly up the rough white walls as the log fire burnt greedily away in the hearth. Astonished by what she saw, Violetta gradually realised why the receptionist had said that working down here, deep in the bowels of the chateau, was almost a punishment. On a sultry summer evening like this, Violetta thought, the kitchen was as hot as hell and looked like some scene from Dante's Inferno. Even without the added threat of this sadistic chef, it would not be a pleasant place to work.

'*Viens ici, toi!*'

She turned at the angry shout and tried not to stare as Badger approached her, his furry black and white mask sitting in an ungainly way on his shoulders. Wearing a stained chef's apron tied twice about his waist and with slim legs clad in the usual black denim jeans, Badger stared at her with his hands on his hips. His French accent was extremely strong.

'You were meant to get down here nearly an hour ago. Look at this mess. There's no one to help me. Am I expected to prepare a three-course meal on my own?'

'I'm sorry.'

'You'll be sorrier if you don't please me,' Badger said sharply. 'So what sort of whore has he sent me tonight?'

The chef seemed amused by the revealing nature of her outfit, cruel black eyes gleaming through the eye slits in the badger mask as he gestured for her to turn around and display herself. She obeyed him without comment but flushed hotly, knowing herself to be practically naked in these narrow strips of material which passed for a dress. The stiletto heels were so high they forced her up onto her toes, her breasts thrust forwards and her entire balance so strained that she could not walk even a single step without swaying her bottom in a provocative manner. After Mandy's warnings about this chef's reputation for violence, Violetta had been considering how to handle his temper without risking unnecessary pain and humiliation. Yet she knew perfectly well there was no hope of persuading him to treat her with respect, not when her body was on such open display. No wonder he seems so amused, she thought desperately, feeling the dress shift as she turned away to face the roaring fire. Her every movement, however slight, threatened to dislodge the strategically positioned strips, possibly exposing an erect nipple or the tantalising reddish triangle of hair between her legs.

'Now spread your legs further apart and bend over,' Badger demanded, and the secret laughter in his voice made her stomach clench with an odd mixture of fury and apprehension. '*Vite, vite!*'

Violetta hurried to do as she was told, even bending to touch the kitchen floor without being asked, its cracked terracotta slippery with grease beneath her fingers. Her sense of humiliation deepened. No doubt he would be able to see everything now through the gaping slits in her dress: the smooth swell of her bottom, the inviting pout of her labia, and above them, obscene in its exposure, the small dark hole between her parted buttocks. There was a silence during which she held her position faultlessly, leg muscles aching from the strain, while excitement began to mount inexorably inside her. Was he going to punish her for being late? Or did he plan to use her body first? Her thoughts were chaotic, whirling around in her head as she waited for him to break the silence, her breathing more laboured as she struggled to keep still.

She heard him approach and instinctively leapt up in pain as something hot and rigid scalded her bottom. Before she could escape, though, his hand on her neck had forced her back into position, one muscular knee nudging her legs apart again. Violetta scrabbled at the floor to maintain balance, her calves taut and her bottom throbbing with pain. This time the chef abandoned all pretence of subtlety and inserted his unseen instrument of torture between her thighs. It was thrust hard against her sex and the fragile skin of her labia.

Unable to control herself, Violetta jerked away in instinctive agony and she cried aloud, begging him to stop. But she must have hit his arm with that involuntary movement because there was a sudden clatter of metal and a ladle dropped to the floor beside her, still steaming with some clear liquid, presumably hot water from one his pans.

'*Voyons, qu'est-ce que t'as fait?*' He swore angrily in French, knocking her to the floor. 'Now see what you have made me do. Clean up that wet floor immediately. Someone might slip.'

'But I haven't got . . .'

His foot pushed her face onto the filthy terracotta. 'Stop whining and use your tongue, slut. That's all it's good for.'

Her cheeks scarlet with humiliation, Violetta found herself closing her eyes and obediently licking the floor like some pig cleaning out a trough. This was the sort of punishment Mandy would enjoy, she thought miserably, but it did not suit her. Even suffering a repeat of that agony between her legs would have been preferable to this disgusting task. But when the tiles under her face were clean, it became clear that her trials were not over yet. Violetta tensed, listening hard. She could hear his footsteps moving around behind her lowered body, presumably walking back to his oven and then returning to where she was now kneeling up expectantly, lips and chin covered in thick grease, her body trembling with shock at this rough treatment. Badger had brought something with him, possibly some kind of saucepan, but she could not see it properly from this angle and had not been given permission to turn around. Her stomach clenched in fearful apprehension. There was a faint smell of burning and she even could sense heat approaching the exposed skin of her back and buttocks. Violetta felt like bursting into tears at the injustice of her position, but with a strenuous effort she managed to control herself, realising that a tearful outburst might only make the chef angrier still. But what had the chef taken off the stove and why did he seem so angry with her? Apart from arriving in the kitchen slightly later than ordered, she had done nothing to deserve these punishments.

'Hand me that ladle. Now stand up and face me.'

She obeyed him instantly, keen to see what he was carrying. But the sight was less reassuring than when she had been able to see nothing, only smell it. He was indeed carrying a saucepan, unlidded and steaming, into which he dropped the metal ladle. The contents of the saucepan appeared to be the remains of thin greenish-white strips of cabbage, floating in water which still bubbled slightly from the stove.

The heavy black and white badger mask tilted and swayed, nodding towards the thin strips of fabric covering her chest. 'Pull that aside and show me your breasts.' When her fingers had moved to do his bidding, exposing her high pale breasts and stiffening nipples, the chef stared at them in silence for a moment. Then he nodded again, this time lowering his gaze to gesture greedily at her covered crotch. 'Now down there, whore. Show me your cunt.'

'Please . . .'

'Do what you're told!'

His voice was like a whip and Violetta hurried to obey him, her fingers shaking now as she guessed that he must be intending to hurt her. Yet there was no anger in his voice, only a suggestion of amusement. Was the man playing with her? Her face was hot as she pulled aside the strips of material covering her sex and spread her legs a little, lewdly pushing out her hips to allow him to see her properly. She found herself wishing Mandy and Heidi were down here in the kitchen with her so she did not have to bear the brunt of these punishments alone. Then the realisation tore through her that Stag must have sent her alone on purpose, perfectly aware of this man's vicious nature and knowing how she would be made to suffer at his hands. Her cheeks paled with anguish. Did the chateau owner enjoy her pain so much that he would deliberately expose her to it in such a callous way? Stag's vast reservoir of cruelty towards her seemed to know no bounds. He claimed to be an obsessive fan of her mother's erotic work, yet it was almost as if he had invited Violetta to his chateau merely in order to break her.

She refused, however, to give these men the satisfaction of watching her crumble at their feet like some abject fool. Violetta faced the chef with her head high, allowing his eyes to feast on her bare white breasts and the reddish triangle of hair between her thighs, the full labia pouting and damp as always. If these men thought she would shatter and disappear under their onslaught of cruel punishments, they were greatly mistaken. She had more pride in herself than that, she thought determinedly.

Yet in spite of her resolve to suffer in silence, the first burning splatter of cabbage against her breasts made her cry out, unable to prevent her lips opening in shock.

'Silence!' Badger exclaimed with sudden rage. 'Or you will face an even greater punishment for disobedience.'

Furious with herself for that display of outright cowardice, Violetta set her teeth and raised her head again. His ladle dipped back into the saucepan and removed another piece of watery cabbage. But this time she was prepared for the agonies of scalding food against her skin and suffered the next few minutes in a bitter tight-lipped silence. Her breasts reddened and steaming from the hot water, she stood like a statue, looking him straight in the eyes with as blank an expression as she could muster. He could hurt her as much as he wished but Violetta refused to dissolve and fall away from the high standards she had set for herself. If her mother had been able to cope with the most physically and mentally agonising of tortures, she reminded herself sternly, there could be no excuses for any weakness on her part.

Still, her eyes stung and watered as Badger shifted position, watching her face with deliberate malice, and slapped one long strand of boiling cabbage against her sex, and then another, even hotter than the first. The tip curled around her inner thigh, both edges coming into contact with her unprotected sex. Intense pain made her soft labia quiver and her nerve-endings scream. Yet she still did not react to this torture, hands linked behind her back and her breasts thrust out in a position of complete subservience as she waited for his next blow. It hurt, yes, but the pain had to be endured. A few days ago she would have run screaming from the cruel agonies this man was inflicting on her breasts and sex, but now she wanted to accept the challenge that had been thrown down, embrace it like a lover and succeed in spite of her sheltered upbringing. For this was yet another part of Stag's stringent testing process and she would not fail this time.

The chef stood back at last, dropping the saucepan and kicking it aside. As it fell and rolled away, the last of that boiling water spattered against her bare ankles and shins. The pain was excruciating. Yet still Violetta forced herself to remain silent, her teeth clenched so hard they were like steel pins holding her body together.

'Now take off the dress.' Badger dragged at the strappy shoulders of her dress, impatiently exposing her breasts. Through the eye slits in the mask she saw his eyes gleam along the pale shining skin beneath his fingers, though she could not be sure whether that was with malice or admiration. 'Come on, hurry up and take it off. You work naked down here or you get my belt across your arse.'

She lifted her hands and began to remove the dress, her eyes fixed on a small dark spot on the far wall of the

203

kitchen. For a man like Badger to see the apprehensio
in her eyes would be an appalling self-betrayal. Th
metal studs, positioned discreetly at the nape of her nec
and down in the hollow of her back, felt stiff an
immovable at first. Her fingers awkward, she struggle
with them in silence, finally getting them to yield an
release the fabric. When at last the dress was nothin
but a pool of coiled black straps on the floor, Violett
stepped out of it and stood naked in front of him. Ther
was a moment's impulse to cover her breasts and se
with her hands, but she fought it, knowing how such
gesture would only demonstrate her vulnerability an
provoke laughter in this man. It was better to hide he
weakness behind a facade of strength and risk a mor
severe punishment than she could take, than to allo
him the satisfaction of witnessing her fear.

Clapping his hands together with impatience, Badge
gestured for her to turn around, presumably so he coul
admire her naked body from the rear. After a shor
silence, he spoke again. This time he sounded almos
impressed. 'I think you have not been sunbathing mucl
It's still very succulent, very white, your skin. *Comme d
lait.*' His laughter was guttural. 'Like a warm bowl c
milk.'

She stood still while the man walked around he
running a finger lightly across her tortured nipples.

'Look at that now, see how they stiffen. *C'e.
merveilleux.* You are a natural, just as Stag told me. Bt
you don't make enough noise.'

He slapped her breasts hard, one by one, and watche
the firm skin bounce in response. In spite of the pai
Violetta made no sound at all. The black eyes narrowe
on her face, noting the clenched jaw and the tightl
sealed lips. His voice lowered to a warning snarl.

'I like to hear a girl cry out when I strike her. To so
and whimper. Maybe even fall to her knees and beg m
to stop. But you . . . you do nothing. You say nothin

204

'Perhaps I do not hurt you enough? Is that it, *ma petite Anglaise*? You like the game a little rougher?'

The next slap caught her off guard and Violetta fell onto the hard terracotta floor, automatically clutching her hot skin. The hand dropped back to her side immediately but not before he had seen it and laughed. He dragged her back up by her red hair and she cried loudly at the pain, not bothering to hold back anymore. What was the point? If this man wanted her to make a noise when he hurt her, Violetta would oblige him. But she would emphasise each sound so that he knew she could stifle it if necessary, that she was exaggerating her pain for his pleasure. Though such a tactic, she realised with sudden irritation, would make this man even angrier than before, when she was making no noise at all. For he would suspect her of laughing at him and his slaps would merely increase in intensity.

'That's much better, my eager little slut, but I must prepare dinner before eight o'clock,' he said, dragging her to the other side of the kitchen. 'The meat is nearly done. You can help me with the vegetables.'

Violetta took the long fat courgette he handed her and glanced about for a chopping board, uncertain of what he expected. There was another fierce slap across her right breast and she yelped.

'I'm sorry, I don't . . .'

'The skin must be softened before cooking. So fuck yourself with it.' When she hesitated, staring at him in shock, he snatched the courgette away and shoved it between her legs. 'Come on, get it right up there. *Vite, vite.*'

Her cheeks burning with shame, Violetta found herself spreading her legs and squatting slightly to accommodate the vegetable's sizeable girth, her fingers slipping on the cool green skin as she forced it inside. Temporarily losing her self-control, she could not help emitting a cry of satisfaction as the courgette slid inside

with remarkable ease and stretched her aching sex
Filled with chagrin at such a display of sluttish behav
iour, she tried to remove the offending vegetable a
once. But Badger encouraged her to push it back in an
even took hold of its knobbly end, pressing upward
and helping her to accept almost its entire length in he
tight channel.

'Now pull it out again,' he grunted, his spicy breath
in her face. He gave a triumphant shout at the cream
whitish smear left along the vegetable as it was remove
and Violetta wished she could disappear into th
shadows, her embarrassment mounting steadily when
the chef took away the courgette for chopping and
replaced it with a smooth purple aubergine.

This time Violetta tried to refuse the vegetable befor
it had even entered her but Badger made it clear she wa
his slave to command. He picked up a large metal fish
slice from the butcher's trolley by his side and slappe
her buttocks until they burnt. After six or seven strokes
she moaned in defeat and agreed to do his bidding
Squatting once again with her legs spread apart for eas
of access, Violetta grimaced with discomfort as th
gleaming bulbous end of the aubergine stung her labia
Once she had several inches of the monstrous vegetabl
lodged inside, he bent to examine the skin around he
sex, stretched so thin it felt as though it would rip. Sh
hissed as his fingers probed at the engorged entrance
begging him to let her pull out the aubergine, but he
pleas only seemed to excite him. He straightene
without removing it and squeezed her sore nipples, sti
reddened from the boiling water, pinching them unt
the blood had almost stopped flowing there. Her hea
fell back and Violetta heard herself groan with intens
pleasure, feeling her juices begin to ooze around the fa
purple aubergine and loosen it.

Stooping again to examine the contours of he
tortured sex, the masked man swiftly realised what wa

appening. There was satisfaction in his laugh. He
aught her dripping fluid on his fingers and lapped at it
hrough his mouth slit. The cruel bulge under his apron
welled in instant response.

Violetta was placed on her back over the damp
vooden surface of his butcher's trolley, her head
anging down over the edge. Badger straddled her face,
ushed his apron aside and unzipped his black jeans.
he fat penis that came into his hand was already rigid,
transparent slither of pre-come coating the wedge-
haped glans. Violetta had no time to think or protest,
nstinctively moistening her lips in readiness as he
ositioned his cock between them and shoved himself
nside.

'Suck me, whore,' he commanded her in a thick voice.
His eyes closed as she obeyed. '*Que c'est bon!*'

Slowly, he dragged his glistening penis out and then
orced it back in almost to the hilt. The veins stood out
n his tattooed forearms as he held her head still
eneath him and kept her throat tilted back to facilitate
reater depth of penetration.

'Come on, you can swallow more cock than that.
out au fond . . . take it right to the back now.'

Violetta gagged on his penis and tried to pull away,
ut his grip was too strong. So instead she concentrated
n regaining a sense of balance, anything which might
elp her feel in control of the situation. Her body was
o high on the butcher's trolley that her feet were
crabbling to touch the floor. With his thrusts jerking
he trolley and sliding her backwards and forwards, she
ould no longer hold the aubergine securely in place. As
er excitement grew, her sex became wetter and hotter,
nd the vegetable inside began to slip. The end result
ad been obvious as soon as he lifted her into this
wkward position. She gave a muffled moan as Badger
fted her even closer to the root of his penis, feeling
hose internal muscles clench down hard to expel the

aubergine and knowing there was nothing she could do to prevent it.

Seconds later, they both heard the fat slippery aubergine tumble and bounce across the terracotta floor. His angry exclamation was followed by a coarse finger and thumb pinching her nipple, punishing her until her eyes watered. With his penis thrust so deep into her throat Violetta could not cry out in pain, though she tried unsuccessfully to twist away. But it was futile to pretend his rough treatment was having no effect on her. She might be struggling against the invasion of his penis but her sex pulsed between her thighs, aching to be entered in a betrayal of her hidden nature.

He withdrew from her throat and turned her over uncerermoniously, his knee forcing her legs even wider. Her bottom cheeks were dragged apart and she squealed at the sudden intrusion of his fingers there. The disapproving sound he made under his breath frightened her, especially when she heard him taking another pan from the stove.

'Your cunt may be dripping, slut, but your arse is a little tight. I think you need . . . *ah oui, peut-être un soupçon de . . .*' She tensed as a trickle of something warm and slimy ran down between her spread buttocks and moistened the secret whorl of her anus. 'Pesto!'

Tensing at the unexpected stab of pain, Violetta drew her breath in sharply and stared straight ahead at the far wall of the kitchen. With the help of the pesto sauce he had dribbled around the hole, something hard and narrow had just entered her anus. Then he positioned himself between her legs and Violetta felt an odd sensation, almost as though her rectal passage were being gradually filled with fluid, and realised with a shock that he must be administering some kind of enema. What she had felt earlier must have been a length of tubing, or perhaps a small funnel, inserted into that tight orifice to provide a channel for incoming

quid. There was a powerful smell of pesto sauce in the
r and she could not help wondering whether that was
hat he was using, her mind reeling at the thought. She
uld hear his heavy breathing now as he concentrated
1 the task, standing behind her with a saucepan in his
nd which he rested occasionally on the smooth
hiteness of her back, making her jerk as the warm
etal base touched her skin. Violetta did not want to
ake him angry, so she stayed as still as possible while
e chef fiddled above her, his fingers often moving
tween her buttocks to adjust the position of what now
lt like a metal funnel. But the sensation of fullness
came more and more unpleasant as the minutes
ssed. In the end, Violetta found she had to bite her
to stop those muscles from cramping and pushing
wn instinctively, expelling this intruder just as she had
pelled the aubergine from her sex.

The funnel was abruptly removed and Badger stepped
oser between her legs. Violetta gripped the edges of the
tcher's trolley as she realised what was going to
ppen.

'Push back hard,' he muttered, dragging her cheeks
art and leaning forward. '*Plus fort, fort, fort.*'

Her bottom almost exploded as Violetta pushed
ckwards as hard as she possibly could and felt the
arm liquid come squeezing out in all directions. Then
e gasped and her eyes closed on a sharp wave of
citement, the thick rigidity of a penis pushing into her
ck back passage. Not content with his brutal and
miliating treatment of her so far, the man in the
dger mask was going to bugger her now. To her
nazement, though, it did not hurt. The fluid running
it of her anus seemed to have provided ample
brication for his fucking, although the squelching fart
his first withdrawal made her cheeks turn scarlet with
nbarrassment. But the chef did not seem to notice,
pping her firm buttocks and shoving his penis back

209

inside again. He quickly built up a rhythm, her buttoc
cheeks and the tops of her thighs slimy with what sme
like pesto sauce as he thrust forcefully in and out of h
rectum.

'*Parfait . . . ça marche*,' he grunted, his voice straine
with the effort. 'Keep pushing back.'

Ashamed to find herself aroused by such appallin
treatment, Violetta turned her hot face into t
butcher's trolley. But she could not escape the burnin
sensations in her stretched sex, rubbed against tl
wooden trolley at each thrust and so highly sensitised l
her ordeal that every nerve in her body was no
screaming for release. Violetta had tried her best
resist but she simply could not hold back an orgas
much longer. Then his hand dragged at her hair, pullin
her head up as he forced her thighs even further apa
almost lifting her away from the trolley. Her boc
writhed helplessly under his thrusts, large hairy bal
slapping repeatedly into the raised mound of her se
That extra stimulation proved too much for them bot
Badger dug his fingernails into her slippery buttocks an
bucked his hips, grunting like a wild animal as his spur
shot deep into the tight invitation of her anus. She d
not want to come like this, she thought fiercely. Not
such a filthy and untamed manner. But within secon
her groans had become sharp anguished yelps
pleasure and she too spasmed into a violent and almo
never-ending orgasm, her rectum gripping and the
releasing her tormentor.

'*Pas mal*,' he panted, a note of satisfaction in h
voice. He straightened and handed Violetta a clea
white apron to tie around her waist, ignoring h
shuddering gasps of pleasure. 'Now don't just lie ther
enjoying yourself. Take those plates upstairs to t
dining hall. *Vite, vite, vite*. The Master and his gues
are waiting.'

* * *

he rest of that evening seemed to pass in a blur for
oletta. Sometimes she was down in the shadowy
tchens with Badger, sucking his penis before licking
t the dirty pots, or she was upstairs in the vast
ndlelit dining hall with Stag and the others, bending
er the table to display and offer up for use her
etched pesto-green anus.

She caught Heidi's wide-eyed astonishment as Stag
id the young blonde across the scattered remnants of
eir dinner, raised her thighs almost to her ears, and
cked her until she cried out at his brutality. Violetta
is ordered to bend and touch the floor directly behind
eir working bodies, her sex entered by Crow while she
izzled against her master's buttocks and licked his
us. She did not protest but performed her task in
ent submission, eyes closed as the tension began to
ow again inside her body. Somewhere across the
gh-ceilinged room, she could hear Mandy being
afted forcibly from behind by both Jackal and Fox. A
w moments later Mandy gave a muffled scream and
uddered into an intense orgasm. When she turned her
ad in curiosity, Violetta saw her friend hanging off the
r end of the dining table, her mouth practically
allowing Horse's large penis as he stood above her
ad. Belly-down on the polished surface, her face
ight red with effort, the excitement of accommodating
o men in her back passage at once and one in her
roat had obviously been too much for the receptionist.
The scene was incredible, an orgy of proportions she
uld only have dreamt about in the past. Their groans
d gasps filled the dining hall, the only other sound the
ip of sweating skin against skin and the occasional
atter as someone clumsily knocked a dish to the floor.
ie ought to have been disgusted by such a crude
ectacle, yet somehow the obscenity of this evening's
tertainment only excited her more. It was almost
conceivable that she could have changed so much in

211

such a short space of time, Violetta thought, closing her eyes again. The deliciously liquid sensations inside her sex intensified as Crow neared his climax and began to thrust like a crazed man, gripping her hips with painful fingers. She was no longer recognisable as the naive traveller who, a mere ten days or so ago, had considered herself a slut because she had succumbed to sexual desire and fucked a stranger on a train. Now she bent willingly to let this masked man penetrate her from behind, groaning with barely concealed pleasure as her tongue rimmed Stag's puckered anus. The only explanation, she realised, must be that this desire had always been inside her, waiting to be uncovered and explored.

There were tears in her eyes later, when Stag raised his whip above her slick raised buttocks and marked her properly at last. The agony she suffered lifted her high above the others, her cries so plaintive it felt as though she were dying. Yet Violetta slid to the floor afterward in a state of delirious joy, aware that she had found something she understood and wanted forever ... the pain, this pleasure, and never quite knowing how to separate the two.

Ten

'I can't believe it's nearly the end of the season,' Mandy complained, closing her eyes as the sunshine flowed over her spine and naked buttocks.

She and Violetta were lying together on sun loungers by the swimming pool for the third afternoon in a row. Usually Mandy would have been kept busy in the chateau office, but business seemed to be drying up as the summer wore on. It was such a scorching day they could almost fry eggs on the patio, she thought wryly. Yet in less than one month most of the guests would have left the chateau and only the staff would remain in residence until next spring, apart from for the odd winter guest. She sighed and stared dismally over the dancing pool. It would be so dull once Violetta had gone home to England.

'I shall really miss you when you leave.'

Violetta shrugged at her unhappy tone, sitting up and stretching as if she had been asleep. She squeezed a little sun cream out of the tube, massaging it carefully into her breasts. The pale skin shone in the sunlight, her breasts swaying with the gently rhythmic motion.

'I can't stay here for ever, Mandy.'

'Why not?'

Her friend smiled. 'I've got a job back home and quite a nice little flat in London. If I stayed here I'd end up with nothing.'

'But I already told you how easy it can be. There's n[o]
need to go back to any of those things. You could as[k]
Stag for a job and ... and ... we could share tha[t]
bedroom in the attic. It would be so cosy, just the tw[o]
of us.'

'But what sort of job?' Violetta shook her head. 'Let[']
face it, he doesn't exactly need another receptionist.'

'That's true. But he often needs someone to entertai[n]
his guests. The diffident ones, you know. To get dresse[d]
up and visit them in their rooms. There are always a fe[w]
who who don't like to come down and mix wit[h]
everyone else. Especially in the winter. You could off[er]
to do that.'

'Prostitute myself?'

'It wouldn't be like that, honestly. Don't you want t[o]
serve Stag? To stay here over the winter and pleas[e]
him?'

'Yes, but ...'

Swinging herself off the sun lounger, Mandy kne[lt]
down beside her friend and stroked her arm. 'I've don[e]
it myself, you know. Though I'm not as good as yo[u]
would be. You're a natural.'

Violetta bit her lip. 'I don't know. It sounds like th[e]
wrong sort of thing for me.'

'But it can be so sexy.'

'Taking my clothes off for a stranger? I don't s[ee]
anything particularly sexy about that, to be frank.'

'For God's sake, Violetta. Haven't you learnt an[y]
thing at all over the past couple of weeks? You have t[o]
see this with different eyes. For a start, it isn't abo[ut]
"taking your clothes off", like you're some cheap who[re]
in a parked car. When you're serving your maste[r]
there's a purity about it.' Mandy paused and drew [a]
sharp impatient breath, seeing the disbelief on he[r]
friend's face. 'Look,' she continued, 'I performed f[or]
some of his guests in the past and a few of the men ju[st]
beat me, that was all. They only wanted to mark m[y]

214

kin. Others wanted to go a bit further. Use my mouth, my arse, you know the score. Sometimes it hurt, OK, but I still felt in control the whole time. It was always *my choice*.'

'You chose . . .'

'To serve my master as he desired, yes.'

A loud whinnying noise from the stable block made them both turn and stare, surprised. There was never anyone in that area of the chateau during the hottest part of the day, when most of the staff and guests were sleeping in their rooms. Violetta started to speak, but Mandy hushed her, still listening. The whinnying sound came again, this time higher and more panicked. One of the horses seemed to be in trouble. Not sure what to do, Mandy glanced up at the silent shuttered windows of the chateau. She ought to investigate, she told herself sternly, though it felt a little odd to be wandering about the chateau grounds without any of the men around. During the siesta, she and Violetta had rarely ventured any further than the swimming pool.

'Maybe one of the horses has got loose and is frightened,' Violetta murmured, meeting her eyes. 'Shall we go and check?'

Arm in arm, the two girls walked cautiously towards the stable block. They had not bothered to bring any towels and their naked bodies shone in the sun: breasts, belly and buttocks slick with tanning cream and catching the light as they swayed. It had been so lovely and peaceful beside the swimming pool but Mandy did not feel comfortable on her own here with Violetta. There was a dusty breeze breaking through the range of cypress trees along the ridge and her mouth felt dry. The stables were not far from the chateau but those few hundred feet felt like an incredible distance today. What if they needed to call for help? They could be attacked out here and no one would hear them. Security was very tight at the chateau, but she knew people did sometimes climb over the high walls in the summer to peek at thei goings-on. Mandy bit her lip, aware that she was a littl scared. Perhaps she should have alerted Stag about tha odd whinnying noise. After all, they were not properl equipped on their own to deal with an intruder.

When they reached the quiet stable block, Mand glanced along the row of wooden half-doors, each c them safely closed, but could see nothing out of th ordinary. Then she realised that Prince, Stag's imperiou white stallion, was not peering over his box in th sunlight as he normally did when anyone came into th stable yard. She pinched Violetta's arm and pointe ahead, gesturing her not to make a sound. Her frien nodded, slightly paler than usual. Then the two girl crept towards Prince's box, treading silently with thei bare feet through the loose straw and dirt of the yard.

Prince stood towards the back of the stall, his ta whisking with some violent emotion. For it was n intruder who had caused the stallion to whinny s loudly, but the new girl, Heidi. The young blonde wa lying on her back in the mounds of straw, her shor leather skirt pulled up to her waist and the fingers of on hand working feverishly between her thighs. Peerin over the half-door to the stall, the girls could actuall see the pinkish tip of her clitoris gleaming with the fluid of arousal, rubbed back and forth between the blonde' soft shaven labia. Heidi was almost like a wild anima completely absorbed in this urgent drive towards re lease, slamming her bare buttocks up and down again the straw as though she were being mounted in he imagination. But mounted by what, Mandy could n help wondering? A human or another animal? She ha to stop a moan escaping her lips, aroused by the sight c this young blonde on her back in the straw, hair tousle and bare thighs glistening with sweat from her efforts.

Heidi exhorted herself in German as she came close to orgasm, her guttural oaths echoing around th wooden stall. Standing almost immediately above her writhing body – a position which put the girl in danger of serious injury if he kicked out – was the muscular white stallion, his own excitement at her behaviour only too evident. Yet Heidi seemed oblivious to the potential danger, her high-pitched cries soon breaking the silence as she climaxed, head thrown back and both thighs splayed as she enjoyed the last intense throes of her orgasm. In response, Prince tossed his head and whinnied loudly, turning around in his stall and neatly lifting his hooves clear of her thrashing body. It was almost as though the stallion had been trained to witness such lewd behaviour and understood how to restrict his movements to prevent injury. The damp thighs beneath him finally closed and Heidi looked up at the horse with a wickedly lascivious smile.

Mandy coughed, and the young blonde scrambled hurriedly to her feet, jerking her short leather skirt back into position as she realised who had been watching her and what they must have seen. 'Enjoying yourself?' Mandy asked her maliciously.

Heidi flushed at the sharp tone but raised her chin defiantly. She looked from one girl to the other and shrugged, tidying her clothes as she came to the stall door. 'So what if I was? You two are just jealous.'

'Don't be so ridiculous,' Violetta said incredulously. 'You're nothing but a hormonal little teenager and you've only been here a few days. Why on earth should we be jealous of you?'

'Because Stag prefers me to you two. You're too old for him now. He fucks me all the time and gives me special presents for being so good. He gave me this skirt today . . . and . . .' Heidi bit her lip, frowning. 'And he told me I could come down here and visit his horses any time I liked.'

'Too old?' Mandy spluttered.

Violetta laughed. 'We're the right age for a man like Stag, actually. We're both in our early twenties, our

217

skin's perfect and we know how to pleasure a man. Oh yes, and we don't have any spots."

'I don't have spots!' the German girl hissed.

'Really?' Violetta said, peering closely at the blonde's face as though she had noticed several blemishes, though Mandy could see perfectly well that the German girl's complexion was smooth and clear.

But her ploy worked. The blonde picked up a handful of soiled straw, throwing it at the two girls with a howl of uncontrolled rage. That was the excuse Mandy had been looking for. She unlatched the stable door and leapt inside, dragging the German teenager to her knees in the straw and slapping her hard. Both girls struggled together for a few seconds, then Heidi sank her teeth into the hand holding her by the neck and Mandy screamed, letting go instantly. Aggrieved, she aimed an unsteady kick at the kneeling blonde, still rubbing at the small red puncture marks left in her skin.

Prince wheeled about the stall in alarm, whinnying and kicking out at the sides, and Violetta grabbed hold of his bridle. While the other two girls rolled furiously together in the straw, she led the excitable stallion to the far corner of his stall and tried to calm him down. By that time, still infuriated by the 'too old' comment, Mandy had pinned the blonde down with her powerful thighs and was tormenting her. But when she foolishly sat back on her heels to rest, Heidi managed to break free and stagger to the stable door, calling for help in a tearful girlish voice. Seizing a handful of straw which stank of horse manure, Mandy stuffed it into Heidi's mouth from behind and spun the girl to face her, amused by her disgusted grimace. Then she forced the arrogant blonde back onto her knees with a whoop of triumph.

'Not too old to win a fight, though, am I?' she said, gesturing to Violetta to pass her some old rope hanging on the stable wall. Then she tied the blonde's hands roughly behind her back and bent her struggling body over a metal food trough. 'Sweetie, could you hand me that riding crop? The nicely oiled one that Stag likes to use on his girls when they misbehave. We're going to teach little Miss Germany a much-needed lesson in manners.'

Heidi tried to cry out as she realised what was about to happen, but the damp straw wedged in her mouth muffled the protest.

Mandy did not give the blonde any time for apprehension, though, too aroused by the thought of the pain she was about to inflict on her. Her hands pushed the leather skirt up and dragged the minuscule thong to mid-thigh. Then she raised the riding crop and brought it down smartly on the tanned bottom cheeks in front of her. Heidi's buttocks jerked and she uttered a muffled yelp, struggling to get away.

'I can't hear you apologising,' Mandy said sternly. Heidi grunted something incomprehensible through a mouthful of straw. 'That's not good enough, little girl. You have to learn your place.'

Mandy gave the younger girl another stroke with the riding crop, taking pleasure in the way her firm body writhed against hers. 'For a start, you can't give yourself airs and graces when you've only just arrived.'

The little blonde grunted again, shaking her head like a wild animal caught in a trap.

'You want me to take the straw out of your mouth?' Mandy asked solicitously. 'I'm not sure. What do you think, Violetta? You want to hear an apology? Oh, all right.'

'Stop it . . . oh please! That hurts!' As the mouthful of straw was removed, Heidi was able to moan at last, wriggling from side to side as the riding crop came down yet again on her red-striped bottom.

'So, do you understand who the boss is now?'

The girl sobbed, nodding her head violently. 'I'm so sorry, mistress. I didn't mean to . . .'

Her sentence dissolved into a broken incoherent mixture of German, French and English as she begged for mercy from the two girls standing above her. Yet Mandy thought the little slut seemed more aroused than hurt by this punishment. Indeed the moans became gradually more soulful and the little blonde began to rub her exposed crotch against the metal trough. Her breathing was ragged by the time Mandy raised the riding crop for the sixth and final time, wishing she had an excuse to beat Heidi for longer, but knowing that she had already marked the young girl's skin quite considerably.

'OK, you can stop crying now,' Mandy said, throwing aside the riding crop and untying the girl's hands. 'I won't hit you any more. Just don't make me cross again.'

'No, mistress.' Heidi's greedy fingers went straight to the exposed lips of her sex, rubbing herself furiously. 'I mean, yes, mistress.'

That beating must have really aroused her, Mandy thought, watching her captive in astonishment. Indeed it took no more than five or six tugs of her erect clitoris for the German girl to reach another noisy climax. As her orgasm peaked on a high scream, the blonde sank onto her knees in the straw, black leather skirt still scrunched up around her waist and the lowered thong leaving a white pressure mark around her tanned thighs.

Mandy licked her lips as she watched, unable to take her eyes off the shaven glistening labia peeping out from between those juice-slick fingers. As if by remote control, she even found her own hand slipping between her thighs and locating the erect bud of her clitoris, beginning to stroke herself in time to the other girl's moans. She finally climaxed as Heidi lay face down in the straw and raised her tortured bottom with its scarlet and white stripes for the other two girls to admire.

All three girls were so absorbed in their excitement that none of them heard the footsteps crossing the stable ard. But Prince, pulling hard at the hand which held his bridle, dragged Violetta across the stall towards the open door, his loud whinnying alerting the girls to trouble.

Outside in the sunlit courtyard stood Stag, watching them through the doorway with his hands on his hips. Their master did not look particularly amused as he took in the red-striped bottom of the young blonde, Mandy's soaking fingers and her friend's guiltily flushed cheeks.

'*Mais qu'est-ce que vous avez fait ici?*' he thundered. 'What have you done to Heidi?'

Before any of them could manage an answer, Stag had strode into the stable and given Mandy a slap which sent her reeling backwards into the straw. 'That's for your disobedience. Heidi, pick up the riding crop and give my receptionist twice the number of strokes she gave you. And make each one harder than the last.'

'Yes, master,' Heidi whispered, reaching for the riding crop.

Mandy cringed naked in the straw, waiting for the inevitable agony on her bare skin once Heidi raised the crop. Out of the sun, the stable suddenly seemed very cold. She was trembling with fear, yet she felt almost as sorry for her friend when Stag swung back towards Violetta, his eyes like chips of black ice behind the antlered mask.

His voice sounded deeper and harsher than ever before. 'It was foolish of you to risk angering me again, *ma belle.*'

'Please don't punish us.' Violetta stumbled backwards, her eyes huge in her white face. 'We didn't mean to make you angry.'

But Stag seemed unmoved by the desperation in her voice. Mandy could not remember when she had ever seen him so furious. Instead, he took Violetta by the arm and dragged her back towards the stable door.

221

'Your mother would never have made such a stupid mistake. I expected much better from her daughter.'

'What are you going to do with me?' Violetta cried, struggling in terror and glancing back over her shoulder at the other two.

'It wasn't her idea,' Mandy began to say but her voice fell rapidly into silence as her master shot her a freezing glare. Then the crop came down on her own white buttocks and she screamed, pushing both hands between her legs to comfort herself. Violetta and her unfair punishment were promptly forgotten. The crop came down twice, three times, four times, and her moist sex started to ache. God but this little blonde has a heavy hand, she thought breathlessly, sweat dripping from her forehead into her eyes. Five times, six times, seven times, maybe even eight, until the stable dimmed to a pale blur and Mandy writhed on her bed of straw like some animal in the last throes of labour, seized by an orgasm almost too powerful for her own body.

Dazzled by the intense sunlight, Violetta found herself thrown to her knees in the stable yard. Silently, as though responding to some secret signal, the other masked men from the chateau had appeared. They formed a ring around her, those animal and bird masks suddenly more menacing than ever before, dark sinister eye-slits and cruel beaks turned in her direction.

Terrified, she shielded her eyes and stared from one mask to the other, her skin clammy even in the dry heat. From their silent air of anticipation, she guessed that today must represent the culmination of her training. The rough white gravel hurt her knees but she made no attempt to move. Her stomach tightened with an odd mixture of fear and exhilaration. Whatever was about to happen had been planned ever since her arrival at the chateau. Or perhaps even before that day, Violetta realised with an uneasy feeling of inevitability . . . while

222

she was still in London and that invitation had landed so unexpectedly on her doormat. But how could Stag have been so sure that she would accept and come here?

'I was right about you from the beginning, *ma belle*,' the Frenchman said, taking a step backwards as though deliberately removing his protection from her. A ripple of excitement ran through the waiting men, their increasing arousal obvious to Violetta as she remained on her knees at crotch level. 'You need a firmer hand than the others if you are to realise your potential.'

'My . . . potential?'

'To be a true submissive.' His voice dropped lower, his tone intimate. 'To become your mother's daughter at last.'

'I'm nothing like my mother,' she said instinctively, shaking her head. 'I've tried so hard to obey you the way you expect. But I can't be a true submissive, Stag. It's just not in me.'

Stag stared back at her without speaking. The silence dragged on interminably, her body beginning to tremble as Violetta sensed his deep and unappeasable anger. Then the Frenchman seemed to shake himself awake, gesturing abruptly to one of the waiting men. She heard footsteps crunch on the gravel as someone approached her from behind. Still on her knees, Violetta turned slightly, her eyes widening in panic at what she saw. Jackal was standing directly above her, a deer mask in his hand. Its dark furry head had a look of terrified submission and Violetta suddenly knew that it was intended to be worn by her.

With obvious satisfaction, Stag watched her expression change to fear. 'Prepare her for the hunt,' he said harshly.

She shook her head, crying aloud as her hands were dragged painfully behind her back, but the men ignored her desperate protests. Crow pulled her head back by her long sweat-drenched hair and Jackal slipped the mask down over her face. Instantly she was plunged into a hot damp darkness. Through the narrow eye slits of the deer mask Violetta could only see by turning her head from side to side, as she had seen Crow doing before. The claustrophobia and lack of control were too much for her. She could hear feet on the gravel, then a scream of sympathetic protest, and realised that Mandy had been brought out into the stable yard. Her friend must have seen the deer mask on her head and realised what was happening. But no one could help Violetta now. This was to be her own personal trial: the last test, the final torture which would reveal how much or how little she had learnt over the past fortnight. Her heart began to race as she tried to second-guess their next move, peering unsuccessfully into the dazzling sunlight for clues. The mask was bad enough but what other torments had the Frenchman planned for her?

Stag was speaking now though his words were muffled, somewhere close behind her as she was pulled to her feet. Her heart clenched in fear at his last callous order.

'We must wait until darkness falls before loosing the dogs. Tie her up in the kennel so the animals can recognise her scent.'

Then he turned on his heel and disappeared, leaving her in the cruel hands of his men without a backward glance. There was no one to protect her now. Even Mandy had vanished, presumably taken back to the chateau for yet another relentless session of whipping. But Violetta had no time to pity her friend, yelping and stumbling as Jackal dragged her by the hair towards the far end of the stable block. As he kicked open the wooden door to the kennels, its foul stench made even her captor recoil for an instant, exclaiming angrily in French before shoving her forward. After the brilliant sunshine of the stable yard, it felt almost cold inside the low-roofed dog kennel. By turning her head carefully from side to side, she was just able to make out the confines of her dimly lit prison. Terrified by what might lie ahead, Violetta began to shake uncontrollably as she was tied to a post in the centre of the kennel. Her bare feet ached from the effort of trying not to make contact with its concrete floor, blackened with piles of damp filth and excrement. The whole place stank of stale urine and dirtied straw.

When his men eventually left her alone, closing and locking the wooden door behind them, Violetta found herself plunged into a cold darkness punctuated only by a few pale strips of light filtering through gaps in the walls and roof. At first she spent some time struggling to loosen her tied hands, listening to shouts and the muffled sound of barking from outside in the stable yard. But the bonds were too tight and she had to give up, painfully realising that she could not possibly escape. Then a wooden partition to her left was suddenly raised and three powerful-looking Alsatians – presumably the same guard dogs who had chased her that morning in the chateau grounds – poured through the narrow gap into their kennel, barking and snapping at each other as though they had not been fed properly for days.

The largest dog jumped up at her with a snarl and Violetta screamed, jerking back in the deer mask. The last thing she felt before passing out was his paw dragging across her erect nipple.

She came back to consciousness with an icy splash of water on her breasts and belly, crying out as she straightened in shock.

'Stop whining and wake up, bitch!'

The man was standing behind her now, loosening her tied hands. Dazed and blinking, she tried to turn her head to see him but the mask was too heavy. She could not place the voice either, though that strong French accent was familiar. One of the masked men from the chateau. Possibly Crow, from that sudden hint of irony in his tone. He kicked out as one of the dogs sniffed at her legs, warning it in French to keep its distance. One of his hands slipped below her bonds and stroked the pale trembling curve of her bottom.

'It's time to come out and play.'

Her neck was stiff from being in one position for so long. How many hours had she been left here in the kennel? The wooden door stood open now but there was no sunlight outside. Night must have fallen while she was unconscious. Violetta tried to speak but her lips were dry and cracked. She moistened them a little, clearing her throat.

'Where's Mandy gone?' Her voice sounded croaky. 'What are you going to do to us?'

'You should be more worried about yourself, slut. That eager little whore loves the punishments we give her.' The man pulled her free from the post and she was able to see him at last, stiffening in alarm as she recognised Badger. 'We've got something special planned for you tonight.'

'Special?'

'You don't know? Stag didn't tell you?'

Violetta attempted to shake her head but the deer mask felt like an iron band around her temples. 'Tell me what?'

'Tonight we go hunting.'

She was dizzy and confused. 'Hunting for what?'

'We hunt for deer tonight.' Badger pushed her naked body out of the filthy kennel and into the yard. The dogs ran out of the door behind them, barking excitedly and pawing at her skin again. The chef cupped her breasts from behind, stroking the painfully aroused nipples with a grunt of satisfaction. 'And you are the deer.'

There was a sudden blast of horns and Violetta whirled, confused and frightened, to see the other masked men coming into the courtyard. They were shouting and whooping like savages as they advanced, great flaming torches raised above their heads, the acrid smell of the smoke burning her nostrils. The dogs ran into their midst, baying and slavering as they milled about the men's feet. There were whiskers and beaks and claws in that crowd and above them, swaying gracefully as ever, the dark tines of an antlered stag.

For a moment she thought they must have come to seize and kill her, like a human sacrifice in some ancient ritual. But as the men came level with them, Violetta found herself caught up in that wild pack and dragged forwards, like a flower tossed onto the surge of a wave. Pulled away from the stable yard and into the open fields, she was taken through rough grass on her bare feet to the edge of a shadowy slope.

There was an urgent voice in her ear. 'Run down the hill towards the woods as fast as you can. And don't look back. You will have three or four minutes before the dogs are loosed.'

'No!' she cried in terror.

Clawing at the heavy mask, she suddenly realised there was no way to release it. They must have fastened it into place at the back of her neck, she told herself urgently, but could not find the straps to undo the mask. Someone was shouting behind her, urging her on to run. She was too panicked to recognise the voice. It might be Mandy, she thought suddenly, her eyes widening. Yet before she could search for her friend in the darkness, another hand had pushed her forcefully in the back and Violetta found herself lurching forward down the slope with someone pursuing her for the first few steps.

'*Vas-y, dépêche-toi!*' It sounded like the Frenchman now, so close she could almost feel his hot breath on her skin. 'Run for your life, *ma belle*, and don't look back.'

Somewhere behind them, Violetta heard an excited whining as the guard dogs were brought out into the chateau grounds. Seized by a sudden primeval terror, she stopped trying to look for Mandy and began running down the slope in earnest. The deer mask weighed heavily on her neck. Violetta crooked her head to one side in an attempt to see her way through the useless eyeholes. Yet only the ground flashed past in a brownish-green blur, confusing her. She felt almost dizzy now. Where were the woods? Three or four minutes, he had said. That was all the time she had before the dogs were loosed to pursue her.

Her bare feet stumbled over the rough ground, her unrestrained breasts bouncing painfully. Beginning to tire, she slowed for a few seconds to listen and the terrible echo of their distant baying boomed through her mask. Then a shout went up amongst the men and her stomach clenched in sudden terror. The dogs must have been released. Violetta turned and ran towards the trees, all the time listening for the sound of paws thudding through the darkness.

She came back to consciousness in the woods, lying naked on her stomach while the three dogs bayed viciously around her. Her breasts were crushed against the dry soil. The deer mask was still clamped tight about her neck. Violetta rolled gingerly onto her back and stared up through narrow eye slits, her every movement accompanied by growls from the watching dogs. The menacing shadows of pine trees towered above her in the darkness. Beyond their strange shapes, the night glittered faintly with stars.

She closed her eyes, remembering the hot breath on her skin, several huge dogs dragging her down with their heavy paws and her scream echoing through the woods. Yet the dogs had not attacked her as she had feared. They were merely holding her there for the men.

Violetta tried to sit up, and instantly there was a large Alsatian in her face, lips drawn back from snarling teeth. 'OK, I'm not going anywhere,' she said shakily, lying back down on the earth.

It was not long before the men followed the dogs into the clearing and found her lying there. First she saw the flicker of burning torches amongst the trees, then heard the men stumble over fallen branches in the darkness, snapping dead wood with their boots as they moved forward across a thick carpet of pine needles. When the torches were raised to reveal her pale nakedness, held down by the three dogs, one of the men shouted triumphantly, 'We've got her!' and within seconds Violetta had been seized and dragged back to her feet. Their hands moved over her body in a wordless silence, their occasional laughter and grunts somehow more intimidating than any threat could have been.

She tried to see who each man was, but it was too difficult to turn her head from side to side while they surrounded her so closely. One man gripped her by the left breast, leading her forwards like an animal in harness. One of the others spread her sex lips open with his fingers, exploring her damp interior with lewd French comments and even thrusting two or three fingers deep inside. Some hung back in the shadows, watching their games from a distance. But all the men laughed when she swore at them, struggling to escape. Forced down onto hands and knees on a long stone altar in the centre of the clearing, she glanced about for Stag but could not see properly through the eye slits in her mask. Kneeling there in the torchlit darkness, Violetta became very aware of her own vulnerability, the men standing close by, and the dogs, leashed now and howling with frustration, mere yards away under the pine trees. For the first time she felt genuinely scared. The rules of the chateau seemed to have changed tonight. These men could use her in any way they wished and there was no one here to protect her.

Soon a whip was produced and Violetta hissed with fear, seeing the black leather gleam in the torchlight as it was raised above her body. The whip descended across her naked buttocks and she sucked in her breath on a sharp cry of pain. It came down seven times, each lash more agonising than the last. Dimly, she felt their rough hands parting her thighs so she could be lashed on her exposed sex. Her moans grew more plaintive as seven more lashes were administered there, the thin leather tail of the whip stinging and cutting those fleshy lips until she nearly passed out with the pain. But when her body slumped, the men raised her with relentless hands, slapping at her breasts and buttocks until she was conscious again. It seemed there would be no escape from this night of punishment.

Several of the men came to stand around her in a semi-circle, laughing and joking crudely about her obvious arousal. Then Violetta cried aloud, feeling the hot unmistakable splash of liquid against her sore buttocks as the men urinated on her from both sides. The weals from the whip lashes throbbed agonisingly as the urine splashed her buttocks and she heard their laughter again, one of the men even directing the last of his warm jet towards her exposed sex. A deep sense of humiliation overwhelmed her and she tried to wriggle away, restrained by several hands clamped round her wrists and ankles. Yet even as Violetta struggled against them, her eyes stinging with tears, she knew that she had been aroused by their vile behaviour. There was something deep inside her which responded to this terrible humiliation, her sex on fire and aching for more. But it seemed that their entertainment had come to an end.

One of the men covered her nakedness with a thick deerskin, fastening it around her throat with a short silver chain. Then they moved silently back into the shadows, leaving her alone on the cold stone altar. Violetta ought to have seized that opportunity to escape but her legs were trembling and her eyes stung. She had no energy left to run. Instead, she laid her head down on the altar stone, finally allowing her eyes to close.

'Do not despair, *ma belle*. This is your final test.'

It was Stag's voice behind her. Violetta froze, listening to his husky words echo around the clearing.

'You have been given the mask of the Deer to wear. You have run before the hounds like a wild animal and now you have been caught. It is time to accept your place among us. *Tu comprends*? Tonight you are the deer and I am the stag.' He knelt behind her and she felt his hands lift the thick deerskin away from her buttocks. 'Now you must submit and open yourself to me. It is the way of nature.'

The shadow of those vast antlers danced before them both in the torchlit clearing as he knelt up, stretching his hands along her belly towards the full curve of her breasts. Violetta moaned in glorious anticipation, her nipples hardening and stiffening into peaks before his fingers had even touched them. Her hands and knees hurt on the altar, yet her sex moistened with excitement as he moved closer. Instinctively she shifted the balance of her hands on the stone and raised her buttocks towards him. She felt the heat of his naked thighs pressing against her buttocks and realised he must have removed his clothes while the others were placing the deerskin about her shoulders. His fingers reached down to stroke her and those secret lips guarding her sex began to open of their own accord, filling with warm blood and inviting him further in. Suddenly it felt like a dance, the two of them moving together in a series of silent steps like a ritual.

'Is the deer ready for the stag?'

Violetta groaned under his roughly searching fingers, unable to conceal her arousal. Her sex was dripping, they could both feel the honeyed juice running down her inner thighs.

He answered his own question without waiting for a reply. 'Stay silent if you wish, but the deer is ready here ... and here ... and in there.' There was a note of pleasure in his voice as he explored the damp contours of her sex, probing the interior with two or three leisurely fingers, and then tracing the outline of her anus. 'Now pull open your cunt lips for me. Offer yourself as your mother would have done.'

Violetta shook her head in the heavy deer mask, even though she longed to obey his command, to pull herself open and beg for penetration. But some instinct made her continue to fight against that desire, in spite of the weakness she felt as his hands explored and tormented her body. It was as though she had taken on the role of the deer in her mind and feared what might happen if she gave in. She even found herself shivering at his touch, her voice dropping to a plaintive whisper.

'I can't.'

'Offer me your cunt, *chérie*. There is no point pretending you do not want me to enter you. Your body has already betrayed your desire.' The Frenchman's voice was insistent. His hand moved quickly and slapped one of her breasts, making her gasp as it swayed. Both breasts hung down like ripe fruit, swollen and aching as he handled them roughly. 'I can feel these nipples, how erect they are. No, don't try to hide them. Your mother would be proud of such responsive breasts.'

Acknowledging the shameful truth of his words, heat scalded her cheeks beneath the deer mask. The Frenchman was right yet again. She could no longer avoid this moment of surrender, not when her body was displaying such indisputable signs of arousal. No longer bothering to argue with him, Violetta reached back with trembling hands and pulled her sex lips open for her master. She no longer felt like Violetta. Perhaps she was becoming her mother. Even the lips of her sex felt unfamiliar, as though they belonged to someone else, some hungry slut eager for abuse. She wanted to deny that they were hers. But there was no way to hide those pouting lips from the circle of onlookers. They hung down between her thighs, engorged and already slick with her own lubricating fluids, a visible demonstration that Violetta was willing to submit to their domination.

'C'est bon. Now do you submit completely?'

A thousand shouts of 'no' resounded in her head, but she knew the only answer which would bring them both satisfaction. Violetta struggled with the desire to rebel again, biting her lip so fiercely she could taste her own blood. Her sex felt heavy and liquified, and all she wanted was to feel that probing cock-head force its way between her lips and up inside her belly.

'Do you submit completely?' he repeated.

His hand jerked at her loose strands of hair as though they were reins, painfully yanking her head back in the heavy deer mask until her throat ached with the strain and tears of painful joy filled her eyes.

'Yes, yes,' she sobbed. 'I submit to you completely.'

'Good girl.' There was a deep satisfaction in his voice. Yet still he did not enter her. 'And who is your master?'

'You are,' she whispered, almost to herself.

'Je ne t'ai pas entendu . . .'

'You are my master, Stag.'

He groaned and drove himself inside her sex with one forceful thrust. Her body leapt forwards with the impact, slamming against the stone altar. Yet Violetta found herself sobbing with pleasure, her mouth gaping wide as she was forced to take his sex again and again. The Frenchman held her in a vice-like grip, his entire being focused on that intense pumping motion between her wide-spread thighs. Stag leant forwards to squeeze her breasts and Violetta arched at the pain, feeling her inner muscles respond with a long ripple of sexual excitement. Her orgasm was so close now, every thrust of his body seemed to bring her nearer to the verge.

He was pinching her nipples so fiercely now they were becoming numb. Violetta hissed with pain and tried to twist away but he was too strong for her. When he suddenly withdrew, she thought he must be angry with her, but he merely repositioned the head of his penis at the puckered opening to her anus and pushed against the tight sphincter. The pain was intense at first but her tortured ring finally yielded to the Frenchman's inward thrust, dragging at the thick shaft of his penis as he withdrew once more. She must have needed a little lubrication, for the chateau owner pulled her bottom cheeks further apart and rubbed the damp head of his penis against her anal opening before trying again.

Violetta remained motionless and submissive, head down on the stone altar, eager for her master to use her anus. She did not have long to wait. Using the muscular power of his buttocks and thighs, Stag forced his penis back inside the tight ring of muscle and began to pump in and out of her rectum. Her gasps of pleasure grew louder as his thrusts increased, and when the Frenchman pushed himself in to the hilt, her anal passage felt stretched to its full painful capacity. Yet far from wishing he would withdraw, Violetta found herself moaning with intense pleasure each time the head of his penis pushed against the back walls of her rectum and raising herself even higher for his thrusts. Indeed, she could hardly believe her own lewd behaviour, writhing about on her hands and knees while this beast-like man entered and enjoyed her most intimate part.

Panting, Violetta finally surrendered to the heat in her belly and sobbed her need aloud. 'Please . . . oh please.'

'Please, what?'

'Please may I come, master?'

'It is not your place to ask such a thing, Violetta. A slave must be patient and wait for permission to be given.'

As though to signal the end of that discussion, the Frenchman moved his iron hands up to her hips and continued to ride her anus in a concentrated silence. Her knees scraped against the stone altar and her entire body was stinging and aching from the whipping she had received earlier, yet she had never felt so alive. Her thighs and buttocks began to tremble with the strain as she fought, head down in her mask, to hold a perfectly submissive position. Yet the chateau owner was right, she thought wildly. This was the way of nature. She was the deer now and he was her master, the stag.

The other masked men must have moved closer for she could hear their low groans now as they masturbated beside the altar. Turning her head in the heavy deer mask, she suddenly realised that Crow was right beside them both. He had unzipped his jeans and was jerking feverishly away at his penis, watching the scene of copulation in front of him. The large red head glistened as his hand slipped up and down the shaft. Turning her head to the other side, she saw Jackal doing the same, his penis already oozing with pre-come as he wanked. She could not see the others but heard a quiet groan as someone came nearby, spattering her naked back with his semen. Violetta panted with excitement and raised her buttocks to meet Stag's thrusts. As if in response, the penis inside her rectum grew even thicker and harder, indicating the approach of her master's orgasm.

'Now you may come, my little whore, my idol's daughter,' the Frenchman groaned. '*Vas-y, petite.* Come on my cock.'

Her sex expanded fiercely with blood at his words and she cried aloud, her scream of pleasure almost deafening inside the confines of the mask. Violetta gasped for air in the hot breathless space as her muscles clenched, driving both of them to the ultimate pleasure. Stag roared with satisfaction, almost crushing her body as he drove into her rectum for the last time. She felt his balls tighten against her sex as he came and experienced a wonderful sense of her own power. Violetta had served her master well and now he was taking his full satisfaction inside her.

His orgasm shot itself deep into her bowels in a series of powerful spurts and the masked man collapsed on her back, panting as though he had just run up a mountainside. Violetta hung there on her hands and knees, shaking under the hot deerskin as she supported his weight. When her master finally pulled out, she felt his sperm trickling slowly from her sore anal ring. Violetta looked up through the eye slits of her deer mask and saw Jackal tensing as his own spunk jetted out onto the ground nearby. The man on her other side also groaned, shooting his load simultaneously. Some of the white stream fell onto the altar stone. On impulse, Violetta reached out and took some of that spunk on her trembling fingers. Then she reached between her wide open legs and smeared it into her soaking cunt lips, writhing deliciously as she rubbed her clitoris and enjoyed the explosion of another orgasm.

It felt like hours later, but was probably only minutes, when she felt warm hands straighten her body and release the heavy deer mask from her face. She blinked for a moment, dazed by the sudden light as she moved her head stiffly from one side to the other. The wood stood silent now, the clearing emptied of his men. Only one torch remained, wedged between two stones beside the altar. As the light from its flame streamed crimson over her face and throat, Violetta looked round to see Stag standing beside the altar stone. He was still wearing his mask. The antlers swayed gracefully as he put a hand to her face and brushed away the tears.

'Are you crying with pleasure or pain, *chérie*?'

Not sure at first how to answer him, Violetta stared wonderingly into those strange dark eyes. Then she whispered: 'Both, I think.'

'That's a good answer.'

The Frenchman sounded amused and perhaps a little impressed at last. But she felt impressed too. They both knew how much she must have learnt to produce such an answer. Violetta closed her eyes, remembering the pleasurable sensations this man had given her. Her raw skin throbbed from repeatedly taking the whip, her anus sore and still oozing spunk from where he had relentlessly buggered her. How wonderful to turn her back on her old life in London and enjoy a new incarnation in this chateau; the Deer with a hunger to match that of her master. Violetta had always refused to believe she could be like her erotic film-star mother. But it was not too late to learn about her own sexuality, to explore this innate submissiveness which had lain hidden for so many years.

'Must I go home now, master?' she whispered. 'I want to stay here at the chateau. I want to serve you.'

The antlered mask tilted to one side as he considered her question. The deep voice was serious. 'That's an interesting offer, Violetta, but it's not as easy as that. My chateau is no place for the uninitiated.'

'I'm prepared to work, master.'

'But are you prepared to play the role of the deer with my other clients? To be beaten and taken by a series of strangers? If you choose to stay, that is what I may demand from you.'

'I understand.'

'And would you allow us to film your punishments, so that everyone can enjoy the sight of your white skin taking the tawse?' He laughed, his gaze slowly wandering over her bruised and weal-marked nakedness as Violetta crouched before him on the altar. 'This I cannot believe, that you could ever take such genuine pleasure from pain as your mother did.'

'But I already do, master.'

The Frenchman paused, meeting her eyes thoughtfully. 'So you claim to have learnt the way of submission?'

'Yes, master.'

'*Alors* . . .' He shrugged, straightening up. 'In that case, perhaps it is time we were properly introduced.'

He lifted both hands to his throat and, to her amazement, began to unfasten the great antlered mask of the stag. Violetta stared up at him, her mouth dry as she waited for her master to be revealed at last. In her imagination he had a thousand faces. But what would this elusive man look like in reality? But Violetta gasped in shock as the mask fell to the ground and the chateau owner looked back at her with dark sardonic eyes. She recognised him instantly. It was the attractive stranger from the train, the one who had pushed her into the toilet cubicle that first day in France and entered her without any preliminaries. No wonder she had found his husky voice so familiar when they first met. The scheming bastard had been inside her less than an hour before.

'You!' she stammered. 'But how . . . why?'

'It was a complete coincidence. I was on my way back from Paris and we happened to be seated in the same compartment. I recognised you straight away, *naturellement*. You have a strong look of your mother. It got me hard just looking at your mouth. I had not intended to fuck you there on the train, but you spread your legs so easily.'

'That's not true!'

The Frenchman frowned for a moment, his silence menacing. '*Je vous en prie*? I didn't catch that.'

'Erm . . .' She hesitated, flushing. 'Nothing, master.'

Stag lifted her chin with a cruel hand, staring down into her eyes for what felt like an eternity. She felt his fingers bruise her delicate white skin and shivered with delight. 'I thought you had become a true submissive? If you are to remain here with me, *ma belle*, there is still much you have to learn about the art of obedience.'

'Yes, master,' Violetta said gratefully, and turned her head to kiss his hand.

NEXUS NEW BOOKS

To be published in April

THE INDISCRETIONS OF ISABELLE
Penny Birch writing as Cruella

Isabelle is a young student at Oxford, well versed in the giving of flagellation and in the Sapphic pleasures the city affords. When her ageing scout, Stan Tierney, lets slip that he knows about a long-established society of lesbian dominas, Isabelle is drawn in. As Isabelle investigates, together with her girlfriends Jasmine and Caroline, it becomes clear that she will have to endure a comprehensive round of sexual humiliations if she is to get close to the mysterious society.

£6.99   ISBN 0 352 33882 2

STRIPING KAYLA
Yvonne Marshall

Now in their mid-thirties and settled into married lives, former debutantes Charlotte, Imogen and Seona continue to enjoy each other's company as playmates, an arrangement of which their husbands are only too happy to approve. But the ghost of 'Kayla' – the mysterious and cruel courtesan whose identity Charlotte herself once adopted – continues to haunt them. Imogen is convinced that the girl who is no doubt being currently trained as Kayla should be made aware of the dark nature of the project she is involved in. Charlotte is secretly thrilled, having sorely missed the dominance she enjoyed for so long. Can she resist returning to this world of bizarre flagellant delights?

£6.99   ISBN 0 352 33881 4

EMMA ENSLAVED
Hilary James

Emma, having been denied every dignity by her mistress Ursula, is now required to sacrifice something even more precious; access to her own pleasure. Introduced to a world where the bizarre has become the everyday, confined under her skirts and desperate for the unique attentions of her beautiful, strict guardian, Emma learns what it's like to be denied release from her torment.

£6.99   ISBN 0 352 33883 0

NEXUS BACKLIST

This information is correct at time of printing. For up-to-date information, please visit our website at www.nexus-books.co.uk

All books are priced at £6.99 unless another price is given.

- - - - - ✂ -

Please send me the books I have ticked above.

Name   ....

Address   ....

          ....

          ....

          .... Post code...................

Send to: **Virgin Books Cash Sales, Thames Wharf Studios, Rainville Road, London W6 9HA**

US customers: for prices and details of how to order books for delivery by mail, call 1-800-343-4499.

Please enclose a cheque or postal order, made payable to **Nexus Books Ltd**, to the value of the books you have ordered plus postage and packing costs as follows:

   UK and BFPO – £1.00 for the first book, 50p for each subsequent book.

   Overseas (including Republic of Ireland) – £2.00 for the first book, £1.00 for each subsequent book.

If you would prefer to pay by VISA, ACCESS/MASTERCARD, AMEX, DINERS CLUB or SWITCH, please write your card number and expiry date here:

....

Please allow up to 28 days for delivery.

Signature ....

Our privacy policy

We will not disclose information you supply us to any other parties. We will not disclose any information which identifies you personally to any person without your express consent.

From time to time we may send out information about Nexus books and special offers. Please tick here if you do *not* wish to receive Nexus information.   ☐

- - - - - ✂ -